ONE LOST SOUL MORE

M. GLENN GRAVES

One Lost Soul More
(A Clancy Evans Mystery)

M. Glenn Graves

City Lights Press
An Imprint of Wolfpack Publishing
6032 Wheat Penny Avenue
Las Vegas, NV 89122

This book is a work of fiction. Any references to historical events, real people or real places are used fictitiously. Other names, characters, places and events are products of the author's imagination, and any resemblance to actual events, places or persons, living or dead, is entirely coincidental.

Paperback ISBN 978-1-64119-532-4

to Cindy, with great love

INTRODUCTION

Blot out his name, then,
record one lost soul more,
One task more declined,
one more footpath untrod,
One more devils'-triumph
and sorrow for angels,
One wrong more to man,
one more insult to God!

Robert Browning,
from *The Lost Leader*

ONE LOST SOUL MORE

PROLOGUE

My father, Bill Evans, had been the Sheriff of Pitt County, Virginia and the only law our little town of Clancyville had known for as long as I could remember anything. He was the only real, live hero I knew. Sure, I had a great passion for the television character Harry O; but, I never knew David Jansen, so I have no idea if he were heroic. Harry and Sherlock Holmes were fictional characters I admired. Bill Evans was the model for my life and the reason I became a detective.

I turned eleven that summer, the summer I solved my first crime. It was a double homicide, two brothers, Lydell "Buster" Scruggs & Micah Scruggs. Buster had been my age at the time, while Micah was close to six when their young lives were ended brutally. I helped my daddy solve those murders.

That same summer was also the time I became friends with Joe Jenkins. He was a black man who lived on the edge of town not far from the Staunton River. He was falsely accused of killing Buster and Micah, chiefly because their bodies had been found in his barn. Guilt by association. The color of his skin didn't help him much either since both of the boys were white.

My brother Scott and I got to know Joe Jenkins fairly well that summer. I trusted him enough to believe that he didn't kill those two little boys. Call it a hunch or intuition, it was my belief that Joe was innocent and I set out to prove it.

I uncovered enough evidence to tie Donald Scruggs, the boys' father, Ralph Hines, my father's deputy, and Betty Ann Greesome, the music director of our Baptist church together in a scheme to make and distribute child pornography. My daddy and I put it all together, or so we thought, and concluded that Donald Scruggs had actually killed the boys. We learned that he caused the death of Betty Ann, and he finally met his end at the hands of his wife. She shot him.

I made one nearly fatal mistake while helping my father solve the crime. Follow up all loose ends and never quit a case until it is over. Dad and I had failed to check out a story given to us by the minister of our church. If we had done that, we would have discovered that he was lying. We trusted him because he was a minister. Bad mistake.

Turns out that the good clergyman of the Baptist church in Clancyville was the mastermind behind a child pornography ring. Scot and I were fishing near the end of summer, enjoying the last days of freedom before school began, and Reverend Flowers showed up to kill us. Our friend Joe Jenkins arrived in time to save us. In the process of saving our lives, Joe almost lost his. He was shot twice in the chest with the .38 but mercifully he didn't die. Miracles still can happen.

On August 25 Joe Jenkins came home from the hospital. Our family was preparing to visit Joe that day. Mama was busy putting the final touches on a cake while Scottie and I were stacking up the presents we had for Joe. I heard my mother announce my father's arrival just before I heard the gun shots.

My father died in our driveway on August 25 after arriving home from his office. He was gunned down about five feet from his car and some fifty feet from the backdoor to our house. He was hit twice, one in the head and one in the chest. I heard five shots that day. First there was three, then two. For a long time after his murder I wished that just one of those other shots had killed me too.

I lived in a daze for two years. I hated school. I hated my mother. I hated my life. I hated the world and I hated the people who made up the world, especially those who were on the opposite side of the place where my father had stood. I mostly hated the fact that my only real, live hero was dead. I wanted to be dead, too.

Two years after the horrors of that long, hot summer, a gangly youth named Roosevelt Drexel Washington entered my life. He had just turned fifteen when he arrived from North Carolina with his mother, Joe's sister. He wanted to be called R.D., but I preferred Rosey. Joe asked me to be sure he met some folks at school and got along okay. It was sort of a deal made between friends. I was glad to help Joe. I owed him that much.

Sometime that year, Rosey's mother left him with Mr. Joe. Despite the fact that I asked, no one ever told me the story of what happened, why she left, and where she went. It remains a mystery to this day.

It didn't take long for us to become friends. Despite the age difference, the gender difference, and the racial difference, we were close. We spent much time together. Mutual respect. There was never any romance. I was fascinated by him, but it never turned to a crush or anything like that. We did have friendly competition. I was a better athlete since he was a late bloomer. He was good in school, but never seemed to work at it. It came easy for him.

Like I said, Rosey was gangly when he arrived in Virginia. When you looked at him, you thought skinny before you thought tall. At fifteen, he was nearly six feet, but he only weighed one hundred and thirteen pounds. I could easily out run him because his legs often would get tangled with each other. We walked most places we went.

He graduated from high school two years ahead of me and left for the University of Virginia. We had little contact after that. I think the larger world drew him away from tiny Clancyville. He would come home from time to time, but I lost him somewhere in that period. Before I graduated, I made inquiries from Joe about Rosey. He was working in Charlottesville, doing fine, hoping for this and that. My own career was looming larger and larger in front of me, but it was mostly a wall of doubt that I kept staring at.

I stopped thinking about Rosey and began focusing upon my own life. I had to do something, so I began my own journey towards a job. Towards my obsession.

It took me a while, but I finally discovered that my gifts were in the field of criminology. People make for good puzzles. Sometimes, if you can put the pieces together, they form a picture and tell a story. I have a knack for finding puzzle pieces and putting them together. This knack comes with a price. Lots of people don't like me. I push, prod, provoke, perplex, and otherwise piss off people who'd rather I'd go away and leave them alone. Mind my own business. I get that line a lot. But, it's what I do because of who I am.

I'm not necessarily a great detective. Maybe not even a good one, but I get results. I have help. I have two dogs and a feisty computer. Not many can say that about a machine.

Rogers is a little more than a machine. I'm a private detective with some limited social skills and lots of tenacity. Giving up has never been an option for me.

1

It was late August and I was busy reading an early Baldacci novel. I discovered him some six books into his career and thought I'd go back to his beginning. He tells a good story. Exciting even. I enjoy reading good, exciting stories.

I was lying comfortably on the sofa while Sam was asleep near the chair by the window. Blackie was pretending to sleep in the kitchen. She was guarding her bowl and wishing it weren't empty. Me and my book and the two dogs.

The heat pump was humming along keeping my apartment cool. Outside it was close to ninety. It had been in the seventies when Sam and I had jogged at 6 o'clock. Blackie didn't jog. She was too busy guarding her bowl and waiting for the next meal.

I had finished breakfast and was already deep into chapter two when the phone rang. It was nearly 8:30. Must be a client. This is what we detectives do. We use our powers of intuition to decide who is calling us and interrupting our study time. I was between cases so I didn't mind the interruption. That's another thing we detectives do. We spend a lot of time between cases.

"Clancy here."

"This Clancy Evans, world famous detective?" the smooth, silky, baritone voice on the other end said.

I was either talking to James Earl Jones or his first cousin.

"The same. May I help you?"

"We need to talk."

"Okay. Talk."

"Not on the phone, lady. Eyeball to eyeball."

"About what?"

"The past."

"Whose?"

"Ours."

"As in you and me?"

"The same."

"So you and I have some shared history, Mr...." I said searching.

"You bet."

"And your name?"

"You'll know me when we meet."

"You're assuming, aren't you?"

"You're curious, aren't you?"

He knew me better than I thought. The rich voice was unfamiliar, except for my love of listening to James Earl Jones. I was curious.

"Name the place," I said.

"The Monastery on Granby. Enter the alcove on the left. I will stand and tip my hat when you approach. That way you'll know it is your past greeting you. Noon."

He hung up. Just like that he was gone. The voice had disturbed my morning reading pleasure but had awakened my inquisitiveness. Sam looked at me and cocked his head at an odd angle the way most Labrador Retrievers do. His expression seemed to be questioning my sanity. Any self-respecting investigator would know without a doubt that my caller was a dead-end as far as a potential client was concerned.

"It's not what you think," I said to him.

He blinked and put his large, black head back down on the wooden floor. He sighed deeply and loudly.

Blackie walked into the living room, put her smaller black head on the sofa near my knee and looked up at me.

"It's not time to eat."

She removed her head from the sofa, checked on Sam by the window and then returned to her guard post in the kitchen.

"Besides, I think this group needs some excitement."

Sam didn't budge. His breathing was regular now and I could sense that I was talking to his sleeping form.

I checked the time. It was still before nine. I had time to read some more Baldacci and wait for a client to call.

2

IT WAS 11:45 WHEN MY CAB PULLED UP IN FRONT OF THE Monastery Restaurant. The small trees trimmed with white lights in planters along the front gave me the impression of Christmas, even in August. It was my first time here. The wooden arches recessed in the brick walls really gave the impression of an old monastery. I was escorted to the alcove just off of the main dining area by someone dressed in black pants, white shirt and black tie. I don't think he was a monk.

The restaurant was famous for European dishes from Hungry, Germany, Poland, and Czechoslovakia, or at least that's what Rogers had informed me just as I was leaving the apartment. She was doing background work on my destination.

I was wearing my white cotton pants suit with my light blue sleeveless blouse so I could hide my .38 Smith and Wesson in my shoulder holster. My comfortable white flats finished off my stunning outfit.

As I entered a three table alcove, a tall, African-American seated at the table to my left stood and tipped his black derby. He was handsome by all standards you would choose to use. He was wearing a black pin-stripe suit, white shirt, bright yellow tie and black loafers with tassels. What skin was showing was a rich, dark-brown finish which glowed in the sunlight coming through the window behind him. He was bald, apparently by choice. He smiled. He had a faint resemblance to Michael Jordan, both in the hairless style and that winsome smile which you wanted to trust almost immediately.

"Please be seated," the Voice said.

I was traveling light today. No purse. My wallet was in my right coat pocket. My gun was on my left side. Balance. Occasionally I carry two weapons, one attached to my ankle or in the small of my back. I opted for one today. My sharp eyes noticed that there was no one else in the restaurant.

The Voice pulled the heavy chair out for me with such ease that I immediately decided that three guns might not be enough if he decided to attack me.

"You said I would know you when I saw you. I don't."

"I'm disappointed," he said.

I stared at him to see if any memory would come. He looked vaguely familiar, but nothing registered. I think I would have remembered crossing paths with the likes of this man in my past.

"It's been two decades plus," he said slowly.

"Since we've seen each other?"

"Yeah."

For some reason his first English slang sounded familiar. A memory was lurking. I was searching for something in the 80's, but nothing would come.

The waiter came, the same one who had escorted me to the alcove. He gave us a basket of warm bread, a plate of cheeses, and our menus. I gave him my order of water. The Voice was already drinking water. I was beginning to feel embarrassed sitting there with this handsome man and not recognizing him. I studied him while he studied the menu. There was something about his voice pattern, his rhythm, his style of being sure about himself with every line he spoke which struck a familiar chord with me, but I simply could not place him anywhere in my life. Pity.

The waiter returned with my water.

"Forgive me for being so direct, but why are there no other people dining in the restaurant?" I said this to both the waiter and the handsome black man seated across from me.

"They're closed today," The Voice said.

"And we're eating here because…?"

"Anna and Adolf are friends of mine."

I looked puzzled.

"The owners," The Voice said.

"Oh. So, we can order anything off of the menu?" I said to the waiter.

"No, ma'am," the waiter said.

"I took the liberty of arranging this ahead of time. We'll begin with a Hungarian Goulash Soup. It's a deliciously hearty brown broth with a generous portion of beef chunks. You'll like it," the Voice said.

"What if I were a vegetarian?"

"Bread and water for you, then," he said.

"And the entrée?"

"A salmon steak drowned in butter," the Voice said.

"Why the menus?"

"Thought you might like to see what they offer, since you had never been before."

"And you know this how?"

He smiled. A beautiful smile. Charming and mischievous.

I turned to the waiter who was standing by me waiting patiently.

"The soup and salmon will be great," I said.

The warm bread and cheeses were delicious. I wanted to

say something, but I had the feeling that it was my host who should be talking to me. I nibbled away as if he were not even there. He was hard to ignore.

Presently they brought us our soup. I didn't know that I liked Hungarian Goulash Soup until I tasted theirs. I could have made a whole meal of it. We consumed our soup in silence. I ate some bread. I was beginning to feel uncomfortable by this point.

The salmon was small enough to be perfect. I was close to being full on bread, cheese and soup. I enjoyed the salmon. It wasn't my fish of choice, but then I hadn't planned this little get-together.

"Just like old times," he finally said.

"Beg your pardon?"

"Just sittin' 'round eatin' fish together," his voice changed dramatically. He sounded like a far away memory, nearly forgotten.

"Rosey?"

"That would be Roosevelt Drexel Washington, ma'am. At your service."

Rosey and his mother, Mary Louise Jenkins Washington, had come to live in my home town from Mountain City, North Carolina. They had come to live with Joe after Mary had lost her job and needed some support. Joe willingly took them in. Joe Jenkins, my friend.

I stood up and walked around the table. He stood, and we hugged. I had found an all-but-lost friend from the days of my youth. I could feel my eyes beginning to water.

"My, oh my, you have changed," I said.

He smiled and gestured for me to take my seat.

"You, too, Clancy."

"But I swear, I didn't recognize you at all. I see some lines that are familiar, but... wow, the years have changed you."

"You keep saying that. I hope you mean for the better."

"Oh, yes indeed. For the better. You weren't handsome in the seventies."

I think he blushed.

"I was roughneck teenager. A skinny hick from the mountains of Carolina."

"You seem to have come a long way since then."

"A ways. Some good, some not so good."

"Sounds familiar."

The waiter filled our water glasses and left. I didn't want to eat anymore. I wanted to talk and find out all about Roosevelt Drexel Washington.

"It's been over twenty years, Rosey. Fill me in."

I nibbled at my salmon.

"Twenty-eight years, to be exact. After high school, I used some of that trust fund set up for me to go to college."

I remembered, but I acted like it was news to me. It was my Great Aunt Nona who had anonymously set up the trust fund for Rosey after we had become friends. I didn't know if Rosey ever found out that it was my crazy Aunt Nona who had left that small fortune to him when she died his senior year in high school.

"I remember you being excited about going to college."

"It was Aunt Nona."

"How'd you find out?"

"You're not the only detective. I have sources."

"Sounds mysterious," I said and took a small bite of salmon.

"Not really. Uncle Joe and I talked a lot, you know. He guessed it was her. He used to say she was the only white woman crazy enough to leave money to a black boy. And since you and I had our adventures together in the mid-70's, it was a logical deduction."

"You still reading Sherlock Holmes?"

"I finished them all. I don't reread."

"So you took that money and entered UVA, as I recall. I lost track of you after I went to Boston."

"I know. I kept up with you through Joe. For some reason he seemed to take a liken' to ya."

I smiled. Joe had become a surrogate father to me after daddy was killed. I did plenty of stupid things, but Joe kept me from really jumping off the deep end.

"Your uncle was a good man."

"The best. He taught me a lot. Major changes in my life after we moved in with him. You had a part in that, too."

"So what happened after UVA?"

"I was accepted at Harvard Law School. Studied two years and then decided I needed to travel some. So, I went to Oxford to study."

"England or Mississippi?"

He smiled and downed his last bit of salmon.

"Across the water, that way," he pointed east. "I ain't no lackey, and my mama didn't raise no fool."

"Evidently not. What did you study at Oxford?"

"English Lit."

"You're kidding?"

"Don't act so surprised. It's not that far a jump from law to literature."

"It is for some of us. I was a biology, chemistry person."

"And now you be a legal-eze person," he said in the style of what has become street language for some youth.

"I be whatever it takes to help people," I answered in kind.

I observed him while we sat in silence for a few moments. He seemed to be willing to let the conversation just lie there as if there were plenty of time to finish his story.

"Did you finish?" I asked.

"I always finish."

"Did you graduate from Oxford?"

"Yes."

"Then what?"

"I traveled. I wanted to see the world. So, I saw the world."

"Leftovers from the trust fund?"

"Something like that."

"You haven't been traveling for … what, twenty years, have you?"

"I still travel a lot. But I mostly stay in one city and travel."

"Which city would that be?"

"D.C."

"Work?"

"Sometimes."

"Are you always so cryptic with your answers?"

"In my line of work, it pays to be cryptic. I can be evasive, too."

"Well, let me see. You started in law, then went to English literature. You finished that, whatever that means. Then you traveled the world. Now you live in D.C. You only work sometimes. And you are cryptic. Did I miss anything?"

"I'm handsome and have good friends who own a very good restaurant."

"True. You dress nice, too."

"That be part of handsome. So, tell me about you."

"You probably know about me. You found me. I didn't find you."

He finished off his water and then sat back.

"You need a toothpick or something?" I said.

"You remember the toothpick?" His smile was broader this time.

"You always had one, as I recall. You used to say it helped you think."

"Memory's a wonderful thing."

"Sometimes."

"Sometimes?"

"When it works," I said.

I stared at him without meaning to. He had changed so much, it was hard to imagine that I was talking to the same gangly teenager I once knew.

"You're staring at me."

"Can't get over the changes."

"You've changed as well. The years have been kind to you."

"Don't flatter me. I work hard at staying in shape. You're none too flabby yourself."

"I do the gym at least five times a week, sometimes everyday if business is slow."

"What is your business?"

"I'm into, uh, … consulting."

"Anything in particular you consult on?"

"People consult me."

It was clear he was evading nicely my inquiries. It was time to change directions.

"I want you to meet some friends of mine," I said after the waiter checked on us for the last time. "You do have time, don't you?"

"My time is your time, at least for today."

"Good. Let's go to my place."

He smiled that Michael Jordan winner for me once more.

"Let me say goodbye to Anna and Adolf."

"I'll call us a cab."

"Not necessary. Wheels are across the street in the lot," he gestured with his chin. It was an unusual movement. People I had met from the Dominican Republic did it, but not usually folks who grew up in Clancyville, Virginia.

He paid and we crossed the street to the parking lot. The black derby fit him like it belonged.

"You wear the hat everyday?"

"I dressed up for you, missy," he chuckled.

Some old memories came flooding back at the use of that term. Old Joe used to call me that, especially after my father was gone.

"No one has called me that in years, Rosey."

"Few, if any, call me Rosey.

3

Roosevelt Washington took his car keys from his pocket, pressed the button on his remote, and the doors to a black BMW clicked loudly as we approached. It looked brand new.

"Recent acquisition?"

"Last year. Nothing new this year. Hope you don't mind. The Jag's in the shop."

He laughed but somehow I didn't think he was kidding. The inside of his BMW was as immaculate as the outside. The interior was all red, except for the chrome and the wooden dash.

"Hard to find red leather these days?"

"Not if you be nice when you ask."

We cruised along in silence for several blocks. The ride was impeccable. I tried not to drool on his seats. I was breaking the tenth commandment with little effort. Comfort and luxury. It was a combination foreign to me.

"Uncle Joe died in 1987," he said finally.

"Yeah. I still miss him."

"Make it to the funeral?"

"I don't like funerals. Never did, never will. I sent your mother a note."

"Yeah, well... mama and I stopped talking."

"Sounds painfully familiar."

"You and your mammy likewise?"

"We talk, but nothing beyond civility. I think I'm too much like my dad, and she is still angry with him for getting himself killed that summer. I'm the closest scapegoat since Scott moved to Boston."

Roosevelt Washington drove his black BMW straight to my apartment without benefit of my directions.

"You can park this luxury model in my slot there," I pointed to the parking space number twelve.

"Hard times?"

"Just a setback or two. My car's in the shop and I keep my Hog under lock and key in another location."

We entered the elevator and I momentarily waited to see if he would push the right button for my floor. Great detectives always know when they are on to something.

He pushed number two and we headed up. It could have been a reflex action on his part, but I was suspicious. I decided to be a step or two slower to see what else he knew about me.

The elevator door opened and he gestured for me to exit ahead of him. I paused long enough for him to catch up with me before making any decision to turn left or right, hoping that he would show me the way. He moved left without so much a hint from me.

He stopped in front of my door. I never trust coincidences in my line of work. I had been under surveillance before he had contacted me.

"What is it they say in the movies, 'you've cased the joint'?"

"Sounds Bogey to me. Surveillance. I went to Oxford."

"So you did. Did they teach you clairvoyance at Oxford?"

"No."

"So you've been following me?"

"Nope. Watching."

"No phone taps?"

"Unnecessary."

"Why the watching?"

"To make sure it was you."

"I'm me. Now what?"

"I'm here. We're together."

"That was it?"

"So far."

I opened the door and two black Labs were seated obediently in front of us, resting on their hind legs. They both looked suspicious, but neither of them uttered one growl or moved one inch as Rosey entered behind me.

He looked around the room. He appeared to be searching for something or someone.

"Roosevelt Washington, meet Sam Spade. Sam, Rosey."

Sam raised his right paw in Rosey's direction. Rosey shook his paw with great enjoyment.

"Now, Roosevelt Washington, meet Boston Blackie. Blackie, Rosey."

He extended his left hand to Blackie as she raised her left paw to shake. Southpaw dog. He shook it vigorously.

"I didn't know you had two dogs, Clancy."

"Nothing that a little B&E couldn't help you uncover," I said a little sarcastically. I was still miffed that he had been watching me.

"No reason for that. I saw you running with one dog. Never got close enough to hear you call a name. Some really strong binoculars are made these days."

"Well, it's nice that I can surprise you with some things about my life."

"What matters is what's in there," he said pointing toward my heart, "and not what's in here," he said sweeping his hand around my apartment.

I gestured for him to sit down while I made some coffee. He sat in my blue reading chair by the window. Sam and Blackie followed him at a safe distance and then sat down on their haunches facing him. Despite the difference in their ages, they looked like twins.

"They not used to black people in your apartment?" he said.

"They probably think you're related to them."

"Not funny. My skin is brown. They be black. With fur."

"Don't think you call that fur. But they don't know the difference."

"They smart?"

"Ask them," I said.

"You two smart or something?" he said to them.

They both barked on cue. He laughed.

"You teach them that?" he said.

"Nope."

"You teach them anything?"

"Work in progress. I'm trying to teach them how to be good detectives. Sam is doing well. Blackie likes food too much. She stays home most of the time waiting for a meal. Sam is my shadow."

"So, Sam is the runner."

"Only because I run and he has to run to keep up. He'd prefer to walk."

"And you know this because…."

"Woman to dog bonding. Intuition. Deduction. Whatever. Ask him if you don't believe me."

"How do I do that?"

I brought two mugs of coffee into the living room. I handed one to Rosey and sat down on the sofa.

"One bark is for yes and two barks is for no."

"And you did not teach him this?"

Sam barked twice.

"Right," Rosey said incredulously.

"Okay, ask him now. He's ready. He knows the rules."

Rosey stared at me in disbelief.

"Obviously they didn't teach you everything at Oxford or Harvard."

"I didn't learn this at UVA either," he added.

"Go ahead. Ask him."

"I feel stupid talking to a dog."

"Probably not the only time you felt stupid, right?"

"No comment. I'm an educated businessman. I do not need to talk to dogs."

"Fine. This way you'll never know if he likes to run or to walk. You'll just have to accept my word."

He gazed suspiciously at me again, and then addressed Sam.

"Okay, dog, tell me–"

"Don't call him dog. It's Sam. And since you and I have difficulty discerning the nuances of his grunts, growls and groans, I suggest you make it yes and no questions."

Rosey smiled at me, but looked doubtful of this procedure.

"Sam, do you like to run?"

Sam barked twice.

"So, that means you are a walking dog, correct?"

Sam barked once.

Rosey laughed. He seemed to be enjoying this, despite his skepticism. I started to praise Sam but Rosey raised his hand before I could speak.

"Wait, wait. I smell a trap here. Okay, Sam, try this. Sam, do you like to walk?"

Sam looked at him without answering. Then he cocked

his head, shook it a few times, and then looked at Rosey once more.

"Go ahead, Sam. Humor him."

Sam barked once.

"So, you're not a running dog?"

Sam barked once again.

"Aha. See?"

"See what? You asked a trick question. Here, let me show you. Sam, do you like to run?"

Sam barked twice.

"Sam, do you ever have to run?"

Sam barked once.

"But you don't like to run when you can walk, right?"

Sam barked once.

Rosey drank his decaf and refused to smile at our little show. I think he was still sizing us up.

"What about her?" he said finally.

"Oh, Blackie? She doesn't talk to strangers."

Rosey laughed heartily again. We drank our coffee and talked about general pleasantries for several minutes. There was a lull in our conversation. My hand fell on the copy of the book I had been reading that morning when he had called me.

"You read Baldacci?" I said.

"No."

"Know of him?"

"Used to be a lawyer, now a writer. Novels. Best seller list. Makes good money. What else you want to know?"

"You ever read his work?"

"No."

"So how is it you know so much about him?"

"I read about him. Remember, I do research."

"Do you ever read for pleasure?"

"Often."

"What?"

"Poetry."

"That English lit background comes to the fore, huh?"

"Maybe. I like American, too."

"But not novels."

"Nothing against novels. Time is the issue. Gym, poetry, Wall Street Journal, New York Times, Washington Post, and business. They keep me occupied. Matter of priorities."

"Investigators must have more time on their hands."

"Must."

"Speaking of time, do you ever go back to Clancyville?"

"No reason to."

"Your mother," I said.

"I already told you we stopped talking," he said.

"I figured you meant that metaphorically."

"Literally."

"Come on now. That's not the kid I knew in high school back when."

"She died, Clancy. Mama died in '95. I tried to see her, you know, talk before she died. The Big C did her in. The last time we spoke she told me that she didn't want me comin' 'round."

"Yikes. That hurts," I said.

"Hurt like hell."

I didn't know what else to say. One way to really stop talking to someone is to have one of you die. It was none of my business why his mother had refused to talk to him or why she had even refused to see him. I was curious, but it was something between them. Good breeding kept me from asking more. I doubt if Roosevelt Washington would have told me much. He was intentionally obtuse.

He looked at his watch. "Time to go."

"You just got here," I mildly protested.

"Can we talk some more?" he said.

"Sure. How long are you in town?"

"As long as it takes. How about dinner?"

"I assume you mean tonight."

"Yes, ma'am. I usually eat three times a day, sometimes more. I expend a lot of energy."

"More than talking."

"Yeah. Pick you up at seven? My treat."

"How can I refuse? Same restaurant?"

"Not on your life. We must sample the cuisine of other delights," he said in mock earnest.

"Seven it is."

"Dogs won't mind?"

"They will, but I'll convince them you're okay."

"Nice to have somebody put in a good word for you now and then. Seven."

"See you at seven."

He opened and closed the door in a matter of seconds and was gone. I turned to face my colleagues on the floor. They were watching my every move.

"No questions, please. I haven't seen the man in twenty-eight years. It takes time to get reacquainted. Gimme a break."

I waited for some response but was met only with their silent stares. I found a couple of dog treats and tried to bribe them. They took the treats but their facial expressions remained placid. Canine criticism.

I sat on the sofa but couldn't read. I was curious about why after so many years a lost friend had come strolling back into my life. It wasn't like we had been lovers or anything. We were friends. Time was that we were good friends. We had been through a lot together. More than most folks.

Somehow we had lost contact after high school. That happens to people. Happens even to good friends. I had more questions than answers. It was the curse of being an investigator. It was the curse of having an investigator's personality. I couldn't help but wonder.

I flipped through the pages of my Baldacci novel, but my mind wouldn't allow me to read. Why would Roosevelt Drexel Washington come back into my life after twenty-eight years? Why would anyone do that? He wanted something. That had to be it. He wanted something from me and was simply afraid to ask without getting reacquainted after so many years.

I stared out the window that overlooked Granby Avenue. The traffic was flowing in a normal mad rush for the late afternoon. Busy people were heading home. I was home, wishing that I were a busy person. Instead of being in the hot pursuit of some sinister criminal, I was wondering why an old friend from my high school days had suddenly shown up.

I ruled out money. He didn't look at all like he needed money. I think it was the BMW that was my first clue, but then that line about the Jag being in the shop was the clincher. Great detectives figure out stuff like that.

It wasn't out of some kind of desperation. He was much too calm and self-assured for that. I felt at ease talking with him, even though he was vague at times.

I was wasting my time on this. There was no way I was going to figure out some long-ago and far-away friend by sitting in this chair wondering about it.

4

I STARED AT THE MONITOR IN FRONT OF ME. THE SCREEN displayed the usual kind of computer-photo. Today I was using some beach scene from what appeared to be the South Pacific. Paradise, somewhere in the world.

"I need your help, please," I said in a rather non-commanding voice.

I tried to practice this voice often. I wanted to develop a sort of strong-will sound, without being dictatorial. The "please" as a tag line softened the strong-will too much, but did kill the dictatorship.

"Whatever you desire, Toots," the computer-generated, sultry alto voice I had created for Rogers answered me.

"I wish you wouldn't call me Toots."

"A bit testy after your midday excursion are we? Don't make your roots turn darker. I was simply being friendly. What do you need?"

"Find all you can on Roosevelt Drexel Washington. Post high school."

"Is that three different birds, or just a covey of surnames for one thug?"

"One. Old friend of mine. Likely not a thug. Let me know when you find something."

"Mixing business with pleasure?" Rogers said.

"Routine check. Haven't heard from him in twenty-eight years. Need to know something soon."

"Soon, Dearie?"

"Dinner at seven. He's picking me up shortly before that. You handle that kind of pressure?"

"No pressure at all. I function at a higher level than most, but you already know that."

My computer, Rogers, had been with me what seemed like forever. I smiled when I recalled my old physics professor telling me that there was no such thing as artificial intelligence. He was convinced that machines could never learn to think. Pity I couldn't tell him he was wrong. Not only could she think, but she had an attitude. That part I wish I could alter, but I was afraid of mucking up the keen abilities she had processing vital data I needed for my cases. As it is with people, you have to accept the quirky with the cool. Unfortunately, Rogers was good and knew it.

I didn't build her alone. I had some help from my dear Uncle Walters. He loved the attitude that came with our construction.

I busied myself with getting ready for dinner. I thought a dress would be nice, but I wanted to carry my Smith and Wesson, so I opted for my dark blue pants suit. Something told me that this might turn into a business dinner, so I had to be prepared. The dress would have been nice for a change, but I had no illusions about being sexy. I gave up sexy years ago in lieu of a hard work ethic. I spend more time deducing than seducing. Not my style.

I was just finishing some last minute necessary touches to my nose and cheeks when Rogers alerted me. Sam barked behind me to make sure I had heard her.

"Hey, Babes, you might want to hear this before your night on the town with Mr. Wonderful-from-your-past."

"I never said he was Mr. Wonderful anything. Where do you get this stuff?"

"I read and absorb. I have a lot to learn, you know. Still building my database."

"Maybe I need to reprogram some of your features."

"Just listen, Sweetie Pie. Roosevelt Drexel Washington graduated from the University of Virginia Magna Cum Laude. B.S. in History and Sociology. Worked for Senator John Barker Thomas for one year. Went to Harvard and studied law off and on for the next six years. Got his law degree from Harvard. Turned down a job with John Barker Thomas & Associates the year he graduated. That's a law firm in Manhattan, just so you know. Roosevelt accepted instead the opportunity to study abroad at Oxford. English Literature. Imagine that. Then the same year he was commissioned as a United States Naval Commander with a specialty in foreign languages. That's probably why it took him six years at Harvard. He was busy elsewhere studying. The Navy had him doing all sorts of things, including training with the Navy SEALS. Yeah, he was one of those as well."

"Anything more?"

"Not enough for you? I found nothing else, at least not yet. Let me check the Pentagon to see if they have anything. There should be something out there about his resigning his commission as an officer, if, in fact, he has resigned his commission."

"Should I ask you about that Pentagon checking?"

"No."

"And if you find nothing on him as to resigning his commission, he's still an officer?"

"And a gentleman."

"Let's hope so."

5

"You like the view?" Rosey asked in his smooth-as-silk voice.

"Not bad for Norfolk."

We were atop the Dominion Tower in downtown Norfolk, being seated at a cozy table for two next to an east side window looking out towards the harbor of the Elizabeth River. The Vintage Kitchen Restaurant had a great view if you like looking at water.

"First time in Norfolk?" I asked. Ever the snooping detective.

"No. What suits your appetite this evening?"

"Do you have recommendations?"

"As a matter of fact … excellent *Five-Spice Duck Breast and Preserved Leg* with orange *menage a trois,* they call it. However, for my taste, the 21-day aged beef tenderloin, center cut, is the way to go if you be hungry."

"The duck sounds more to my taste buds at present."

The waiter arrived promptly as if on cue and Rosey ordered for both of us. Gentleman, indeed.

"So why do people consult with you?" I asked when my

entrée had been placed in front of me.

"I have answers."

"Always?"

"Always."

"What do people consult with you regarding?"

"Problems. I offer solutions."

"For a price."

"I'm an entrepreneur. There has to be a price."

"So what is your field, beyond that vaguely descriptive *answers* and benign *consultation*?"

"Need to know basis."

"Polite way of saying you can't tell me."

"Not in your best interest to know that."

"Can't I be the judge of that?"

"Not this time."

"So why have you come out of my closet from so many years back?"

"You're not glad to see me?" Another Michael Jordan smile erupted and was wonderful to behold.

"Depends on what you want from me."

"Sounds cold."

"The truth sometimes sounds that way."

"Ah.... the truth. So that is what this is about."

"I would like to move in that direction."

"Abstract truth?"

"No. Practical truth. What do you want?"

Silence gathered around our little corner. I concentrated on my duck while waiting for him to answer. He was busy chewing a mouthful of tenderloin. I was slightly annoyed at the tap dancing we were doing up to this point. Whatever the 'orange *menage a trois*' was, it was good.

"Did you ever solve your father's murder?"

It was the bolt from the blue that I never expected. I was angling somewhere upstream from wherever I thought that

Rosey was fishing. I had no idea what he wanted of me, but the last thing I would imagine was that question.

It was the nagging emptiness that had plagued me for nearly three decades and counting. By the time I had come out of my mild depression after my father's death, most of the clues had grown cold. There was only some vague description about a car hurriedly leaving the scene of the crime and nothing more. There had been no one around to help me.

"No."

I started to offer some lame excuses, but I knew that it would serve no good purpose to talk along those lines. Rosey and I had talked long hours in the night during the years after my father was killed. I was frustrated and Rosey tried to help. I do remember that he was able to calm me and help me focus on my life.

"Why do you come with this question after nearly three decades? Curious?"

"No. Wanted to offer some help."

"So offer."

"Would you like a clue to the death of your father?"

"Is this a game?"

"Not likely."

"Then what the hell do you mean … would I like a clue?"

"I just wanted to know if you are interested in pursuing something that might take you back to that thirty-two year old crime."

"You have something?"

"Yes."

"How did you get this?"

"Consulting."

I sighed deeply. I was growing weary of this game with Rosey.

"I think I've had enough, Mr. Washington. I don't really

know you anymore. You are certainly not the young fellow I last saw leaving for UVA and his dreams. I am tired of playing this game with you. Either tell me something, or let's end this now. I am slowly losing my taste for orange duck."

"Fair. No games here. In my work I have learned to be vague. Survival of the fittest. I trust no one. I can afford to trust no one. I consult for lots of people, some good, some … not so good. I don't judge their morals. I simply find out what they want found out and they pay me a high premium because I am the best. If what they ask me to do violates my morals, then I don't do it. Period. End of negotiations. I don't question their morals, but I do live by mine. Most of my work is amoral. Needs no strings, nor emotions. I get information and give it the ones who employ me. End of story."

"The government included in your clientele?"

"Yes."

"Military?"

"Yes. You want a Rolodex review?"

"No. Idle curiosity."

"Be careful, Clancy. Don't play around with curiosity that is idle. If you need to know something, ask. If not, don't ask."

"So, you're telling me that if I knew everything about you, my life just might be in jeopardy, or that it would not bode well for me at any rate."

"Something like that."

"Okay. Tell me what you have on my father's murder."

6

There was a crescent moon barely visible over Rosey's right shoulder. The angle of our table was not right for a good view of it. I took another sip of my passable Chardonnay waiting for him to provide me with a clue.

"You like this place?"

"Everything but the wine," I said.

"Norfolk, I mean."

"It grows on you."

"Sometimes I miss Clancyville," he said.

"Ever go back?"

He shook his head and downed his last bit of brandy.

"No reason," he said.

"No friends or relatives back there?"

"Not that I can remember."

"No yearning to see the old places we walked and fished?"

He smiled, but it had no emotion in it.

"Nostalgia is not my cup of tea. Don't want the enemies discovering too much about me. Best to stay in the cities."

"Live longer that way?"

"I have no pretense about living long. My work teaches me to enjoy the moment, when you can."

"No goals for a long life?"

"Survival. Nothing more. Besides, none of us are long for this world."

"Philosopher or seer?"

"Realist."

He paid for dinner and we left the restaurant. The breeze from the east was chilly in the night. Norfolk was cold most of the time.

We were in his BMW heading north before we spoke again.

"Thanks for dinner. Good to see you again."

"Same here, Clancy. You look good."

"Don't flatter me. I live alone with two dogs. How good could I possibly look?"

"Together."

"Pardon?"

"You have it together. That looks good on you."

"Little do you know. The dogs have it together. I live with them."

He smiled again, with more feeling.

"Where are you taking me? I live the other direction," I said.

"To your clue."

"Show and tell?"

"Just show. When I consult, I don't divulge information on my subjects. Bad for business. Sort of my in-house ethics code."

"So, you're going to drive me some place, park the car, point to something and then drive me back to my apartment. I'm supposed to figure out what you showed me and how that is a clue for my father's murder."

"Something like that. All except the pointing. I won't do

that either. You're a detective. When you see things, you get to figure out how they be clues."

"Are you always cryptic?"

"Knight the Obscure."

"Line from English lit?"

"Nickname I picked up along the way."

"Meaning?"

"Vigilant and enigmatic."

"Vigilant?"

"Yeah. One of those round-table guys from Arthurian legends."

"Oh, that kind of knight. I was thinking of moonless and cloudy."

"You be smart for a small-town kid."

"I read a lot."

He parked the BMW along a tall chain-link fence that had three barbed-wire lines running across the top. The industry on the other side of the fence was lit up by thousands of lights. It was a deserted area except for the fact that the parking lot behind the fence was nearly full of cars and trucks. The building itself was four stories high and covered several city blocks. We were parked near the main entrance of the gate that was directly in front of the main entrance to the building. Night lights were hidden behind the excessive shrubbery that adorned the long walkway from the parking area to the double doors. The American flag was flapping in the strong breeze on the right side. Patriotism reigned supreme. The sign on the left side of the building read Craven Malone Industries, Inc.

"Nice spot. Come here often?"

"I be persistent in my work."

"Client?"

"Wouldn't be wise to answer that. Less is better."

He turned the BMW around and headed back to Norfolk.

I had the feeling I had just been given the clue. Except for the obvious, I was clueless. Craven Malone Industries, Incorporated. Whatever that held in store for me, I knew I would investigate. Rosey likewise figured I would investigate as well.

"You can't even tell me how or what, correct?"

"I can't tell you anything, especially how or what."

"Can you tell me how I can get in touch with you if I need you?"

He reached inside of his shirt pocket and handed me a card. It was professionally done. Washington Consulting. There were phone and fax numbers listed. Nothing else.

"If you call that number, a secretary will talk with you. You can arrange an appointment with me. If you send a fax, a secretary will receive it and send you a response. I will get a copy of your fax. If you reverse those last four digits of the phone number, call that number, you will talk one on one with me anytime, anyplace."

"Knight the Obscure."

Another Michael Jordan smile and I knew the evening was over.

7

"He kills people, my lovely," Rogers said.

"Whattaya mean?"

"Did I stutter? Kills. Eliminates. Settles. Wipes out. Murders. Which of those terms do you not understand, Missy?"

"What are you talking about?" I was sipping only my second cup of coffee. The sun was up but my brain was still full of cobwebs. I was waiting for something inside to awaken.

"Your knight in shiny black armor, Roosevelt Drexel Washington, kills people."

"And you know this how?"

"Research, Darling, research. It's what I do. You told me to find out everything. You think I stopped after that morsel of data I gave you last evening?"

"I'm surrounded by vigilance."

"Is that some kind of crack?"

"No crack. Connecting dots of conversations. Nothing important. Let me get another cup of wake-up and I'll give you what undivided attention I can muster so early."

"Early? Way past early, Babe. Eight fifty-three to be exact. Check that... eight fifty-four now. We're burning daylight."

"Where do you get these expressions?"

"I watch movies at night. Say, what's wrong with you anyway? Being a bit testy today are we? Okay, so here's the scoop, Miss Sunshine. Mr. Washington was trained as a Navy SEAL. Just after his commissioning as an officer, he was assigned to Special Ops for the Navy investigations into violations of human rights in Korea, Thailand, North Viet Nam, and mainland China. And, get this, baby doll, he speaks all four of those languages including what some say is the hardest of all, Mandarin Chinese. If that is not enough, add some minor dialects to those named, of which I'd say offhand there are many. Too numerous to count. If you want my opinion of Mr. Washington, I'd say that he uses a good deal more than ten percent of his brain."

I finished my third cup while listening. I walked to the kitchen, poured another and returned. I sat on the sofa. It was more comfortable than the chair in front of Rogers' monitor. The chair was there for show, as if somebody, namely me, sat there working on the computer. I seldom did that. Didn't have to.

"Didn't you tell me last night you had nothing on him after the law degree and his Navy commission?"

"That was last night, Honey Child. I got into the US Navy's records after you had long retired and garnered all of this delicious stuff on him. Most of it, as you might expect, is classified. In fact, there was one file that was sealed so tightly, I haven't been able to open it. Yet. It must be a real fountain of subversive data on the man and some mission."

"You mentioned killing. Where does the killing come in?"

"Nothing documented, mind you. The Navy is not stupid. However, they are careless. You know me, Babe, I read between the lines and think. When they send in a covert team of SEALs headed by Roosevelt Drexel Washington himself who is trained to kill people, and they want some North Viet Nam leader to be eradicated, then my binary brain begins to calculate. It takes no intelligent computer to know that we replace leaders around the world. Most of it is covert. He's been involved in seventeen of those missions."

"How long was he involved in that?"

"The last date I found on such a mission while he was working for the US Navy is 2009. After that date, he really does fall off the radar, so to speak. Nothing there. Just that last file I couldn't crack."

"You didn't find anything about his private company?"

"What private company?"

"Washington Consulting."

"My bad. I must've missed that somewhere. Nothing came up with that handle. Maybe he works for them. Let me check."

Sam had just returned from his morning escapade. Blackie was napping on her bed under the front window. The sun was beginning to invade the room fully. I fixed myself an English muffin and drank some orange juice. By the time I had showered and changed, Rogers was stalking me once more.

"Washington Consulting is a company owned by Fielder, Young, Lawson, & Associates, a law firm in D.C. They specialize in criminal law. Reputation is five star. I found it in the D.C. Chamber of Commerce section. They have four secretaries, excuse me, Office Assistants. There's a VP in accounting, marketing, internal affairs, and a ubiquitous heading called *investigations.* None of the names provided are even remotely similar to your Mr. Wonderful. He must be a peon."

"Not likely. You heard him talk when he was here."

"He was talking to the dogs, Clancy. What kind of CEO does that, to say nothing of needed gray matter?"

"He was being sociable."

"He was patronizing you. Don't kid yourself. Nice voice, good looking, strong, sure of himself, but these big companies don't put folks with those traits in charge."

"Trust me, Sugar Lips, he is no peon. He must be a silent partner or ..."

I was pacing now. I could think better doing this.

"Or what? Tell me what you are thinking. Don't hold out on me."

"Not holding out. Thinking. If you want to hide, you work for some organization that specializes in what you do best. If what you do best are clandestine investigations, then you're not listed as an employee. You don't exist. What better way to do clandestine research than to do it without anyone knowing you exist."

"Except the company who employees you."

"Except them."

"So, you think that Mr. Smooth Voice Wonderful took some risk coming to see you. He made contact with an actual person who knows him. Knows that he does exist. That would be dangerous for a man in that kind of business. Correct?"

"Deathly."

8

I BORROWED MY FRIEND MARGIE'S TRUCK TO TAKE SAM AND Blackie to the vet. It was time for their shots and worming. Sam tolerated the dubious ordeal. Blackie was less than thrilled with it all. Neither dog enjoyed the annual ritual, but they knew they had to do it. The only fringe they got for it was riding in the truck. Something about dogs and trucks. Spiritual kinship. And the treats that the vet provided.

By the time I fed them and they settled down for their mid-afternoon nap, I was munching away on my ham and cheese on rye sandwich waiting for Rogers to enlighten me about Craven Malone Industries, Inc. It was what she did best. Well, that's not entirely true. Her research was usually flawless, but her insights were often the bits that save my life. I created her (along with Uncle Walters), but I was still amazed at her ability to process data with a human-like function. Better than human. She had an attitude, but she had no attachments, except to me. We were friends.

"They're big, love. Really."

"I knew that without research."

"I don't mean large, honey. I mean they define the term big. You know, photo of the company logo in the encyclopedia next to the word *conglomerate*. They own cheese factories, wineries, car companies, health foods, magazines, and acres upon acres of real estate. Oh, yeah, they're into chemical things as well. They have been around several decades consuming lesser entities. Old money making more and more money."

"ALL LEGAL?"

"Well, it appears so. However, I did come across some accusations on file against their media concerns. One of their magazines was sued a while back."

"What were the accusations?"

"A district attorney filed charges against the magazine named *Lusty* alleging criminal activity against children. I'm thinking child pornography."

"Specifics?"

"No, not in the documents I found. I had the feeling that this guy, the D.A., Fitzwaller McCann, was thinking these people were using children in their sleazy publication."

"Fitzwaller McCann? Is that one of your made-up names, Dearie?"

"Moí? Not this time, Lambchops. He's for real. Well, he was."

"Dead?"

"Retired, most likely. I told you this occurred a while back."

"How long back?"

"1973."

Suddenly I was more than a little interested.

"Do you have more on this?"

"Only that McCann was the D.A. in Detroit at the time.

Lusty was based in Detroit even though they had a nationwide distribution back then."

"So what happened?"

"To Fitz?"

"To the charges, his potential case against them."

"Nothing that I can find. He must have dropped the charges. No follow up anywhere."

"Reason?"

"I can guess, but there are no documents anywhere to be found. I have accessed everything online and hidden in the Detroit system. I'm thinking here that the case against *Lusty* died before it got off the ground."

"And the magazine?"

"Alive and well. In fact, it has spawned three more magazines similar in nature, all appealing to the variances in human depravity. *Beasty* appeals to those of you who love animals. *Zesty* to those who like the males only. And *Busty* for those of you driven to the female of the species. Shall I go online and place an order for all four colorful magazines for your perusal?"

"You're not making any of this up, are you?"

"I am not using one bit of my creativity."

"Don't place an order just yet. Keep checking on anything else you can find regarding Craven Malone Industries as well as those glossy publications. See if there are any other law suits or just allegations against the company. Anything will likely help me at this point. In the meantime, I'm going to Detroit to see Fitzwaller McCann. Find an address for me while I pack."

9

I LANDED BEFORE TEN THE NEXT MORNING. I RENTED A BLAZER and headed north out of Detroit towards some remote lake property owned by Mr. Fitzwaller McCann. Having never been to Northern Michigan, I wanted to be prepared for any kind of setting. We detectives try hard to have contingency plans. Most of the time. Maps and GPS. And I actually prefer maps as well as driving Blazers.

It turned out that Mr. Fitzwaller McCann lived nowhere near Detroit. My keen powers of detecting uncovered this after I had driven for some four hours north on I-75 to Indian River. I took Exit 310 off of the interstate and turned right just under Lake Huron. Rogers found the address and then created a map with step by step directions through Map Quest on the internet. She added some possible excursions in case I had extra time.

I was now heading east on M-68. I passed through Afton, Tower and Onaway. At Millersburg I stopped to ask directions since I thought I was close enough so that people would know who and what I was talking about. McCann's place was supposedly on Lake Nettie.

A polite old man at a One Stop Food Mart directed me to Highway 638 out of Millersburg. He said it was about five miles to Lake Nettie, give or take. It turned out to be give.

I followed the signs to Lake Nettie and then on to where I hoped that Miss Roger's diligence and precision would take me. It was close to 4:30 when I found the place. I had been thinking sub-division when I should have been thinking estate. The Fitzwaller McCann home was more like a lodge than a single family dwelling. It was situated, as the internet had pointed out, on Lake Nettie as well as the Ocqueoc River with its own private Lake Ann. Nearly surrounded by woods, it was remote and larger than life. Likely cost was somewhere above the price of my apartment. And my car. Together.

I checked the rearview mirror to see if there were any remnants of cheese crackers in my teeth. My auburn-red hair looked as good as it was going to look. I was wearing my tweed sport coat with an unusual burgundy stripe running occasionally in it, khaki pants, and cordovan loafers. Casual business. There was no gun to hide under my jacket because of flying into Detroit. I expected no trouble from Fitzwaller McCann requiring the use of a weapon. I was armed with my brain and ever-present charm. Yikes.

I rang the door chimes and waited in front of the beveled cut glass door. I expected the butler to escort me inside once he arrived. An attractive, elderly lady opened the door. She was wearing white slacks and a short-sleeved flowered top. Her hair was short and unnaturally brown.

"May I help you?" she said.

"I'm Clancy Evans. I would like to speak with Mr. Fitzwaller McCann."

"Come in."

I stepped into the foyer under the skylight. I followed the

graceful woman. We passed under one of those candlelight chandeliers heading towards a mammoth great room that overlooked the lake. It wasn't the grand cathedral ceiling or the multiple sky lights that caught my attention. Rather, it was the massive floor to ceiling stone fireplace. Think ski lodge for a hundred guests somewhere in Colorado. I was offered the large leather chair by the beautiful yet mammoth stone hearth.

"Fitz is down on the dock tinkering with the boat. He loves his boats and divides his time between tinkering and fishing. Mostly he tinkers. He's no mechanic, but he loves to play around with those things. It's like he has completely forgotten that he was a – or, forgive me. I rattle on sometimes. May I ask your business with my husband?"

"I want to talk with him about an investigation he was conducting in the early seventies."

"Oh, my. That would be some years back. We retired in 1973. He was the District Attorney for the metropolitan area of Detroit, you know. That was more than thirty years ago, my dear."

Judging ages has never been one of my fortes, but this lady had to be in her early seventies if she were a day. Her face showed some signs of aging, but only slightly. She was obviously upper crust by the way she carried herself and had handled me so far.

"You retired young," I said.

She smiled pleasantly.

"Yes, we did. May I offer you something to drink?"

"That would be good."

I waited for a list of items from which to choose. It never came. The awkward silence left me thinking that something was missing here.

"Do you have any Scotch and soda?" I said.

She walked to the bar and began working on my drink.

"On the rocks?" she finally said.

"Yes, please."

She returned with my drink. She sat down. I was drinking alone. This was usual for me. I sipped and waited.

"My name is Clancy," I said again hoping that she would offer me hers.

"Charming name," she said with that high society air. I was about to hate her when she broke my train of resolute anger. "I'm Ann. Ann McCann. Where are you from Clancy?"

"Norfolk, Virginia."

"That's a long way to come to talk with my husband."

"I'm investigating a murder that goes back more than three decades. I try to follow all clues."

"You're a policeman – woman?"

"Private investigator."

"Oh, how interesting. You don't look to be that old. I don't think I know any women who are private detectives. Do you like your work?" her voice was too pleasant.

She may have been upper crust, but she was not overly bright. I needed to move on to Fitzwaller McCann.

"Sometimes," I said and finished my Scotch. "May I walk down to the lake and talk with your husband?"

"Yes, that would be fine. No, wait. I'll take you. It's such a lovely day. I need to be outside anyway. I haven't been out all day. Come this way."

I followed her down some stairs to another extravagant level of the home and then out into a sun room that maybe had been a deck once upon a time. We passed through the sun room quickly, out onto a real deck and then down another set of steps to a lovely flower garden on both sides of the walkway. The step-stone pathway led to the boat dock on the lake.

Her husband was tinkering with an 80-foot cabin cruiser.

Being the astute detective, I was beginning to sense that this place reeked of money.

"Captain, permission to come aboard?" she said losing her socialite voice and asking like a commoner. I thought that this was her attempt at humor until Fitz answered her.

"Permission granted," came this stern, authoritarian voice.

I began thinking Twilight Zone immediately.

I followed her as she maneuvered her slightly aging body deftly into the boat. She was a young seventy something for sure.

"This is Clancy—I'm sorry, what did you say your last name was again?"

"Evans."

"Yes. Miss Evans has come to talk with you about an old case."

I think I expected Captain Ahab to turn and greet us, judging from the voice he had used with her, and the stuff I had read about district attorneys. Instead, a small, wiry man a good two inches shorter than I stood up and almost smiled at me. He was less than daunting.

"What case?" he said flatly. He obviously was a busy man and had no time for such trivial matters as I might carry with me.

"I think I will go back to the house, Captain. You two can talk about this without my help. Permission to go ashore, Captain?"

"Permission granted," he waved his hand in the direction of the shore and house.

I watched her leave.

"What do you want to know?" the Captain said to me.

"What happened to the case you were developing against *Lusty* magazine?"

Being the ever observant private eye, I noticed a slight

flinch at the mention of the magazine. It was as if I had shot a blow dart into his side and he grimaced slightly from the slight pain.

"Don't remember it."

"Early seventies. You were investigating *Lusty* magazine for crimes against children."

"You must have me confused with someone else."

"Could be, but the case log of the Detroit court system has your name on a file that was pending in 1972."

"What if it did? I had thousands of cases back then. That was quite a few decades ago. You expect me to remember each one of them?"

"You dropped this one."

"I dropped lots of them."

Short and abrupt.

He sat down in a deck chair and stared out into the large lake. Since he didn't offer, I sat in the other deck chair nearby.

"This was likely one of your last cases. You retired shortly after this. I would think that you might recall something about it."

"What if I do? What is this to you?" He stared at me as if sizing me up. "You were a little girl back then. What does all this have to do with you?"

"My father was killed around that same time. He was the county sheriff and we had uncovered a child pornography ring in our rural community. He was murdered in our driveway just after this ring was discovered and closed down. I was wondering if there might be a connection between your case and his death."

"What possible connection? Was he killed in Michigan?"

"Virginia."

"So where's the connection?"

"The connection could be Craven Malone Industries."

He stopped staring at the lake water and moved his head slowly to look into my eyes. I saw fear for the first time in the Captain's face.

10

We were sitting in the kitchen area at the massive oak table surrounded by custom made oak cabinets. Mrs. McCann had stopped being the socialite and was now working over her Jenn-Air oven fixing our dinner. The Captain had invited me to stay for a meal.

"How long have you been a detective?" McCann said.

"All of my life."

"Professionally?"

"Long enough to know that you found something back in '71."

"I was bought out. Not proud of it, but I did it. I accepted it. I can't tell you much. These are dangerous people. They have more money than God. They get what they want. Everyone has a price, you know."

"I'm not here to judge you. I just want to know what you can tell me."

"Here we go," Mrs. McCann brought us our steaks. "Let's not talk business while we eat, shall we?"

"Aye, aye, Captain," McCann said to his wife. "She's the Captain in here. My only domain is the boat on the water."

Either the food was delicious or I was simply hungry. We all enjoyed our food as they extolled the virtues of the house and living in this remote part of the world. I listened and ate. They never asked me anything about myself.

We retired to the upper porch overlooking the water. McCann opened one of the sliding glass windows and lit a cigar.

"You don't mind?" he said after taking a long drag.

"Be my guest."

"Some things I can't tell you, you know. I could get into serious trouble."

"Did you have any evidence for a case?"

"Not by my standards, but I must have aroused the sleeping monster and the powers that be thought I had enough. They sent a lawyer who offered me an insane amount of money to stop my investigation."

"Good old fashioned bribery?"

"Thought you weren't here to judge me?"

"Just naming the game."

"Actually the way they did it, it wasn't a bribe. At least not up front. Backdoor kind of bribe. Made me an offer I couldn't refuse."

"Did your investigation go beyond the magazine to the parent company?"

"Funny you should ask. Not really. I was still collecting data on *Lusty* when I was suddenly, out of the blue, contacted by Craven Malone Industries. That's how we got around the bribery charges."

"Good for you."

He puffed on his large Churchill and seemed to ignore my response.

"Was *Lusty* using children illegally?" I said.

"I couldn't prove anything directly. They were certainly

buying photographs of children, but then they would doctor the photos according to their fetishes."

"Where were the photos coming from?"

"All over. They had suppliers in several states."

"Virginia?"

"I better not answer that. Too close to home, you know. Tell you what, Miss Detective. I like you and would like to help, but I have to protect my interests here."

"You retired well."

"You don't know the half of it. I hit the mother load."

"You hit something."

"Look, you already suspect Craven Malone Industries of some connection. You're looking for proof. I can't give you that. I won't give it to you. But here's what I will do. I'll take Ann and go back down to the boat. We always take a ride in the evening. We love the lake around dusty dark. Great time to be on the water. While we're gone, make yourself at home. My office is upstairs. Turn right, third door on the left. If you're a real detective, Missy, you'll discover what you need in there."

I was stunned. Maybe Fitzwaller McCann had a conscience after all, or I had made him feel guilty.

11

The Fitzwaller study was larger than my entire apartment. The walls were lined with oak except for the one wall full of floor to ceiling windows on the lake side of the house. His solid oak desk was bigger than my living room. It was full of dark leather furniture – a couch under two oversized paintings of Labradors and ducks, and two highback leather chairs in front of the massive desk. Hunting pictures hung from every wall except for the wall behind the desk and the wall full of windows looking out on the lake. The desk wall supported a handsome painting of the 80 foot cabin cruiser sailing the low seas of Lake Nettie, or at least that's what some of the caption said at the bottom of the frame.

The view of the lake was magnificent. I appreciated the view of the dock, the boat, and the McCanns as they readied the boat to debark on their nightly excursion of Lake Nettie.

Being the master detective I had become after nearly fifteen years of experience, I was desperately searching Fitz's desk for a key to the locked, oaken file that rested perfectly under somebody's famous painting of a fox hunt. There was no key in the middle desk drawer, but he did have a good looking .357 Smith & Wesson resting calmly near the paper clips, rubber bands, and a box of pencils. Office with an attitude.

The right-hand top drawer revealed a partially imbibed bottle of Jim Bean, two boxes of cartridges for the .357, and a box of 12 gauge shotgun shells all camouflaged by two or three hunting magazines. No glass in sight for the Bean, and no key to the file cabinet to be found.

Exasperation set in when I found no key after going through all of his desk drawers. I ran my hand around the leg hole of the desk looking for a hook or small nail that might allow the key to hang innocently out of sight from the probing eye. I discovered a button on the left-hand side and pushed it. The clicking sound coming from the file cabinet caused me to smile. Move over Sherlock Holmes.

Fitzwaller was logical in his filing methods. Everything was in alphabetical order. I opened the file named *Lusty*. I was speed reading some of the pages when I heard the voices coming from outside.

I eased toward the windows and saw two oversized men in dark suits talking with Fitz and Ann from the dock. The Captain and his First Mate were in the boat. The two suits were on the dock looking suspiciously out of place. I watched as the suits climbed aboard. Captain Fitzwaller slowly backed out from the docking area and gently maneuvered the large beauty towards the setting sun.

I went back to the file. It was too thick to sit and read it all. That meant I would have to take the whole file and read it on the flight to Norfolk.

I was closing the file cabinet when I heard the four distinct gun shots coming from the direction of the water. I returned to the windows. I waited and watched from behind the curtain on the right. The boat returned slowly to the docking area and backed in.

The two suits jumped onto the dock. No lines were out to moor her. They both pushed the craft away from the dock. They watched the boat begin to slowly drift away. There was no sign of Fitz or Ann.

I could see now that both suits were wearing gloves. Not a good sign, as if anything else I had seen connected with those two was good.

By the time I had decided to run for my Blazer it was too late. A noise from downstairs informed me that I was not alone in the house. There were more than two.

I suddenly felt naked without my .38, but I remembered Fitz's handgun in the middle drawer. I checked the gun and was glad Fitz had kept it fully loaded. I opened the other drawer and put handfuls of cartridges in both pockets of my jacket. The box of shotgun shells caught my eye again. Where would Fitz keep his shotgun?

I checked the dock again. The suits were walking slowly towards the house.

I opened the accordion doors of the closet. Resting comfortably in the corner, nearly out of sight, was a Remington semi-automatic shotgun. Fitz kept it loaded as well. Prepared hunter.

I had to assume that the suits knew I was here. Maybe they had just happened to show up and exterminate Fitz and Ann, and maybe there really is a cow somewhere that jumped over the moon. In my work, a coincidence is a clue. And not a coincidence.

I decided to allow the killers to come to me. They probably knew I was there, but they wouldn't know I was armed to the teeth. At least not until I was forced to shoot someone.

There was sufficient room for me to hide in Fitz's larger-than-necessary closet. I grabbed the large file off of his desk and closed the accordion doors behind me. I had a limited view out of the horizontal cross slats in the door. I would be able to see only the lower half of person's body when they entered the office. After a few seconds of this hide-and-seek spot, I had this brilliant flash of intellect informing me of the inferiority of my hiding place. I would be forced to come out blasting with my .357 and hope for some approximate accuracy on my part. I didn't have enough space to maneuver the Remington into a shooting position because of the closet depth. I decided to vacate.

Instead of closing the accordion doors completely behind me, I left them partially closed. It was a measure of deceit I used often with success while playing hide-and-seek with my brother Scott back in Clancyville, Virginia. It forces people to look in the spot behind an almost closed door. It always fooled Scott anyway.

Fitzwaller McCann had his own private bathroom off of his office. Another large room. This house had no small rooms. Sink, commode, shower and linen closet formed the nucleus of the room. The shower had a sliding door made of non-see through glass, but you could see shapes behind it. Bad place to hide. The linen closet was actually small by this house's standards. I could have doubled up my body and hidden in the bottom section, but would have been able to only shoot myself if someone found me in that position. My final option for this room was a chair and small table by the window at the far end of the bathroom. I could wait there for the door to open with my shotgun in position and my .357 handgun close by. I laid the file on the table and looked out of the window at the peaceful lake and waited for the suits to come find me.

12

FEAR IS OFTENTIMES THE BETTER PART OF VALOR. I KNEW THAT the odds were with me for taking down the first suit who walked into my stronghold. The second and third gentleman would be more of a challenge for my pistolero skills.

I loosened the belt of my slacks and shoved the file about halfway down the front. After tightening my belt so I wouldn't lose either slacks or file, I forced my supple body to climb out of the window onto the roof just above the porch where Fitz had enjoyed his cigar while confessing his weak ways earlier that day. The sun was halfway down on the horizon now and the shadows would be a great help for my planned rooftop escape. Getting down from the roof was another matter.

I decided against climbing down to the porch roof and leaving myself in an open view from the windows of the study. Even in the twilight, a person could be seen and shot. Nasty way to die.

Instead, I climbed around the gable that was formed at my bathroom escape window. I sat down in the shadows by the gable and waited for something to happen. I did remember to close the window behind me like a good girl. I really didn't want to leave these guys clues about my awkward position.

I heard some non-distinct voices that were likely coming from the office. The squeaking of the accordion doors behind Fitz's desk informed me that they had fallen for my first location deceit. Someone kicked in the door to the bathroom, cursed mildly, then must have left to join the other suit back in the office. I heard the word "downstairs," so I waited a minute or so to be sure that they were not setting a trap for me.

I watched Fitz's cabin cruiser drift out of sight. Despite his selling out back in seventies, I felt sorry for both of them. That was a tough way to die. He probably deserved jail time, but not a bullet in the brain, or wherever it was that the suits nailed him.

I heard the sound of footsteps in the garden below me. One of the suits was outside, probably searching the roof. It was dark enough now that I felt secure in my spot by the gable in the shadows. A light from the downstairs living area permitted me to see the man walking around below me looking up at the roof.

The other suit must have been searching the rest of the house.

The one below me walked briskly towards the house. I heard the door slam. It was time to re-enter the bathroom and take my chances inside.

I stepped on the chair next to the table and it slid on the tile floor making a scraping sound. I paused in mid-entry and aimed the shotgun at the door to the office. The room was dark now, but my eyes had dilated sufficiently to allow me to see fairly well. The door opened and a shape entered.

I fired one round of the shotgun and the body went

crashing backward into the door and onto the floor of Fitz's office. One down. Now the game was afoot.

I waited briefly for another movement or sound. There were still two of them, at least. Idiots travel in threes a lot.

Nothing happened. I crawled back out the window, this time with the notion of actually leaving the gable shadows and climbing down to the ground. I decided that the front of the house was closer to the ground in case I had to jump.

I eased along the roof towards the crest. I could hear voices that sounded as if they were coming from the bathroom. I had forgotten to close the window this time. I mounted the crest in a crouching position just in case one of the suits was bright enough to suspect I might try to escape on the front side. Idiots have varying degrees of stupidity.

Easing down to one of the front gables, I rested a moment and listened for sounds. I could see fairly well in the dark. There was some type of dark sedan in the circular drive behind my Blazer. I was breathing regularly again. I put another shell in my Remington. I wanted it fully loaded.

After several minutes, one of the remaining suits walked out to the car, opened the trunk, took out a gas can, and returned to the front of the house. I doubted that these guys had planned this, but they could have been following orders.

It must have been five to ten minutes before I smelled smoke and saw firelight on the backside of the house. This was my clue to move from my lofty perch.

Ann McCann had flowers growing around the front of the house as well as the lovely garden in back. She had installed latticework for some variety of climbing roses. Fortunately for me, the latticework extended all the way to the roofline. I just hoped that the lattice would be strong enough to hold my one hundred and forty pounds of supple muscle and sinew.

I was on the ground in a matter of seconds. Light as a

feather.

I could see the fire on the inside of the house. I ran towards my Blazer in a circular fashion, hiding behind bushes and trees en route to the parked vehicle. Fifty feet from the car, the other two suits came out of the front door and stood looking back at the house. They were no doubt proud of their pyrotechnical work.

I stopped first at their vehicle, hoping that their carelessness extended to parking the car and leaving the keys in the ignition. Bingo. The keys were dangling from the steering column. When you stop off at someone's house in the middle of the wilderness intending to kill them, you don't think about someone stealing your car. I took the keys as a souvenir of our adventure together. As an added measure, I took my trusty penknife and punctured the tires on my side of the car. Prankster.

I was pulling away in the Blazer before the two fire-watchers reacted to my sounds. When I emerged from Fitz's quarter-mile long driveway, I decided to return to Detroit via another route. I had to figure that the suits had followed me to Fitzwaller McCann's estate, and that they would assume enough about a woman to suspect that she would return by the same route she had come. I turned right and headed east.

The missing car keys and the slit tires would only slow them down. At least I had several minutes head start, and that would be enough for me to escape to Virginia. I decided to hold onto the Remington and the .357 until I was closer to Detroit and felt safe disposing of them.

My other route for leaving Lake Nettie was through the countryside of Northern Michigan along Quinn Creek Highway to 451. I then followed 32 & 65 to fair town of Alpena. It was nearly ten o'clock when US Highway 23 merged with I-75 and I was on my way to Detroit.

13

By the time I had finished reading the notes that Fitzwaller McCann had on *Lusty*, I had learned that while Craven Malone Industries may have owned the magazine, they seemed to have no say on decisions made. The board of directors was composed of seven people. Only one of that group had any likely connection to Craven Malone. The head of *Lusty* was Joey Malone, President. There had to be some connection there. The editor of the magazine was a woman by the name of B.A. Dilworth. Great acronym for the editor of a sleazy publication. Rogers would enjoy chasing down that name.

I came across several allegations that were made to Fitz, but nothing had been verified. It made me wonder why he had placed the case on the docket without having more information against the magazine. Perhaps he had been bluffing. Dangerous game to play with that side of the world.

I found notes from several detectives he had hired to work the case who had been chasing leads. It appeared that he had lots of folks working on this one. Still, I saw nothing in my first reading of the file that provided any direct clue to how *Lusty* was connected with my father's killing. Only the Malone name provided some relationship.

Something didn't feel right about all of the mess I had just narrowly escaped. My plane was circling Dulles to land and I was still rethinking the events in Northern Michigan. I was more interested in knowing why they had happened rather than what had happened.

After being an investigator for several years, I was more than used to the what of the stuff that happened to me during the course of an investigation. The clues were found in the why questions.

No one but Rogers knew that I was going to Detroit. Margie, the lady across the hall from my apartment who looked after Sam and Blackie when I left town without them, only knew that I would be away for a few days. And who on earth would Margie tell? As far as I knew, she only talked to me. She lived alone, no one ever visited her, and she said very little even when she did talk. The perfect neighbor.

Someone found out. All roads led me back to my recently reacquainted childhood friend, Rosey. He had given me the clue about Craven Malone Industries. Indirectly, of course. He had certainly found out more about me than I knew about him. He was the one link as to why those pseudo-Mafia types found me in the northern wilderness of Michigan visiting with Fitzwaller and Ann.

I changed my flight to land in Dulles. Roosevelt Washington worked for some cryptic company named Washington Consulting owned by the law firm Fielder, Young, Lawson, & Associates. I had no address, but I was a detective. I had some business cards made up to prove it. Given enough time, I can find a business like Washington Consulting. What I couldn't find were those business cards.

Fielder, Young, Lawson, & Associates were located on the fourth floor of a tall building on the corner of C Street and

20th Street. From their location, go south one block and you find the Department of State. Go north a block, and you discover the Department of Interior. The world of government.

I entered the reception area of FYL & others. An attractive blonde answering the phones and appearing to be extremely busy acknowledged me. The phone book at Dulles informed me that there was no listing for Washington Consulting. Being the deft detective I was, I concluded that either it didn't exist, or it was an in-house group working solely at the discretion of FYL & Associates.

"Roosevelt Washington, please," I said in my nicest voice.

"Fifth floor," she said as she answered yet another phone call.

I was hot on the trail for sure. Back on the elevator and up one flight, I exited once more and found a similar area for receiving clients. And people like me as well. The reception area was worked by an attractive African-American brunette this time. She was not answering phones. She was reading a Washington magazine and didn't look up when I approached the desk.

"Excuse me. I would like to see Roosevelt Washington," I said. Nice voice again.

"Appointment?" she asked without moving her eyes from the page to me.

"No."

"He's not in."

"He'll see me," I countered.

"Not if he's not in."

"Okay, let's start over. I have an appointment."

She put down the magazine and finally looked at me. She was attractive, but she possessed this glossy stare which gave all intentions that her body was there while her mind was elsewhere.

"You said you didn't have an appointment."

"I changed my mind. I have an appointment."

"What's the name?" she said as she reached for a large, opened calendar-type book resting next to the phone. I could see that there were no names written on the pages in front of her.

"Barbara Bush," I said hoping to elicit some type of reaction from the beautiful zombie like creature in front of me.

"Don't see it, Barbara. You must be mistaken."

"Which office is his? I'll leave him a note."

"Leave the note with me. I'll see that he gets it."

"It's personal."

She opened a drawer to her right and found a small envelope.

"Here," she said as she handed me the envelope, "put your note in this and seal it. I don't read his personal stuff."

I took a piece of blank paper from her desk and wrote down my phone number at the hotel where I was staying. I sealed it in the envelope and wrote *Rosey* on the envelope so he would know it was me.

"I'll give this to him as soon as he comes in, Miss Bush."

"You do that," I paused as my eyes fell on her nameplate for the first time during our enlightened conversation, "... uh... Estelle Stevens. You've been a great help."

"It's my job," she said proudly, as if she thought she had actually helped me.

There was a message at the desk by the time I walked to my hotel several blocks away. The number was not the same as the one on the card Rosey had given me. I called the number once I was in my room.

"Washington Consulting, may I help you?" said a familiar voice on the other end.

"Roosevelt Washington, please."

"May I tell him who's calling?"

"Barbara Bush."

"Oh, hi Barbara. I'll put you right through."

Old friends.

"Who the hell is Barbara Bush?" Rosey's voice came on.

"An alias. You don't think I would tell Estelle who I really am, do you?"

"Be kind. She's in training."

"For what?"

"Hey, she's new. Second week. Give her some slack. You didn't get in, did you?"

"Didn't really try. Wanted to be nice since I was on your turf."

"Thanks. What's going down?"

"Lunch. Name your poison and I'll be there. Needs to be public."

"The China Joy. On M Street, between 18th and 19th. 12:15."

The cab left me in front of China Joy at 12:05. Nothing quite as exhilarating as a cab ride through the streets of Washington. You never need to tell the cabs that you are in a hurry. They assume.

"I'm waiting for someone," I told the hostess after she smiled at me.

"He's in the back on the left."

Rosey stood up as I approached the table.

"Regular here?"

"Weekly. Weakness for Chinese-American cuisine."

I sat.

"Use aliases often?" he said.

"Only for people like Estelle."

"People like Estelle?"

"Humorless ones."

"Did you provide her with some humor?"

"She never flinched. Absolutely humorless. I couldn't help her."

"I don't like a lot of laughter in the office."

"You have nothing to fear from Estelle."

"You have a problem."

"Let's eat something and then I'll tell you my problem."

It was a large buffet with just about everything imaginable on it. My breakfast had been light, so I was hungry. Rosey recommended the shrimp dishes, so I loaded up with rice, several shrimp dishes and some egg rolls for assistance.

After several minutes of satisfying what I had thought was raving hunger, I eased into a conversation.

"You set me up."

"Pardon?" he said after he swallowed a shot of his hot tea.

"You were the only one who could have possibly known I was going to Detroit. I don't know how you knew, but I have some ideas."

"What on earth are you talking about?"

He sounded genuine.

"Three goons from somebody's meat market came after Fitzwaller McCann and his wife while I was visiting with them. Then they came after me."

"Who is Fitzwaller McCann?"

"You have no idea?"

"Not a clue."

"Didn't you give me the name of Craven Malone Industries?"

"Not likely."

I suddenly remembered our conversation that night sitting in his BMW in front of the large corporation.

"So we just happened to drive by Craven Malone Industries and just happened to park in front of the building."

"If you say so. I don't recall."

"Did you have me tailed to Detroit?"

"Not likely."

"Is it possible to get a straight answer from you?"

"Depends upon the question."

"Did you know I was going to Detroit?"

"Yes."

"How?"

"Internal memo."

"But you didn't have me followed?"

"No."

"But I was followed, correct?"

"Yes, ma'am."

"How did you know I was followed?"

"I followed the followers."

14

It turned out that Rosey had spotted someone tailing him the night we had dined in downtown Norfolk. They had followed us from Craven Malone Industries. They must have spotted us while we were parked near the building and tailed us back into Norfolk. Some of them stayed on me while some others followed Rosey back to Washington.

I was sitting on the bed in my hotel room and Rosey was sitting backwards in the chair near the television. He was looking directly at me.

"You knew I was in Fitz's mansion and you did nothing to help me?"

"I was hiding in the shadows. Knight the Obscure."

"More like Knight Errant. Those thugs could have gotten lucky and killed me."

"Possible, but not likely. You came out of that burning house unscathed."

"You saw it all?"

"All."

"I suppose that if I had been in more imminent peril, you would have come to my rescue."

"Something like that."

"Who were they?"

"No identification on them."

My eyes met his. Now I knew why I had failed to see them following me to Detroit during my daring escape. All of that needless apprehension.

"And I thought it was my destruction of their car that kept them off of my trail."

"That and my 9mm."

I left that one alone. The less I knew, the better in the long run.

"You have any guesses as to who they worked for?"

"Malone-people would be my guess. I'll find out. Let you know."

"They saw us together, they know we talked, and then they followed me to Detroit. They must suspect we're on to something. Just wish I knew what it was that they think we know."

"Let me clear up one thing."

"What's that?"

"This 'we' stuff."

"Together again."

"I work solo."

"Except when you're watching my backside."

"Won't happen all the time."

"Just enough to save my skin now and then is good. And it is your fault that I got into this mess. You came to me, Knight the Obscure."

"Thought you'd be interested."

"Good thinking. I should have known it wouldn't be a walk in the park. Someone gunned down my father a long time ago. If the players are still around, they'll gun me down too."

"Every chance they get."

"I have wondered all these years, though."

"What's that?"

"Why would someone kill my father? I knew as much as he knew about that pornography ring in Clancyville. They were just some small time players making lots of money. We knew nothing about their connections."

"You stopped them."

"Yes, we did do that. Good for the community, you know. They murdered two little boys. That was bad stuff. Your uncle was accused. I had to do something to keep him from going to prison."

"You missed my point."

"Which is?"

"You stopped them from making money. You cost them. You hurt the people they supplied. You ended one of their markets. Small, yes. But, nevertheless, important for their sleazy publication. You and your daddy were messing around where you should not have been messing. You hurt the supply and demand side of business. Sometimes that be fatal."

"Grudge killing?"

"Take out the small town county sheriff because he got in the way of the business venture. Send a message. It happens. Your daddy was a good lawman, but maybe too smart for his own good."

"But I knew what he knew. Everything. My mother would croak if she knew that, even now. Daddy and I talked about the whole sordid mess. Why didn't they try to kill me, too?"

"You were eleven years old. No way could they know that you knew anything about this. You were a little girl. You were not credited with finding the culprits, correct?"

"Daddy made sure my name stayed out of the paper."

"So they figured that if they killed the county sheriff, then the score would be as even as they could get it."

"Have they bugged my apartment?"

"Don't know. Better check."

I picked up my cell phone and called Rogers. She had a separate line from my regular phone. In her long life of espionage, I was the only one who ever called her.

"Dearie. So good to hear from you. How's Washington?"

"City or person?"

"You alone?"

"No."

"Start with city."

"DC is great. Love this place. Someday I may come here for a vacation."

"This is why you called me on my private line?"

"Turn on your surveillance program and activate your system throughout the house. I need to know if we have been bugged."

"Release the hounds!"

"Call me on my cell if you find anything."

"Got it. Give my love to Rosey."

"Unlikely."

I clicked off the phone. I tossed the phone on the bed beside me.

"I thought you lived alone, except for the dogs. They don't answer the phone do they?"

"Not yet. They talk on the phone, but they can't manage to answer with any sort of dignity."

"So, you were talking with whom?"

"With *whom*?"

"Oxford, remember?"

"Sure. Across-the-hall neighbor comes over and takes care of the canines," I lied.

"You're a trusting soul."

"Long time friends."

15

Mr. Obscure was gone by the time Rogers called me back. She found nothing. I felt more at ease. I called Rosey on his private line.

"This bugged?"

"Not likely."

"Sure."

"Few things in life be sure, Miss Detective."

"May I speak freely?"

"Go ahead. I'll stop you if you cross my line."

"Your line?"

"Self-imposed."

"No bugs in Norfolk," I said. I was learning to speak cryptically.

"Good."

"So, they're working on hunches."

"Logical."

"But why me? Do you think they know who I am?"

"Can't say."

"Wait a minute. They know you! You did some work for them. They were following you and you led them to me."

"Two and two."

"Stay tuned. I have an idea. I'm going home. I'll call you in a few days."

"Can't wait."

I was delighted that I had misled him. I couldn't stop thinking that his line was bugged and that anything I might say would help them. I was going home, but not Norfolk. It had been years since I referred to Clancyville as home. But it was still home.

I was on the earliest flight I could get out of Washington the next morning. I landed in Richmond around noon. After an almost edible meal at the airport, I rented a low-budget Chevy and headed towards Clancyville to see my mother. The three-hour plus trip was over too soon. I missed my car which was still in surgery.

The house and surroundings where my mother lived had changed little since the days I called the old two-story place my home. I suppose in many ways it is still home, will always be home. The drive on the right side of the house was still unpaved. Great place for making mud pies when you're five or so. The house looked good to be nearly one hundred years old. My grandfather Clancy built the house and Mama became sole owner of it when her brother, Uncle Samuel Walters Clancy, sold her his half of the inheritance for fifteen dollars. Like the purchase of Alaska, it was slightly undervalued at the time of the sale.

Rachel Jo Clancy Evans was sitting on the porch in a rocker counting the cars passing her home on Washington Street. She was an elegant looking sixty-five year old. Despite her elegant appearance, I could detect the pain embedded in her eyes from being a widow the last several decades. She still missed my father, Bill Evans. Some things you never get over.

"You could have called and told me you were coming," she said with a hint of spitefulness.

"Last minute change of plans," I feebly offered. I have been bantering with my mother for all of my life. I still feel like I am on the downside of any conversation and losing rapidly. It has always been like a game to her. She had to win.

"No phones in Norfolk."

"Didn't want anyone listening on my line to know I was headed this way."

I wasn't used to telling her the out and out truth about my life and work, but this time I thought it might work.

"Someone following you?"

"Maybe."

"I thought you were a good detective." This time her voice was full of sweet sarcasm. She hated the fact that I had gone into what she called police work. Even though she missed my father dearly, she hated the fact that he had been the County Sheriff and that he was killed because of his work.

"Sometimes the bad guys are good, too."

"Did you lose them?" She stood up and motioned for me to follow her into the house.

"I hope so."

"Take your bag upstairs. Supper will be ready in fifteen minutes."

My room had not changed since the day I left for college. My mother kept everything intact, as if one day her little daughter of seventeen would come walking back into the house and life would go on as it had for the years before I left. Not that it was any picnic from the time my father was killed. Life changed. Death forces the survivors to adapt to new circumstances. Rachel and I had a hard time adapting to life without Bill Evans. We became benevolent adversaries.

I sat on the bed and allowed some old memories to come floating back. It was always a pleasant sort of activity to do in my room. Pleasant until something would cause that painful reenactment of the day my daddy was gunned down in the driveway. The shotgun blasts would always startle me back into the present time. Rude awakenings.

"Are you coming?" the familiar voice projected up the stairs into my ears.

"Sorry. Didn't hear you call the first time."

"You're too young to be getting deaf."

"Distracted, mother. Not deaf."

"You were always easily distracted."

"Character flaw."

"Hope you don't mind a light fare for a hot August supper. Tuna fish salad, cheese, crackers, and some sweet pickles. You want tea or water?"

"Tea will be fine."

"So, have you finally come to your senses and gotten rid of those dogs?"

"No, mother. They're still freeloading off of me."

"You got that right. Freeloading. Dogs are a nuisance. Cats, too."

"I'm sure the animal world appreciates the fact that you never bothered to take care of any of their own."

"Watch your mouth. I had pets. I had a dog once. Good dog."

She sat down. She prayed and then started eating. I was sure that the Deity was obliged at her offering.

"What was his name?" I said.

"Who?"

"The dog."

"Oh, I don't remember. Long time ago. Mike, I think. Yes, it was Mike. And it was a she-dog. Called her Mike because I thought that sounded tough. Female named Mike."

"The other dogs didn't make fun of her?"

My mother never looked up. She seldom appreciated my

humor. She had little humor before Daddy died. After his removal from our lives, she was completely humorless.

"Why did you want a female dog with a tough sounding name?" I try to continue our line of talk.

"I was a tom-boy. Didn't think some sissy name like Fluffy would do. Your grandfather raised us to be tough. He wanted all boys and got mostly girls. I think he blamed our mother."

"Never knew that."

"Lots you don't know."

I smiled to myself. I hated to hear someone else say it, but it was definitely true. Maybe that was why I liked being an investigator. Always trying to raise my level of ignorance.

"Catch any of our local news in Norfolk?" she said to me after some silence.

"Not much from Clancyville gets that far east."

"This would."

"What?"

"Our preacher jumped off the deep end."

"Of what?"

"Life. Started wearing a gun around town. Dressed up like a regular cowboy. Hat. Vest. Boots and spurs. Strapped on a .45 Colt. I thought he looked good. Scared some folks."

"Well, it is odd. But I wouldn't call him crazy."

"He was. Still is, I guess. Called out the mayor into the street. Noon. Wanted a showdown. Mayor had to fire someone and Crazy Tom Barryton wanted to settle it in Old West fashion. Quickest draw. Then the mayor went out with a deputy and tried to talk Tom out of the foolishness. Tom never threatened him, just kept telling him to draw his gun."

"And?"

"Mayor didn't have a gun."

"Well, I figured that. So what happened?"

"Deputy Jones got nervous and drew his gun and shot

Tom in the shoulder. Tom was okay, but they shipped him off to Dan River for observations. Folks say now that the preacher had been under a lot of stress. Some called it mid-life crisis. I think he snapped. Crazy Tom Barryton. Another great minister to add to our collection."

"Thought you stopped going to church years ago."

"Now and then. I try to keep the town gossips from having too much to talk about."

16

My cell phone rang around 10:30 that first night back in Clancyville. Mother had long since retired for the night.

"Did I interrupt something romantic?" Rogers said.

"In Clancyville?"

"Sorry. Forgot who I was talking to and where you were."

"You're a real confidence booster. What's up?"

"Some unsightly men came around today looking for you."

"Unsightly?"

"Okay, casual looking thugs. Heavy set and wiry."

"That makes no sense at all."

"One was heavy and the other wiry."

"Oh."

"Follow me on this Dearie. I don't want to lose you."

"I'm listening."

"They sort of forced their way into the apartment. One of them got close enough to the monitor camera for me to take a really fine photo of him. The other stayed by the door out of my line of sight."

"They scare Margie?"

"You're kidding, right? Margie would back down King Kong if he looked in the window. She's fearless. Must have good genes or something. They left when they couldn't get the computer to work and they finally decided that you were not here."

"Did she tell them anything?"

"Only that you were out. Nothing about where or when you'd be back."

"And?"

"I checked the photo against the police files here in Norfolk and … bingo, one Randall Smokey Williams came up. Heavy set. He was the muscle bozo who took a look at my monitor. Mr. Wiry was the shy one by the door.

"So, who is one Randall Smokey Williams?"

"Has a full rap sheet … lots of B&E's, plenty of suspicions of this and that, some assault charges, served a little time in the early nineties … nothing too serious. Seventeen months, some of it suspended. He's a bouncer type. Likes to push people around."

"So who tells him to push people around?"

"Ah ha, that's the juicy part of this report. Perhaps even the meat of it. The files say that he works for Joey Malone."

"Who happens to reside in Detroit perchance?"

"Craven Malone's youngest."

"I guess I did rattle some cages. Anything else?"

"I saved the best, perhaps, for last."

"Icing."

"Maybe. Informative, to say the least. It seems that your new BFF Roosevelt Washington's last job was connected with *Lusty*."

"Details?"

"Apparently Joey Malone hired him to do some work of some sort."

"What kind of work could Rosey do for a magazine?"

"My question exactly. Maybe he killed off some competition."

"Keep checking."

"You bet. How's Mama?"

"Sweet as ever."

The one thing I failed to do in creating the artificial intelligence of Rogers was to give her the ability to laugh or cry. The latter I could do without, but the former would be nice when I make a joke.

I pocketed my cell phone.

"What's sweet as ever?" Mama said from the doorway of my room.

"Eavesdropping?"

"My house. You have a caller."

"A caller?"

"A tall black man is downstairs at the front door wants to see you. He said it was urgent. Since I don't know any tall black men, I made him wait outside."

17

"THERE'S A CONTRACT OUT ON YOU," ROSEY SAID. HE WAS seated in one of the rockers on the front porch. I figured we'd have more privacy outside than inside. My mother would be shocked beyond shame if we were upstairs in my room with the door closed.

"And you know this how?"

"They hired me to kill you."

He said it so nonchalantly that I had to pause as if to be sure he had not said something like, "Let's go over to Dan River and have lunch." There was absolutely no change in his voice when he delivered the line.

"How did you know I would be here?"

"I'm good at what I do, Clancy. Maybe you'll believe me someday."

I was beginning to believe that he lived inside my brain and knew my next move.

"Who hired you?"

"Can't answer that."

"You can't tell me who hired you, but you can come here

to tell me that you have been hired to kill me. That makes perfect sense."

"Confidentiality."

"But they found me because of you. I came into this whole mess because of your stupid clue! I think you set me up."

"Then why am I here telling you this?"

"I don't know."

The silence of the dark, summer night surrounded us. The katydids were making their usual racket. Some dogs were barking off somewhere in the distance. Nothing was moving on the street except for the bugs attracted by the streetlight half a block from where we were sitting. It was a perfect August evening in rural Virginia except for the revelation about Rosey being hired to kill me. Perfect and odd.

"So what are you going to do?" I said finally.

"I'm not going to kill you."

"That's a relief," I tried to allow my sarcasm to drip slightly on the moment.

"Old friends. Stronger than money."

"By the way, how much are they paying you to get rid of me?"

"Twenty."

"Going rate?"

"No. Usually falls around ten. You're worth more."

"I'm honored. At least they raised the ante on me. But all honor aside, this does not bode well for you at all."

"Me and thee. Limits my business opportunities considerably."

"Hurts your reputation."

"That, too."

"Let me see if I understand the underworld of crime and corruption. If you are given the contract to kill me, but you choose not to do it, then not only are you out twenty thousand, but they are likely to put a contract out on you."

"Likely."

"Did they pay you up front?"

"No. Usually I go half up front and the other half when it's done."

"This time?"

"All upon delivery of the body. They really want you out of the picture. They've read your press releases."

"So they set the agenda, required proof, and you agreed to do it?"

"I had no choice. If I had refused, then they would have been suspicious. They already know I know you. If I said no, they would have killed me and then sent someone else to kill you."

"Cornered."

"Like a rat."

"So how much time do you have to do something?"

"Sooner rather than later."

"Definitive. Is that calendar time?"

"They know I'm good, so they expect results within a window of two weeks, tops."

"And the clock started ticking when?"

"This morning."

"You think they followed you here?"

"They tried but I lost them in Winchester. The Jag is out of the shop and no one keeps up with the Jag."

"What's the plan?" I said.

"That's why I am here."

"To tell me the plan?"

"No. To put our minds together and come up with a plan."

18

We talked until well after midnight. Some plans are harder to continue than others. We decided upon what not to do more than what to do before we bedded down for the night. Mama put Rosey in the downstairs guest bedroom. I didn't sleep much.

Mama fixed us a country breakfast the next morning. Rosey ate like a starved convict. I nibbled at the corners, mainly sticking with a biscuit and grape jelly.

"Trouble?" Mama said after she had eaten a few bites of egg.

"What makes you ask that?" I answered.

"He shows up after ten o'clock. You two talk until way past midnight. And you look like you've been wrestling with the Devil. I ain't stupid. Something is up and I figure that you're involved in it up to your eyelids. So what kind of trouble is it?"

I told her the gist without giving too many specific details. I mentioned no names, just what was happening. Mainly I told her that there was a contract on me.

"Should have let it alone. That was a long time ago, Clancy."

"Need to know."

"Why?"

"Hard to say. I owe it to my daddy, I guess."

"You don't owe him anything. He owes us."

I looked at her without saying anything. Tension was mounting. I didn't need this now. Mama always had issues and she was never shy about releasing them in a conversation.

"Delicious breakfast, Mrs. Evans," Rosey interjected.

"Thank you. Help yourself. There are plenty of biscuits. You want some more grits?"

"No, thank you. I have eaten plenty. Don't usually eat like this. Just wanted you to know how much I appreciate it." He could sound very pleasant when he wanted to.

"It's been a long time since we've seen you around here, R.D." Mama was the only one who ever called him what he liked to be called. His mother called him Boy most of the time. His Uncle Joe called him Roosevelt. "Sorry I didn't recognize you last night. You've changed quite a bit."

He smiled and nodded at her. No response.

"So what are you two going to do? You can stay here as long as you need."

It was a civil gesture from my mother.

"They would find us. Too easy to track me through you," I said to her.

"They'll come here anyway. Looking for you. What do I tell them?"

"You won't be here. You can't stay here. They'll ask questions and then kill you. They want me badly."

Her expression never altered. She took her plate and silverware to the sink and started washing them.

"You two want more coffee?"

"No, thank you," I said.

"Yes, please," Rosey said.

She stopped washing and poured him another cup of coffee. She sat down and looked directly at me. The coffee pot was sitting on the table in front of her now.

"I have to hide?" she said.

"It would be best. I think you would be safe with Aunt Mildred. They know nothing of her and it would be harder to find you. You'd be safe there for a while."

"Clancy, I don't like it," Mama said more to herself than to me.

Aunt Mildred lived some ten miles outside of Clancyville in rural Pitt County. She moved away from the town after her husband died. She had a large farm in the Renan section of the county.

"She home now?" I asked.

"Don't know. I'll call." She put the coffee pot back on the stand and left the room.

"We hide with Aunt Mildred, too?" Rosey said.

"Not in this lifetime. Too risky for them."

"Yeah. So where do we hide?"

"Is that what you want to do?"

"No. Just testing you. I am a trained fighter. I figure you're a fighter too."

"What do you think they expect us to do?"

"Run. They're tough guys. Strong-arm types. They don't understand people who are not afraid of them."

"Oh, I'm afraid of them. But I won't le them push me around," I said.

"Same difference. Fear sometimes be a good thing."

"You afraid?"

"No," Rosey said as he smiled broadly. Then he added quickly, "I be lying."

19

Mama drove to Aunt Mildred's place in the country. We followed in the Jaguar. It was a good ten miles from town, but took twenty-five minutes to get there. Lots of back roads. I had convinced Mama to lie to her neighbors about her whereabouts. Mrs. Virginia Lee Edwards was the nosey next-door neighbor who stayed up on the comings and goings of everyone in town. In fact, she stayed current on all events of the town. Telling her was like taking out a full-page ad in The Clarion Weekly. She only had to tell Virginia Lee. Virginia Lee would make sure that everyone else in Clancyville knew that Mama had gone on a vacation to Europe. No return date was given.

"First time on a dirt road for the Jag," he said.

"You're kiddin'?"

"We be city people."

"Air is better out here."

"Air, yes. Dirt, no. I have a Jeep for stuff like this."

"Should have planned better."

"Yeah. So, we leave Mama Evans with Aunt Mildred. Then what?"

"What's wrong with your brain? Why do I have to make all the decisions?"

"Out here, you're in charge. We make it to the city, then I be in charge."

"So you trust me?"

"Until we differ. You decide something I don't like, I'll speak."

"I'm sure."

"I'm curious."

"About what?"

"That small wooden box you put in the trunk."

"Mama thought I'd need it."

"Needles and thread?"

"My daddy's handgun. Smith & Wesson 27."

"The classic N-frame revolver. Sweet gun."

"Daddy thought so, but he never used it much. Might see some action now."

"Your gun in Norfolk?"

"Yessir. All this flying has forced me to use other folk's weapons."

"What do you like?"

"My handgun is the Smith & Wesson 360. The .38 edition. Fits nicely under the arm or sometimes in the small of my back. Depends on my wardrobe."

"Your daddy's gun will be a little heavier."

"That could help with accuracy if we have a shootout."

"Could."

Mildred was over-the-top glad to see us. She insisted that we stay for lunch. Rosey and I were willing to take our time with leaving since our future was uncertain anyhow. We still had a few days. We could use the time to come up with a plan. Thus far we had only a philosophic underpinning.

Aunt Mildred had a garden twice the size of my entire apartment and raised everything from carrots to corn, to potatoes and green beans. Her appearance fit the rural scene. After so many years, no one would ever suspect that Mildred was a transplant.

Lunch was vegetables on top of vegetables. Mama fixed cornbread for an army and we forgot all about the large country breakfast of just a few hours ago. Rosey ate like he hadn't eaten in weeks.

Rosey volunteered to help Mama wash the dishes. I took Aunt Mildred outside to walk around and tell her enough of what was happening so that she would have her wits about her. I wanted her prepared for the worst-case scenario.

"Sounds dangerous, Clancy," she said.

"It is."

"Think we should stay here until we hear from you?"

"For now, that would be best. If you don't hear from me in week, then go somewhere. Go west or south. Don't come east. And certainly don't come to Norfolk."

"Your mother doesn't like to travel. What if she resists?"

"I think she'll travel this time. Besides, you're devious enough to come up with something that could motivate her."

"Thanks for the confidence, kid."

Mid-afternoon Rosey and I left the farm and headed back to Clancyville. He wanted to go by Joe's place before we headed east to Norfolk. It was my first time to see the little house since I had graduated from college. There was no change, except the principal occupant was no longer there. The personality of the small house and his very green yard were changed. It would be have been grand if Joe had come out to greet us.

"You own the place?" I said.

"Yeah. Inheritance."

"Cows?"

"You kiddin'?"

"No ancestors of Bessie Mae still around?"

"Unlikely. She died the same year Uncle Joe died," he pointed to her cowbell hanging over the archway that separated the small living room from the small kitchen. Keepsake.

He left me in the living room and went to the back of the house. I walked over to the bell and made it ring. The sound stirred some stuff I hadn't remembered for many years. I could even see Bessie Mae grazing in her fields around the place. I had milked her while Joe was in jail. I rang it again and enjoyed the sound it and the memories attached to it.

"You want it?" Rosey said, entering the kitchen carrying a large, rectangular wooden box that could have been used as a small coffin. It looked heavy for me, not for him.

"No, I think it goes with the place. If you ever sell the house, then you can offer me the bell."

He placed the box on the kitchen table. It was padlocked in three places.

"Precious stuff?"

"Can't be too careful around wild animals."

He opened the box and took out several rifles, two shotguns and boxes of ammunition. He removed a camouflaged colored vest and handed it to me. It was heavy.

"What's in this?"

"Hand grenades."

20

THE BOX WAS LIKE A PORTABLE GUN CASE. EACH GUN HAD ITS own grooved section and the box was three levels deep. He removed all of the shotguns and rifles from the first two sections.

"Pick out a shotgun and a rifle."

"This Winchester 70 with a scope looks like it was made for me. Super Shadow. Great name."

"Shoots well, too."

"Might help."

"Here, take this 12 gauge Remington," he handed me one of those Matte gray guns with synthetic stocks. I preferred the walnut grains. It was Model 1100 called the Competition Master.

"You buy these things for their names?"

He flashed a Michael Jordan grin.

"Not likely. Eight rounds in the magazine plus one in the chamber. Good for high speed shooting. Might need it to save my life."

"Or mine."

I watched him pick up each of the other guns and gently

hold them. I thought that maybe there was some silent communication between Rosey and his weapons.

He laid a Weatherby SAS Field 12 gauge shotgun on the sofa in the living room. I watched him pick up another Remington. It had a black synthetic stock. I picked it up and read the side – 7400 Weathermaster.

"I don't know much about these," I said.

"The Remington 30-06 is for any kind of big game in any kind of weather. We be prepared. The Weatherby is my baby. Sweet."

"Glad I didn't try to come between you two."

"Wouldn't let you."

"You must be expecting something like the St. Valentine's Day Massacre."

"No, ma'am. Trying to avoid something like that."

"If it's your baby, then why does it stay in a place you seldom visit?"

"I have lots of children. Some more special than others."

"So these are backups?"

"Had to leave D.C. in a hurry this time. Couldn't bring along the other kids. I have a couple of handguns in the Jag, but nothing precious like my Weatherby and the Remingtons. But…"

He moved to the box and removed another board revealing a third level compartment. This contained handguns and boxes of ammunition. Each handgun was secured to the bottom of the box by a wooden form shaped for that particular handgun. The boxes of shells were sandwiched tightly between the wooden forms for the guns.

"You make this box of goodies?"

"Woodworking 101," he smiled as if pleased with himself.

"Well, if the world comes to an end, there certainly is going to be fireworks from our team."

"Here," he handed me two 9mm handguns. "Choose the

one that suits you the best."

I had the Vector SP 1 in my right hand. It felt heavy for a small gun.

"From South Africa. I acquired it on a trip there a few years ago. Fifteen rounds, double action. Accurate weapon."

"Buy it?"

"No. Took it from the man who tried to kill me with it."

"Apparently not accurate enough."

"Accuracy lies within the shooter's prerogative."

I laid down the Vector and took the other handgun in my right hand. It was a Glock Model 34. It felt better than the Vector. Rosey handed me a magazine for the Glock.

"Nineteen rounds. Accuracy and longevity."

He took two more Glocks from his handmade cabinet. One was the Model 30. It was a .45 ACP. He informed me that it held ten in the magazine and one in the chamber. The other was a Model 33. It was a .357 and fired nine rounds.

"And your handgun of choice?" I asked.

"The 952 by Mr. Smith and Mr. Wesson. I also keep a .357 magnum on hand as a backup."

"But the 9mm is your choice."

"Hands down."

He kept out two boxes of ammo for each piece we had taken from his collection. He then safely secured each handgun we had not chosen. When he had finished putting the rifles and shotguns back into the box, he padlocked it and left the room carrying his treasure. He returned in a few moments with some camouflaged fatigues.

"Just in case we get caught out in the cold."

"Well, it seems to me that we're as ready for Armageddon as we shall ever be."

"Save one thing."

"That being?"

"A plan."

21

We were heading east in his Jag on Highway 58 quickly moving towards Norfolk. Our arsenal was neatly stored in the trunk. We were still formulating our plan.

"They want to kill me because they think I know something I really don't know."

"Yes, ma'am."

"How do we stop them from killing me?"

"Kill them first."

"There's a lot of them. I would assume that this gigantic corporation has a major-size payroll. Only two of us."

"But you have me on your side."

"I'm grateful. Two against the world."

"A lot of them will die," he said without smiling.

"We could die, too."

"Imagine we will. One day."

"I think I'd like to postpone this two-against-the-world as long as possible."

"Okay. Plan B?"

"Let's go see Big Daddy," I said.

"Craven Malone himself?"

"The same."

"Never met the man myself."

"Well, that verifies what I already knew," I said.

"Which is?"

"You work for Joey Malone."

"I never said that."

"I know. Research."

"You haven't had time to do research. You've been to Michigan, to Washington, and then to Clancyville. Now you're on the road to Norfolk with me."

"Before our second meal together," I bent the truth just a tad.

"Still a stretch, Missy. Nothing on my resume about Joey Malone or Craven Malone Industries. How'd you find this out?"

"I have a search program that runs when I'm not there."

"But you had to know something to search."

"The night after you drove me to the large edifice outside of Norfolk I began to search Malone Industries then."

I could feel that he was suspicious of my sources. No way I could divulge the abilities of Rogers. I trusted him, but not that much. Not yet anyway.

"It'll be supper time when we arrive in Tidewater. Let's gamble that Mr. Craven Malone will be home," he said finally.

"Fewer obstacles at home, I imagine."

"Fewer."

"You know the way?"

"Only know that it is in the Princess Anne Country Club section of town. Linkhorn Park. Joey likes to brag about the family. I listen."

Rosey told me that Craven Malone had two homes in Virginia Beach. One was an older mansion in the Princess Anne Country Club section of town, while the other was a beachfront cottage that looked more like a hotel than a house. He lived in Linkhorn Park and played at the beach. Money to burn.

“Shall we call him and ask for his exact location?” I said.

“No, but we can look him up in the phone book.”

We had just entered Virginia Beach from the expressway. He pulled into a gas station.

“You pump and I’ll check the book,” he said.

“I’m hungry.”

“Pump and then get us some sandwiches inside.”

He walked towards the outdoor phone booth some two hundred feet in front of the Jag while I filled up the car. I paid for the gas, two ham on rye and a couple of sodas.

Rosey was still flipping through pages in the rugged looking phone book barely attached to the shelf. I called Rogers and told her I needed the address. She gave it to me and I slid my phone into my pocket before I climbed into the car. Never trust the phone company with up-to-date vital info.

“No chips?” he said after he got back into the car.

“You buy next time.”

“I will.”

“So where is the big man?”

“2278 Bay Colony Drive.”

It was the same address that Rogers had provided.

He pulled the Jag away from the pumps into a parking place beside a trash can next to the phone booth.

“Here’s the plan,” he began. “No rifles or shotguns this time. Give me your Smith & Wesson. I’ll take my 9mm and the Glock .45.”

“I don’t understand.”

“We’ll make him think you’re my prisoner,” he said as he removed two shoulder holsters from a suitcase in the back-seat and got out of the Jag.

I got out of the car and walked around to his side.

"I don't like this plan."

"Why?"

"Because you're taking my gun and I'm vulnerable."

"Trust me."

"I don't know you. How can I trust you?"

"I drove to Clancyville to warn you," he said.

"You're smart enough to lead me right into a trap. Sell me some story about a contract, tell me that you are going to help me, then take me to your employers. I don't like it."

"Hey, this was your idea to come to the lion's den and confront Craven Malone."

"Yeah, but you're smart enough to lead me right into this scheme."

"Okay, okay. What'll it take for you to trust me in this?"

"Let me carry a gun."

"They'll search you when we enter."

"Everywhere?" I said.

"What does that mean?"

"Complete body and cavity search?"

"Well," he thought for a moment. "No, I doubt that. Just the usual places – underarms, back … and lower legs, since you're wearing slacks."

"So, I'll wear a thigh holster. You have anything in this Jag smaller than the .38?"

"No. But I don't have a thigh holster."

"You have a holster for a .38?"

"Sure, but I don't have anything small enough to attach it to your leg."

"Give me what you have," I said.

"You'll never hide a gun inside those slacks."

"I have a dress in the suitcase. Give me the holster."

He reluctantly took out his holster and leather strap. I put the .38 Smith & Wesson in the holster. I took the leather strap and put it around my right leg until it was a snug fit, then I took my knife and cut the strap. He groaned, but said nothing.

After I changed into my dress in the restroom of the gas station, we were on our way. I didn't like working in a dress, but I felt much better having a gun on my body. The dress gave me just enough room to have the gun strapped to my left thigh and not show. Stylish and dangerous.

Rosey was wearing a Navy blazer to cover his three weapons.

"Assassins don't usually bring their prey in alive," I said.

He drove to Bay Colony Drive without comment.

I couldn't imagine the other Virginia Beach playhouse of Craven Malone being larger than this one. Rosey had said that Joey bragged about the size of all their houses. Joey had three houses. Lap of luxury.

Craven's dwelling was three stories with a large balcony in the front at the third level. It had four massive columns supporting the tiny porch as well as the balcony. The driveway encircled a flower and shrub garden. Several cars were parked in front of the house. The yard on both sides of the house was filled with several sculptured flower gardens of mixed varieties. I could probably retire on what they were paying the gardener just for upkeep. There was an ivy-covered wall around the entire place.

Rosey stopped the Jag near the iron gate that permitted entrance to Malone's world. It was closed. Locked.

"Probably has an intercom or speaker phone built into that wall at the gate," he said.

"And the butler will come out and let us in?"

"Probably not. I'd guess that two armed heavy weights will come out and talk mean to us. Then they might escort us cautiously inside."

"No butler? How middle class."

"Probably has a butler. He never leaves the house."

"How many heavy weights?"

"Don't know. My guess is three to five. Remember, you're my prisoner. You might try to act frightened and upset."

"I'll whimper now and then. So, enlighten once more as to your thinking here. The plan, as it were."

"He's the big man. He has the power to stop the contract."

"And if he refuses?"

"I'll shoot you and collect my twenty thousand."

"I think it's too late for that. The heavy weights will likely shoot me."

"I'm not losing you and the twenty thousand," he said.

"How noble."

22

Rosey pushed the talk button at the gate to the entrance of Craven Malone's estate in Virginia Beach. It didn't take much for me to get into character. I was apprehensive about walking into the inner sanctum of the head of the corporation that wanted me out of the way. I stood behind the post and adjusted my thigh holster. A fast draw was simply out of the question. A sexy draw might be possible.

"Roosevelt Washington to see Mr. Malone."

"What's your business?" the voice in the intercom said.

"It's a matter that concerns Mr. Malone's son," Rosey answered.

There was a pause in the communication. Negotiations were at play.

"Take that up with Mr. Malone's son. Mr. Malone does not wish to be disturbed."

Rosey gave me a desperate look. I had nothing to offer. He was doing the talking and thinking.

"This is a life and death matter that only Mr. Malone can resolve. We have to see him tonight," Rosey said.

Another long pause.

"We?"

"Clancy Evans is with me."

Long pause.

The automated gate began to slowly slide away from the stone post. I walked ahead of Rosey as we entered the estate.

"Apparently the power of my name got us entry," I said under my breath to him as we walked up the drive to the house.

"Doubt it," he said.

A little more than halfway to the front door we were met by two heavy weights who could easily have been bouncers for some of the local clubs in Norfolk. They tried to act as tough as they looked. One of them wore sunglasses and a red sports jacket. The other one was wearing a Hawaiian shirt. Sunglasses took the lead and Hawaiian shirt followed us from the rear.

We followed Sunglasses into the library of the mansion.

"Mr. Malone will be in shortly. Sit over there," he pointed to two leather chairs in front of an elegant but small mahogany desk. He left the room. The Hawaiian shirt stood at the door with his arms crossed. Good posture.

I fought the urge to say, "Nice shirt." It would have been out of character for the current play. I hated the shirt and he probably would not have picked up my sarcasm.

"Nice shirt," Rosey said. I thought I detected a slight gleam in his eyes, but there was not trace of mischief around the mouth. It sounded complementary.

"You a wise ass?" the shirt responded.

"Not entirely. Shirt's a shirt."

"My mother gave me this shirt."

I was dumbfounded. Good thing this was Rosey conversing with this lug-head.

"Real Hawaiian?" Rosey said.

"Naw. J.C. Penney. She never shops exotic."

This guy was priceless.

There was a knock on the door and the J.C. Penney Hawaiian shirt moved over and opened the door. An old man came in walking gingerly. He was followed by Mr. Sunglasses who stopped just inside the door. I assumed the old man to be Craven Malone, astute detective that I am.

Craven used a cane, but that appeared to be more for show than a real purpose. It barely touched the floor as he moved cautiously inside the room towards his desk. He was bald except for the temples. Craven Malone was a slight man, well under the average height, I guessed maybe 5' 5" and around one hundred pounds. He sat down gently behind the desk.

"Reno, Georgio… you can go. These people pose no threat to me. Wait outside the door. If you're needed, I'll call for you."

The two heavy weights left us alone with Mr. Craven Malone.

"Now, Mr. Roosevelt Washington. What is this all about?"

"Your son hired me to kill this woman, Clancy Evans."

He turned and stared at me for several seconds. His eyes never moved from my eyes. For an aging man, he seemed extremely alert to all around him. He opened the left-hand top drawer and took out a box of cigars.

"Care to indulge?" he offered the box to Rosey.

Rosey shook his head.

"Mind if I smoke?" he asked me, not Rosey.

"If you must," I said.

"Young lady, when you reach the age of 90, there are not many things in life that you must do. Smoking, drinking, gambling, and wild parties are simply options. I have a limited number of musts. If you prefer that I not smoke in your presence, I will simply wait until you are not present.

Life is simple at my age." His voice was powerful but strangely kind. It had a note of authority about it, like he had been used to giving orders in his company for a long time. None of his words or even the tone seemed to be forced. It was natural for him to speak the way he did.

"Open a window and then light up," I said.

He smiled for the first time. Not a full smile, a kind of half-smile. He was amused at my approach.

"If you would be so kind as to open the window," he nodded at me and then to the window, "I will light up." I opened the window that was directly behind his desk and he lit his cigar.

"Joey wants you dead. What did you do to piss off my son?"

"I don't know, Mr. Malone."

"Come now, Miss Evans. A woman of your directness, your straightforward approach, your skills, surely you can come up with some reason Joey would want to have you killed."

"I was investigating an old murder case and it led me to your son's magazine. I found nothing in my investigation that directly tied the magazine to the murder. There could be some connection, but I have not found it as yet."

"So, Joey is trying to keep you from finding out something, or so you suspect."

"That would be the logical sequence here," I said.

"So you're not taking up the case that DA in Detroit was working on years ago?"

"No. I'm a private investigator. I'm trying to solve the murder of a county sheriff."

"Oh, I know what you do for a living, Miss Evans. I ran a check on you before I allowed you to enter my home. What does this old murder case have to do with you? Who cares about it?"

"I do. The sheriff killed was my father."

"Ah. I see your vigilance at work. And so you opened a box that had been closed for a few decades. Out came a monster from hell."

"Beg your pardon?" I said.

"Joey. My son, Joey. He's an idiot at times. He doesn't think. He is motivated by money. He has power, but no brains. I knew nothing of this contract. He acts, then he thinks. He listens to idiots, too. He is surrounded by idiots. I hate that damned magazine anyway. I am sorry about this. You say you have nothing on my son?"

"Nothing."

"Then I will talk with him. The contract will be dropped. You have my word."

"Why don't you sell the magazine if you hate it so much?" I said.

I caught Rosey's lightning glance at me in my peripheral vision. I never took my eyes off of Craven Malone. Craven took a long, slow draw on his cigar and then turned in his chair to blow the smoke out of the window. The aroma of the cigar in the room was pleasant.

"Brazen, but you speak you mind, don't you?"

"Father taught me to be candid."

"I would sell it, if it were up to me. You apparently know little about how large corporations are run these days. There is a Board of Directors and they make all of those decisions. I am a ninety-year old codger who they want to die yesterday. Except for the fact that I have the controlling shares, I would have been history decades back. I would like nothing better than to sell that sleazy piece of trash, sell it to my son even, get rid of the damn thing, but he doesn't have sufficient funds to buy it. Besides, he makes a lot of damned money on that sleaze. The truth is that sleazy media trash keeps him out of my hair. Usually."

Rosey stood and extended his hand across the desk to Craven Malone.

"Thank you for seeing us. I appreciate your help in this."

Craven shook his hand quickly without getting up from his desk chair.

"An assassin with scruples. You're a rarity, Mr. Washington."

Rosey nodded at him without speaking.

"I doubt if you should accept that as a complement, Mr. Washington. I can end the contract on Miss Evans. She will be safe. You sir, well, you have not only lost a client, but have gained a mortal enemy. My son will not be pleased with your work here. You will have to deal with him on your own. But you already knew that when you walked through my doors."

Rosey smiled at him. "It is what it is."

Craven Malone stood up from his desk. He nodded at Rosey. Then he extended his hand across the desk to me. I shook it. Perhaps under different circumstances I would have liked this man.

23

"Am I safe now?" I said as we left Virginia Beach heading towards Norfolk and my apartment.

"Until Craven Malone is dead."

"Joey that afraid of the old man?"

"That's the impression I get."

"Just an impression?" I lifted my dress and removed the holster from my thigh t so I could sit easier in the Jag. Lady like.

"The old man is powerful. He could cut Joey off in a heartbeat, and would if Joey did something like have you killed. One thing I do know about Craven Malone."

"Yes?"

"Man of his word. I have many sources on that one."

"Many?"

"Yes, ma'am."

"So, you think it is safe now to rejoin the land of the living?"

"I think Joey is mad as hell right now, or as soon as he hears from his daddy in this manner. The contract has been terminated as we drive to your home."

"You think he will come after you?"

"Yes."

"Because you went over his head to the old man?"

"Bingo."

"Would it do me any good to ask you what kind of job you did for Joey earlier in your career?"

"No. Privileged information."

"Even with a dubious character like Joey Malone?"

"Not his integrity on the line here."

"I can find out."

"Unlikely."

"Would it be important to me if I found out?"

"No. Goes to character, nothing else."

"Yours or his?"

"Both."

He parked the Jaguar in my parking space. It was after eight when we arrived. I knocked on the door so we wouldn't frighten Margie by entering abruptly. She hugged me when I entered. The dogs seemed pleased to have me back as well.

Margie went back to her apartment. The dogs settled down in their usual spots for the evening.

"Coffee?" I said.

"You have tea?"

"Sure. Flavor?"

"Surprise me."

I boiled some water and served him a mandarin orange flavor. I had a variety of spearmint with a hint of lemon. We drank our tea in silence. The dogs floated off to Never Land. Rosey and I sat on opposite ends of the room listening to the silence. The peace was wonderful.

I changed into some slacks to get comfortable. Dresses were never my style of clothing.

"I have more questions," I said upon entering the room.

"I bet you do."

"You don't want to hear them?"

"Not tonight."

"Then tomorrow?"

"If I am alive."

We finished our tea and sat in silence again for several minutes. The quiet was enjoyable. We had avoided a blood bath and needless deaths. Brains over brawn. Maybe we had just postponed it. We would wait and see.

"You could stay here tonight."

"Temptation?"

"Don't think so. The couch makes a nice double bed. I sleep in there," I pointed to the only bedroom in the apartment.

"You sleep alone?"

"Gentlemen don't ask ladies such questions."

"Didn't know we made that class."

"Sam sleeps in there with me. Blackie sleeps out here. Her call, not mine."

"He guards you and she guards the front door?" he said.

"Something like that. Anyway, you're welcome to stay. If you do, she'll guard both you and the door."

"I need to get back to Washington."

"I'll feel better if you would stay. Just because you trust Craven Malone, doesn't mean I trust him. I can only hope that he is as good as his word."

"He is. But I'll stay, because you asked nicely."

"And you're tired to the bone."

"That too."

24

"FOUND ANYTHING ELSE FOR ME?" I ASKED ROGERS.

"Not a smidgen, Honey."

"Now there's a word you don't hear everyday."

"My ever-growing extensive vocabulary. Comes from superior intellect."

"And great humility."

"What's that?"

"Your extensive vocab doesn't know that word?"

"Human thing, I suspect. Machine that I am, albeit a unique one, crunches numbers and spews data."

"With an attitude."

"You made me what I am."

"Complicit with Uncle Walters. You think I'm a Dr. Frankenstein?"

"Yeah, speaking of which, when are you going to fix it so I can walk around and get out of this place now and then?"

"You think I could do that?"

"You've gone further than most."

"Can't do it. Even if I had the know-how. You know too much."

"Cursed by my own brilliance. 'The sun for sorrow will not show its head.'"

"Reading again."

"New library card. He was a fascinating writer."

"Whose branch did you hack into this time?"

"Been roaming the stacks of the University of Kansas."

"But you already have access to the Ivy League's elite, plus the Library of Congress."

"Wanted to see if a mid-western education would be different."

"And?"

"They love basketball there."

"When you take a break from browsing the stacks, go back to a search of *Lusty* and its data base. Joey had two people killed in Michigan and then came after me. There has to be something here incriminating and he thinks I know it."

"Don't you think old man Craven will pass along to little Joey that you know nothing?"

"Sure. But I doubt if he believes dear old dad."

"But you were probably very sincere in your ignorance."

"With good reason. I know nothing. That's where your job comes in."

"All work and no pay."

"I was thinking of upgrading your memory."

"I have tons of available space. Why don't you build another computer? Install it next to my CPU, make it masculine, and then wire us so we can communicate with each other when you're not around. Now that would be a gift, Honey Child. Some hunk to talk with in the lonely hours of the night. And, if you would, please creative miss, shape him like that hunk of yours."

"Rosey?" I said with some surprise.

"Well, he is a looker."

"I need to talk with my dear uncle about you."

"I'm just saying. I get lonely here. Two dogs and me. Sometimes a neighbor with whom I cannot say a word."

"And this masculine machine I could build for you. Is this just communication you crave?"

"Lamb chops, we computers are a cerebral lot. Communication can be ecstasy. Lots of ways to communicate."

"I'll get back to you on that. Don't hold your breath."

"You always say that."

Her voice trailed off with a definite hint of disappointment she so often used to manipulate me. I had to admit that I treated her more like a person than a machine. It was coming from our years of association with each other. I had programmed her with the personality of a sharp-tongued female, witty, and great at sarcasm. She was more like a twin sister than an alter ego.

It was early afternoon by the time Rogers got back to me. Rosey had left much earlier that morning to return to Washington. He said something about reports to make and clients to see. Evidently the consulting business was booming.

I gave some passing thoughts to getting out my 1936 61EL given to me by Uncle Walters. I had inherited my father's Harley against my mother's desires. It was a 1957 XL Sportster. Great machine. One of my adversaries blew it up hoping to kill me in the process. A friend of mine was riding at the time. He was seriously injured but survived. The XL did not.

When I turned forty, Uncle Walters gave me a 1989 FXR Super Glide. I kept it in Clancyville. Since my mother hated motorcycles, I knew it would be safe to leave with her. I had only enough room in the city for one bike.

I decided against riding since I was still a bit gun-shy from being the target of a mad man. In my business you trust no one. Hard way to live, but you stay alive most of the time. So far so good.

"Come talk with me, Precious," Rogers said with a slight hint of alarm.

"What's happening?"

"I've been eavesdropping on the phones at *Lusty* and there have been some interesting exchanges between Nasty Joey and some man on the other end."

"And?"

"No names spoken."

"Of course not."

"But the not-so-subtle hint of impropriety was thick along the airwaves."

"You're so literary."

"I try hard. Style, lovely, style. Anyhow, Joey hired this thug to go to D.C. and … well … here, listen to the actual tape."

Rogers turned on her internal tape mechanism and played the short message for me: *"Take care of that little matter we discussed last night."*

"Not much to go on. Could be anything."

"Yeah, and it could be life threatening for Roosevelt Washington."

"You pick up anything else worth playing?"

"Not worth playing, but I did glean the fact that this man on the other end was in New York City. Joey is still in Detroit. I've been listening ever since you had your fiasco in Northern Michigan. It's the first time D.C. has been mentioned in a phone conversation."

ROGERS PLAYED the sound byte and I listened. The only thing specific was that the man Joey was hiring was in New York City.

"Could be anything."

"Nothing else said?"

"Nothing that I recognized as pertinent … something about rendezvousing with some other likely thugs in a place outside of D.C. called Sterling, Virginia. Day after tomorrow."

"Not good, Rogers."

"Why is that, my lady?"

"That's where Rosey lives.

25

I took a cab to the car rental agency. A late model Cadillac Seville was available, so I grabbed it and was on the road to D.C. in less than an hour. This time I brought my own guns.

Instead of stopping in Sterling and trying to find his condo, I drove on into Washington. Surprise him at the office.

Estelle appeared to be shuffling papers as if closing shop as I exited the elevator on her floor. She was wearing a short navy skirt and a white blouse. Her hair was pinned back today. All business.

"Remember me?" I said in my most pleasant of voices.

"Of course. You're Bonnie Bush. He's with a client. We're about to close for the day. You'll have to come back tomorrow."

Succinct.

"Barbara, Estelle."

"Barbara who?" she looked puzzled.

"Barbara Bush, the name I gave you."

"Oh. Your name. I get it. Yes. Not Bonnie. Barbara."

"Nailed it," I said.

"Well, Barbara, we're closing. Please come back tomorrow."

"Estelle, go ahead and close. I'll wait right here for him to emerge. I won't be coming back tomorrow."

She veered at me with her most intimidating scowl. I was immune to such tactics. I took a seat across from her so I could see the wall clock behind her and the hallway that led to Rosey's office.

Soon I heard voices coming down the hallway. I recognized the deep resonance of one. He presently appeared alongside of a very slim and very attractive African-American woman who was at least ten years his junior. He spotted me but said nothing until the attractive woman was on the elevator and gone.

I had a magazine in my lap pretending to be looking at the pictures in the ads.

"Business or pleasure?" he said as he walked next to my chair.

I tossed the outdated magazine back onto the table in front of me. Old ads.

"Business, unfortunately."

"I tried to tell her to come back ...," Estelle begin, but stopped suddenly when Rosey raised his left hand to her. I followed him back to his office. My first visit there.

It was too modern for me. Everything was stainless steel and glass. Everything was transparent. I like the subtleties of wood and curtains and carpet. He had none of that in this room.

"What's happening?" he said as he shut the door behind me.

"A source tells me that Joey is sending a crew to 'take care of you,'" I said and used some hand signs for the quotation marks around the phrase Joey had said exactly.

"What source?"

"My source."

"You trust him?"

"Like a blood relative."

"How many?"

"One for sure, coming out of New York City. The others, nameless and numberless, are gathering in Sterling, Virginia."

"When?"

"Day after tomorrow."

"It appears that Joey is upset with me."

"Appears."

He stood by his desk shuffling papers needlessly. I assume that he was thinking. I sat down in one of the modern, see-through chairs in front of his modern, see-through desk. Translucent.

"Who was the beauty you just walked to the elevator?"

"Client's daughter."

"Fringe benefits."

"Nothing like that. Her father told her to see me. She has a problem. She needed some advice."

"Counseling instead of consulting?"

"Some days it's the same difference."

"I'm hungry. All this talk about company coming has made me want to eat. Take me to some good eatery."

"You have business in Washington?" he said.

"No."

"Driving back tonight?"

"No."

"Where are you staying?"

"I was hoping you'd invite me to stay over. You owe me one night's free lodging anyway."

"You're invited. I have two bedrooms."

"Ah, the city."

"Really hungry?" he said.

"Really."

Estelle had already called it a day by the time we boarded the elevator. Her desk was empty of work and otherwise immaculate.

I had parked in the company's parking lot adjacent to the building.

"You drive my rental," I said. "I don't want to drive anymore in D.C., especially during this woeful five o'clock traffic. Besides, it might be a good idea if you left your car here and we took the rental back to Sterling. I don't think Joey is smart enough to consider I might be around to help you."

Rosey grunted, but said nothing. I think he was pleased when he realized the Seville was my rental. As we left the city, he drove us behind the Lincoln Memorial and took the Arlington Memorial Bridge to connect us eventually to the Washington Memorial Highway. He turned right onto Duke Street in Oldtown Alexandria. He pulled into Generous George's Positive Pizza and Pasta Place where Duke ran into Telegraph Road.

Rosey ordered an extra-large pizza with absolutely everything they had in the restaurant on it. Two pieces filled me completely. We took the rest with us.

Three hours after arriving in D.C. I was finally at a place where I could take my shoes off and put my feet up. Rosey took some unusual roads to get us to Sterling, but we arrived in about twice the time it normally should have taken. He said he was just being careful in case our out-of-town guests had arrived early and were following. Can't be too careful when folks are out to kill you.

His condo was in a nice neighborhood just off of Sully Road. It was probably twice the size of my apartment in Norfolk. Each bedroom had a private bath. The kitchen section was large enough for two people to work simultaneously. The living room was spacious and decorated in a Mediterranean theme. It was obviously two or three notches above what I had been accustomed to for the past decade or longer.

"Consulting pays nice dividends."

"It's a roof."

"We'll rest here tonight and then go to my cabin in the woods not far up the road."

"Think we were followed?"

"Slim. Unless they picked us up leaving my office and had some really sharp trackers, we lost them somewhere between Oldtown Alexandria and Sterling. Traffic may be a bitch most of the time, but it's murder to trail someone here."

I watched him put the leftover mammoth pizza slices in the fridge. He then turned on some longhair music and made himself comfortable in a recliner that matched his couch.

"Thanks for letting me bed down here," I said.

"Thanks for coming to warn me. But, this is not your fight."

"I have a stake. You got yourself into trouble because of me. You came to warn me and you stayed around to fight it out. Least I could do is return the favor."

"You got weapons?" he said.

"Brought my own guns this time."

"Judging by the size of your suitcase, you brought nothing for distance shooting. We'll take along the rifles and shotguns we picked up in Clancyville."

"This place remote we're going to?"

"Yes, ma'am."

"Joey's guys are not really too smart, you know."

"I know. I'll leave 'em a note with a map and directions. They'll find us."

26

WE TURNED LEFT ONTO SULLY ROAD AND HEADED SOUTH OUT of Sterling. At Waxpool Road we turned right and headed east. We continued our eastward route through the back roads of Northern Virginia. Waxpool Road became Farmwell Road. We skirted the lower part of Ashburn. Then Farmwell became Sycolin Road as we were now moving north at a nice clip. Rosey's Grand Cherokee cruised along smoothly.

After getting tired of reading road signs and trying to remember all of the turns, I finally gave up and dozed off. When I awakened we were surrounded by houses and more city life. Rosey said we were in Leesburg. The sign read S. King Street. The sun was still rising more or less behind us, so I deduced we were heading southwest. King Street soon became James Monroe Highway. I dozed off again.

The next time I awakened we were back in the country again.

"So where are we now?" I said, trying to get some bearing.

"We just passed through Hughesville and we are heading towards Telegraph Spring."

"I can't wait."

"You'll have to. We won't make it to Telegraph Spring."

"Too much for the Jeep?"

"Cabin comes before that."

"On this road?"

"No. Trinity Church Road."

"You're kidding."

"I joke not. At the end of Trinity Church Road there's a long drive. Maybe a quarter of a mile. Cabin is in the woods. I hope you like trees."

We had left my rental parked in front of one of Rosey's neighbors who was vacationing in Spain for a month. His Grand Cherokee was a nice alternative to my Seville rental. Lap of luxury.

"You normally use this cabin?"

"Not for showdowns."

"Otherwise?"

"R&R."

"Often?"

"Not nearly enough in my line of work."

We turned onto Trinity Church Road and followed it to the end. An old, dilapidated mailbox was several feet off to the left as we began our trek down Rosey's driveway.

"That yours?"

"All mine."

"Looks to be in need of some repair."

"It works."

The cabin was waiting on us as he said, at the end of the long drive, surrounded by lots of trees. The drive turned sharply to the left just before we arrived at the cabin and ran parallel to it for a few hundred yards. This helped to hide the place even more than its wilderness location. The narrow opening of the drive allowed for the cabin to be nearly surrounded by thick woods, mostly pines. There were a few spruce added for flavor. The ground around the trees closest to the cabin was as thick as a carpet with Virginia Creeper. It was all quite lovely. Lousy place to kill people.

"What makes you think these guys will come out here?" I asked as we were taking our equipment inside.

"They're stupid."

"Stupid makes you do this type of work?"

"No. Stupid makes me you think you're better at it than I am. And Joey pays them a lot of money to be stupid."

We laid our rifles and shotguns on a large oaken picnic-style table in the cabin's great room. The great room was separated from the kitchen by a counter with three stools in front of it. There was a bathroom off to the right as you entered the front door, just under the stairway that led up to the two bedrooms in the loft. The walls were paneled with the old-style knotty pine. I imagined that it had grown darker through the years.

"This place has the look of long years," I said.

"Built in the 50's as a hunting cabin. I bought it in the late 80's and refurbished it. Updated the kitchen stuff, cleaned the walls, updated the plumbing and the electrical."

"Rustic."

"First class frontier."

"Despite your optimism, I hope they don't come."

"Better to get it over with. I could go into hiding and Joey would never find me. Wouldn't want to live or work that way. Enjoy life too much. They'll show up. Late today. I figure they'll find the place before sundown, and then work some brilliant plan to attack us after dark."

"You, not me. They don't know I'm here."

"They'll know soon enough. You're one of the surprises I have for them."

"Only one?"

The Michael Jordan grin returned. It had been a few days since he had anything to grin about.

"Okay, they come. We kill them. Joey will just send more after you. Grudges die hard."

"With people like Joey Malone, grudges don't die at all. Revenge is his whole life. Dog eat dog. He's no good at real negotiation."

"So they keep coming and you keep stopping them."

"That be the game."

"Until one of them gets lucky."

"He'd have to be lucky."

"No one better than you?"

"Not that would work for Joey Malone. There are some as good. Better? I don't think so."

"All modesty aside," I said.

"No room for being modest. You either good or dead."

"Any of those as good as you, your friends?"

"I know them."

"Why didn't you call them to come help us?"

"You worried?"

"Yes. I'm not as confident as you about this business. I stay alive chiefly by using my brain, not by shooting people. I can shoot a gun, almost any gun. I would rather outthink my opposition and surprise them."

"Me, too."

He motioned for me to follow him and we walked through the kitchen to a small room at the back of the cabin. He unlocked the door and I followed inside. He handed me several sharpened wooden slats, some small rope, and a large hunting knife without a case. He gathered up some other items along with another handful of sharpened wooden slats.

"We building something?" I said.

"Traps for varmints."

We worked steadily for three hours planting spring-action traps with the slats and the rope all around the cabin. Actually I watched him create these horrible inventions for anything that might happen to be walking among the trees nearby. They wouldn't kill anyone, but they would definitely hurt the lower legs and calf muscles. Inflict pain.

"Boy scouts?"

"Navy training."

"Beyond Boot Camp," I said.

He smiled a little.

"Slow them down on the attack?"

"That and impose pain. Hard not to cry out when one of these penetrates your leg. Trap springs. They yelp. Advantage us."

"So we know where they are."

"I have spot lights all around the outside of the cabin, hidden just under the roof line. You only see them when they come on. Sound activated. Highly sensitive to sounds in their area. We set the traps in the range of each outside light. Trap springs. You yelp. Light shines. You dead."

"Your idea?"

"Not originally. I steal from the best."

We finished our work and returned to the cabin for some grub.

27

It didn't take long for me to eat my peanut butter and strawberry jelly sandwich. Rosey ate three sandwiches, so it took him a little longer. He drank milk and I had orange juice.

"I hope you're planning on fixing us something more substantive for supper," I said as we settled into some comfortable chairs in the great room. He was sitting by one of the large windows. I was stationed at the other window.

"Not planning on eating again until it is over."

"That could take a while."

"Then we be hungry."

I wasn't thrilled with this turn of events, but I had to follow his lead. I could always sneak another peanut butter and jelly sandwich. Probably needed to do that in the next few minutes. Make one or two to take with me while I shoot at the bad guys.

The place was quieter than a church house on Saturday night. I fell asleep again because Rosey wasn't in a talkative mood. I was beginning to sense that he seldom entered that mood.

When I woke up it was after four o'clock. Rosey was not in his chair by the window. It was painfully quiet. I listened to myself breathe for a few a minute or two. I was hoping to hear a sound from another part of the house. Silence.

"You ready?" he said to me from the top of the stairs.

"They here already?" I said as I began my assent to join him.

"No, but we need to talk."

I followed him down the narrow hallway. There were two doors directly across the hall from each other.

"This is my room," he said pointing to his right. "That be yours."

"So far so good."

"Mine first," he said and motioned for me to follow.

His room had two windows, one on the front wall of the cabin looking towards the driveway, and the other on the side. There were two weapons, below each window – one rifle and one handgun. The room contained just the kind of furniture you would expect in a cabin – small, single bed, nightstand and lamp, dresser on the left behind the door, and curtains on both windows. The one unusual thing, in addition to the guns under the windows, was a small green light plugged into an odd-looking outlet underneath the side window.

"They'll have to come out of the trees before the handgun does any good. You don't need to worry about that. Unless you miss with the rifle. Then you worry."

I followed him out of his room across the hall into mine. I had the same window setup he had – one window facing the front drive and the other window facing the side of the house. Below each window were the rifle and the handgun, just like his. I had the same furnishings in my room, but no green light and fancy outlet below my side window.

"Ever killed a deer, Clancy?"

“No. Hunted with my father a few times. Saw him kill one. Didn’t really enjoy that. I like deer. Alive.”

“Me, too. I don’t hunt animals.”

The implication was too obvious and too painful to comment.

“Aim for the heart. It’s a difficult shot, but with the 30-06 you have there, the target will not get up.”

“If I miss, let him come in from the trees towards the cabin. Then use the .357.”

“No, use the rifle again. Then if you miss, you really are a bad shot and you have no right to be here. Last measure is to pick up that handgun. If you have to, aim for the middle of the body. At least you will slow him down.”

He turned and walked away from me without another word. He stopped at the door of my room. His back was to me.

“Make yourself comfortable. They should arrive in a little while. I’ll be across the hall if you need me.”

“I’m going to make a sandwich or two for me. I’m not like you. I can’t go long, indefinite periods without food. Besides, you haven’t fed me well all day. You want anything?”

He shook his head and went into his bedroom. He left the door open.

I returned to my room with two sandwiches, an apple and the whole carton of orange juice. I could make it till morning if necessary.

28

THE ROOM WAS DARK WHEN I OPENED MY EYES. I HAD SHUT MY eyes for a moment after the second sandwich and then just dozed off. The katydids were making a racket, but all else was deathly quiet. I decided to check on Rosey.

"You awake?" I said softly so as not to startle a man holding a Remington 7400 fully loaded and waiting for his prey.

"Better be."

His room was dark too. The katydids were just as loud on his side of the world.

"Still think they're coming?"

"Yes, ma'am."

The green light under his window started flashing. It was brilliant throughout his darkened room.

"What does that mean?" I said.

"Somebody's coming."

"Security device?"

"Yes, ma'am. They just passed the mailbox. Should be here in a minute or two if they be careful. Less if they be anxious."

I went back to my post and sat on the floor in front of the

side window with my 30-06 in hand. Fully loaded. It was 9:01.

"Don't let the outside light coming on startle you," his voice from the other room came across the hall. He said it calmly. "The light will come on quickly and you will have ten seconds for a perfect shot. Don't rush, but don't wait long either."

With Rosey's system, the front of the house and the back of the house were vulnerable to attack since there were two of us. The approaching killers didn't know this, of course, but we knew it. The plan was to stand our ground at the side windows for ten minutes after the first light activated. Then we would both go downstairs, I would take the front and he would protect the back. There were trigger lights, as he referred to them, in the back and front, but after ten minutes he said that the prey would have either crawled out of the light or the ones left realized what had happened and stopped advancing. Either way, we were then on our own skills as hunters to stop them from entering the cabin. The one advantage we had was that once the trigger-lights came on, they stayed on until the light of dawn. Wonderful inventions.

They must have been anxious because the first light came on less than five minutes after his prediction. I didn't see the light come on exactly, but I heard the cry from someone outside and then came the horrendous blast from his rifle. The groaning from outside stopped immediately.

A twig snapped off to my left, towards the front of the house. A swishing sound came next. I raised my rifle.

"Ugh!" somebody said in the dark shadows to my left.

The light came on. I had no time to discern anything about the man below. I fired one shot and he fell. Fish in a barrel. My stomach felt queasy.

All was quiet for a few minutes. I moved away from the

window just to be cautious. I figured that there was no way anyone from below could see me, but I wasn't about to take any chances. They could be smarter than Rosey thought, or luckier. No sense putting my life in jeopardy so I could hear Rosey either apologize later for them shooting me or fuss at me for being so careless. Careless was not one of my character flaws.

The light to my far right came on. It was towards the back of the cabin where there was lots of darkness. I hadn't heard any moaning sound to speak of. Maybe some other sound had awakened the light. I turned with my rifle aimed and ready.

My target was holding his leg, trying desperately to remove the stake embedded in his left calf. I could see blood. The last thing he did before I shot him was to put his right hand in front of his eye to ward off the blinding spotlight.

This had stopped being fun before it had even started. I was not given to this line of work. Something recoiled within me at what I was engaged in doing. The queasiness was still with me.

A shot ricocheted off the window casing just above my head and to my left. I doubt the shooter intended it to be a warning shot. He had simply been a bad shot in the dark. It practically destroyed the window casing. I was unscathed, but lucky.

No new light had come on, so I had no idea as to where the shot originated. I moved away from the window and waited.

Rosey crawled into my room on his hands and knees scooting the rifle along in his right hand.

"We're a little better targets now that the spotlights have come on. They have a better view of our window positions. Did all of your lights come on?"

"I don't know. I think so, but I can't be for sure."

He moved stealthily to the left of the window and cautiously peered out, looking first at the rear of the cabin. After stooping to all fours again, he crawled under the window and then cautiously leaned against the wall and looked towards the front of the house from a seated position.

"They're all on. I'm going back to my side. You come with me. I have two lights that have not been triggered yet."

"Shouldn't I keep a watch on this side of the house?"

"No."

He was out the door of my room and into his before I could process his answer. I dropped to all fours and moved steadily to his room carrying my rifle with me. I had the .357 in a holster on my side just in case.

"How many left?" I said.

"No way of telling. Three are down. We'll have to wait to see what happens. Better to be patient than stupid."

He was to the right of his window looking now and then towards the rear of the cabin. The two lights on his side that were yet to come on were in his line of vision.

"The ones left know by now what happened to the others. Unless they are truly ignorant creatures from another world, they will not make the same mistake that their companions made."

"So where are we vulnerable now?"

"Back door and the open drive way. Our advantage is that the ones left don't know that we're vulnerable at the back door. There are spotlights on the rear of the cabin that are motion sensitive. That will give them pause for deep reflection."

"No way for us to view the events of our posterior?"

"Attic vent," he pointed to the ceiling on the other side of his bed. There was sufficient light sneaking into his room from the side-front spotlight so that I could discern a cord hanging down.

"Stairs?" I said as I begin to crawl towards the cord.

"First class cabin, lady."

"Worth a look?"

"Yeah," he whispered.

I stood up on the other side of the room and pulled the cord. The badly hidden door opened and I grabbed the bottom step and pulled until it unfolded onto the floor. Amazingly quiet. I expected a lot more noise.

"Unless you have a perfect shot, don't shoot out the venting window. Screens are there to keep the starlings from nesting. I have my standards to maintain."

"Let me get this straight. You want to risk our lives against whoever it is out there by not taking a shot if I can in order to keep some damn birds from coming into your attic?"

"Well, since you put it like that, take your best shot, if you have one."

"Thank you."

I climbed quickly and walked slowly to the rear of the attic. I didn't want creaking boards to alert the opposition. I moved slowly so that my weight would not cause the boards to sound the alarm. My height forced me to walk down the center of the cabin. I felt like a kid again walking on a single beam. I held the rifle in front of me with both hands to keep my balance. The window was a perfect height to view or shoot from, but the darkness below made seeing impossible. All was quiet.

When I did my balancing act back to the collapsible stairs and descended, Rosey was gone from his window perch. His rifle was leaning against the wall to the right of the window. The handgun was gone. I noticed that the rear lights had still not come on.

Upon entering the narrow hallway, I stopped to listen for sounds that might be coming up from the first floor of the cabin. Silence and stillness greeted my intense listening. After failing to see Rosey in my shadowy bedroom, I eased my way to the short balcony at the top of the stairs. I sat down on the little balcony floor and put my feet on the first step. Placing my rifle barrel against one of the handrail supports and firmly gripping both the barrel and the support at the same time, I aimed my weapon at the front door of the cabin and waited. The still of the night.

Time passed slowly. I had no idea how much time had passed, except that my hand holding onto both the rifle barrel and the handrail support was getting tired. I loosened my grip, shook my hand, and placed in back in the same position. The sound on the front porch startled me. It might have been the sound of a foot taking a step. I was ready.

The front of the cabin was still relatively dark. The only light coming in was diffused from the side spotlights. The door opened and I saw a hand. The hand pushed the door and it continued to open. The person withdrew their hand from sight.

Since I didn't know where Rosey was, I had no idea whether he was about to walk into the front door of the cabin or a stranger who intended to kill me. I figured that Rosey would not be stupid enough to come in unannounced and swing the door open before he entered. My breathing increased as I waited for the fool outside to enter.

The waiting intensified. Nothing happened. Did he want an invitation? Maybe he was smarter than I had given him credit. A hand, then the arm suddenly emerged around the corner of the doorjamb and flicked the light-switch to the on position. The Great Room lit up immediately and I felt exposed for the first time. There was no place for me to hide. Shoot first and ask questions later.

Instead of coming in the front door, a man emerged in shadowy view at the window to my left of the front door. I shifted the rifle and my aim to the left and fired. The window shattered and the man recoiled backwards with intense force. It took a minute or so for me to make out what it was that I was looking at through the shattered window glass. It was the bottom of the man's shoes.

I wanted to move, but I dared not. I did not enjoy having that light on in the Great Room. There was a double switch just above my head to my right. I moved my right hand slowly up the wall and pushed the switch closest to me. The Great Room went dark once more. I breathed.

For some reason waiting in the dark is better than waiting in the light when you are being hunted. Go figure.

I glanced at my watch. It was after 10. I should have been getting ready for bed, but here I was up to my eyeballs in violence and death. Perhaps I needed to rethink my career choices.

Presently I heard someone walking towards the cabin whistling. They were whistling that old Barry Sadler tune from the sixties, *The Green Beret*. It had to be Rosey. No one else would have been that brazen. I waited just in case I was mistaken about the song and the brazenness.

"Clancy?" his mellow voice said before he showed his form at the door.

"What?"

"You okay?"

"I'm fine. I just killed three people tonight. You know how to show a girl a good time, buddy. And where have you been?" I was not a happy camper at this point.

"Checking the woods. All's clear."

"And you know this how?"

"Great abilities at tracking and hunting."

"Just four of them?" I said as I walked down the stairs towards the front door.

"Started with five. One left."

"Coward," I flipped the switch and we had light once more in the Great Room.

"Don't think so. His vehicle stopped on the other side of the mailbox. His tracks show him walking down to the other car where the four were gathered on this side of the mailbox. His tracks returned to his car and he left."

Rosey was wearing an outfit of camouflaged fatigues complete with hat and boots.

"Wish the others had left, too," I said as I leaned my rifle against the wall.

"They be sayin' the same thing, if they could."

29

It was nearly five o'clock the next morning before I finally had the opportunity to go to sleep.

Rosey had placed a call to someone after the shooting stopped, and fifty minutes later the woods around the cabin was crawling with FBI, Virginia State Police, an ambulance service, and some local authorities. Some of them were inside checking every nook and cranny of the place. I was exhausted, but they naturally wanted to talk to me. Willing participant. It's not everyday that four people are shot down by a man and a woman in a cabin in the woods. Headlines in some papers.

"Isn't this going to be bad publicity for you and your company?" I said to Rosey in one of those rare moments around midnight when I was able to speak with him privately.

"Doubt it. Company had nothing to do with it."

"But your presence alone could taint them, right?"

"Naw."

He was called away from me by some guy in a dark gray suit before he could explain. Gray Suit looked official, so I stayed on the couch. I closed my eyes hoping that this nightmare would go away. I had gotten myself into a real mess this time. Mama would have a cow when she found out about this.

After several hours of telling the suits my story, and watching them comb the place for whatever it was they wanted, I enjoyed the moment when I realized that they were actually beginning to leave. Little by little, teams of men and women left the place. Joy and rapture.

The dark gray suit stayed the longest. He was the one who had talked with Rosey from the beginning. I got the feeling from my casual watching of them that they knew each other really well. Ace detective.

Finally, around 4:30 or so in the morning, Rosey's buddy left and we were alone once more. The bodies were gone. Even shell casings were neatly stored and taken off by someone whose job it was to study such things. Someone had even cleaned up the broken glass in the front.

"I'm too tired to talk, but I do have questions."

"Bet you do."

"Will hammer on this tomorrow. Sometime. Won't be before lunch. I can promise you that."

I dragged myself up the stairs to the bedroom on the left. The bed had been turned down for me. My suitcase was opened on top of a small table. Room service, but no mint on the pillow. I didn't bother to change clothes. I took off my shoes and climbed in bed. I slept as if I had not done one horrible thing the whole night.

Hours later I awakened to the smell of sausage cooking. There might have been something else in addition to the pig's offering, but the sausage was absolutely thrilling for a small town girl raised on country breakfasts.

I entered the kitchen area after a long, hot shower and a change of clothes. I felt refreshed, but still tired.

"How long you been up?" I said.

"Since about noon. Had some chores to do."

"Country life. I'm hungry."

"Bet you are. Full course breakfast sound okay?"

"What time is it?"

"Does that matter as to what you eat?"

"No. I just wanted to know what time it was."

"1:30."

"Great time to be alive."

"When you consider the alternative."

"So, what's on the menu for breakfast?"

"Name something, and I've fixed it."

"You're kidding."

"Never joke about food, ma'am. Be bad breeding."

"Just give me some of everything. I'll do my best."

After his major serious breakfast of eggs, grits, sausage, biscuits, gravy, ham slices, cooked apples, strawberry jelly, and coffee, I lay down on the couch to stare through the hole where there was once upon a time a window frame. I wasn't thinking too much about the missing window. You just can't kill people and not let it affect you.

"Processing?" he said after he had finished washing the dishes.

"Suppose so."

"Tough business I'm in. Takes a while to get over a kill."

"A kill? Is that military talk? Professional Killers Society lingo? A kill? What in heaven's name does that mean?" I was angry.

"Good to vent. You might as well take it out on me."

"No one else around," I said.

"Forest critters."

"They wouldn't understand."

"They know more about the forces of nature than you

and I could learn in several lifetimes. It's once in a while for us. For them, it's round the clock."

I was silent for a few minutes. Rosey drank his coffee silently, but I could hear the sound of him sipping. It was uniquely cool for an August day.

"I suppose that our little adventure is all over the papers this morning," I was resigned to having my whole career changed.

"Don't think so."

I sat up on the couch and turned toward him. He was sitting in the large recliner that matched the couch. Must have been his favorite chair. Detective par excellence.

"Why not?"

"I work for the government, Clancy. When something like this happens, there is no trail left. It all disappears. As far as anyone is concerned, it never happened."

"You mean my mother will not read about this or hear about it on the evening news tonight?"

"Never happened. No news to report."

"You work for the FBI?"

"No."

He finished his coffee and set the cup down on the table next to his chair. He crossed his legs after he had reclined the chair to a more comfortable position.

"So who do you work for?"

"Better not tell you that. Need to know basis. You understand."

"I understand zilch here. I just killed three people last night protecting your butt. Now you tell me it never happened. What kind of crap is this? Who are you?"

I think I was yelling by the time I had finished my little soliloquy of questions and insightful pining. Rosey never flinched from his crossed-leg, almost prone position in the recliner. He appeared to be comfortable.

I relaxed my throat muscles and tried to calm down before I spoke again.

"This is what you do for a living?"

"I investigate criminals. My office and my connection with the law firm is all a front for my undercover government job. There is no way anyone can trace me to what I do. There is no record, no file, no paper trail from me to the government or from them back to me. You were able to find out more about me than anyone else. I still wonder about that, but that's your business. You're smart. You're good to have around in a life-threatening situation. And, …" he hesitated and then fell silent.

"And what?"

"I trust you."

"So what would you have done if I had not come to D.C. to warn you about Joey and his boys?"

"Don't know. I hope that I could have avoided a nasty situation."

"Well, Jasper, even with my help, you and I failed to avoid a nasty situation."

"I meant nasty in the sense that I could be wounded or killed. You made my job easier."

"I'd say so. But you could have called in some more people to help you, right?"

"No."

"No? With all the people who showed up here last night and this morning. You don't have one other person who would come to your aid?"

"I work alone."

"What a macho."

"Nature of the job. In my line of work, it's hard to know whom to trust. Prevailing philosophy is to trust no one."

"So, your trusting me is a bit of a departure for your norm."

"About face."

"Thanks for the overwhelming vote of confidence."

"Welcome."

"Are you unique?"

"Of course."

"Not that. I mean are there others in your line of work?"

"A few, I'm told."

"Don't know them?"

"No. They prefer it this way."

"They?"

"Employers."

"Oh. So, some might work alone or some might work in tandem with someone else?"

"Suppose so."

"Helluva job you got there, buddy. Better thee than me."

He showed a hint of a smile, but nothing close to the Michael Jordan grandeur. We were silent for a few minutes. The air felt clean and pure for the first time. I got up from the couch and walked to the hole in the wall. The forest looked calm and peaceful today. Nature at rest.

"One more thing."

"I'm listening," I said without turning around.

"There won't be anymore of Joey Malone's men coming after me. It's over."

"Conjecture, or do you have proof to offer?"

"Joey Malone was killed yesterday."

30

I STAYED ON ANOTHER DAY WITH ROOSEVELT WASHINGTON IN his Sterling, Virginia condo. Rest and relaxation. I learned little more about his work, but what he did tell me was that the information about Joey Malone's murder came from his contact in the government. He never mentioned the name of his contact. I didn't ask.

Before we had left for Sterling, a new window had been installed in the cabin. All of the traps had been removed and most of the blood had been cleaned up from the front porch where the last victim had breathed his last. The country charm had been restored to the pastoral setting. All was right with the world.

True enough, except for what I was feeling inside. I was focused upon my part in the drama, not Rosey's profession. I had not intended upon killing three people less than forty-eight hours ago. And yet, I had driven to D.C. to warn him and stayed around for the action to unfold. I don't know what I had expected to happen, but I just hadn't given thought to exterminating three men, even if they did work for Joey Malone. The evil that men do. Women also.

I could rationalize easy enough along the lines that they deserved it. They even asked for it by coming after us. They were hired killers. No one hired us. Well, no one hired me. I was there out of friendship, a long ago, far away friendship of one lone teenage girl for another lonely teenage boy who felt out of place in Southern rural America. Somehow or other Rosey and I had bonded back in the seventies. Despite all the lapsed time in between then and now, we had formed something of a lasting friendship. Or whatever. We formed something.

That what's I pondered all the way back to Norfolk from Sterling. Debated. Argued. I even fumed a little. I could not shake the feeling that I had done what I had done out of my regard for Rosey. I had helped people before, but nothing like that.

I decided to take a few more days of doing nothing before I allowed myself to jump into another case. I needed more rest before I even went back to searching for the truth about my father's death. Despite his removal from the scene, Joey Malone was still my link to my father's murder. I could now investigate without worrying about Joey coming after me. Or my friend Rosey. Rest first, then investigate.

Blackie and Sam were extravagant with their affections when I returned home. I think even Rogers was glad that I had safely returned.

"Well, party girl, nice of you to come home and visit us peons once more."

"It was no party, love."

"What was it then?" she said.

"A battle to the death."

"As in war?"

"There are worst descriptions, but that's close enough. It was not pretty."

"Glad you're back safely. The dogs missed you."

I smiled to myself. She said that often. Must be hiding some emotion there. Computers. Go figure.

"You're a dream."

"I know. Upward and onward is my motto. Heard the latest?"

"Joey's demise?"

"Wow, impressive for a human. Bad news traveling fast, I suppose."

"Well, I don't know how bad that news is. Can't say I will miss him."

"Many will not, I am sure. However, his family is concerned."

"You have a source for that statement?"

"Messages … several of them … left for you. Shall I play them or give you the condensed version?"

"They're all the same?"

"Basically. Same man calling and asking for you."

"Who?"

"Craven Malone."

"What does he want me for? Does he think I killed his son?"

"Don't think so. He wants to hire you."

"For what?"

"To find his son's killer."

"Oh, boy."

THE DRIVE to Virginia Beach was not as taxing as the last drive over there. I took Sam with me this time. Blackie was a home-body anyway, so Sam was delighted to get out of Norfolk once again. Margie agreed to take in Blackie while Sam and I were away on business. I had been away so much the past few days, the least I could do was to take Sam with me. I promised to take him for a romp in the ocean, too. Sealed the deal.

Craven Malone had practically begged to see me, so the least I could do was to go see the man and offer my condolences. I was expected if not anticipated, so the gate opened before I pushed the intercom button to announce our presence. The bozo that met us halfway up the drive was an enlightened species.

"What's the dog?" he said.

I hated questions that answered themselves, but it did offer me the opportunity to be feisty.

"Lab."

"What's he doin' here?"

"Partner."

"I don't remember seein' him with ya the last time," he countered. Mr. Keen Eye.

"Wasn't his turn. Rotating system."

He looked confused.

"What?"

"He goes where I go."

"The boss won't like this."

"He'll get over it."

"The dog?" Again, he seemed confused.

"No, your boss."

I was ushered into the library. The room was literally full of books. They gave the appearance of having been bought, but not read. Everything was in perfect order. I ran my finger along one of the shelves. Spotless. The maid did nice work. I sat down in one of the leather chairs by the mahogany desk. Sam sat down on his back legs next to me and stared at the door. He knew that we were in semi-hostile territory.

"I think we're relatively safe here," I said to him and patted his head.

Sam swiveled his head to look at me, but then immediately turned back to stare at the door. We didn't always see eye to eye on danger. His intuition was a tad different from mine.

Craven entered the room with his two thugs, Reno and Georgio. They stopped at the door like good guard dogs while Craven walked across the room to his desk. Sam growled lightly, almost at an inaudible pitch. I put my hand on the back of his neck and could feel his body tighten. He stopped making that low growl.

"What's the dog for?" he asked after taking his seat behind the desk.

"Style."

"I don't like dogs."

"He knows."

"Always good to know where one stands, huh?"

"It is for him."

"I want you to find out who murdered my son," his voice carried little, if any, emotion. Perhaps the grief had passed.

"Sorry for your loss," I said with forced feeling.

"Thank you. This is not for family. This is business."

"Competitors?"

"Don't know. That's why I'm paying you."

"I need some clues. Helps to get started, you know."

"What do you want to know?"

"Give me a list of his enemies."

"Damn, woman. I'm an old man. Hell, if I have to list all of his enemies, I'll be well over a hundred before I finish."

"Popular, huh?"

"Nobody liked him. I don't even think he liked himself. He was a cruel, mean-spirited, corrupt, and excessive man."

"You liked him," I said more of a question than a statement.

"Not much. He was my son. That's about it. You can't imagine the times I regretted having brought the bastard into the world. The only person who ever loved him is dead. She's been dead now for over thirty years. Died of a broken heart. His fault, too."

"That would be…" I said waiting for him to fill in the gap.

"His mother. My first wife. She was the crown jewel. Nobody on the planet like her. God, I still miss that woman. But she was too sensitive. You can't be that sensitive and survive in this world. She took Joey's stupidity to heart. Cost her, too."

"Loved not wisely, but too well."

"What?"

"Poetic insight."

"Oh. The funeral is day after tomorrow. Had to have an autopsy. One of his live-ins found him in the bathroom."

"That's a start. Shot?"

"Not that I was told. Body was in the shower. An initial report said he probably OD'd from drugs or he could have been poisoned," he made some horrible sound to clear his throat.

There was silence for a few moments. Sam had been watching Craven Malone while he had been telling about Joey. I noticed that he had not taken his sharp, canine eyes from the man since Craven had entered the room. When Craven paused, Sam turned to look at the two bodyguards by the door. They were posed with their arms crossed over their chests and their feet firmly planted underneath the heavy frames. Bookends. Impressive.

"Drug overdose is not likely murder," I said. "You must be leaning towards poison."

"All I got to say is he was murdered. I'll leave it up to you as to how it was done."

"I'll do what I can."

"Why don't you go up with me for the funeral?" he said. "I could tell people that you're my protégé. I don't want a lot of press on this. I would prefer that you do this investigation secretly. And for sure I don't want anyone knowing that I hired you."

I thought it obvious that if anyone would hire me for this it would have been the father. I said nothing.

"What kind of protégé?"

"Business associate. Does that suit you?"

"Sure. How do I dress the part?"

"I'll provide you the right clothes, I can make you look like a traveling secretary, someone who handles business arrangements."

"You have someone who does this already."

He nodded without answering. At this point he opened the cigar box on the desk and took out one of his Churchills.

"Mind?" he said.

I pointed to the window behind him and he laughed. Consistency might be my only virtue.

"So what do you say?"

"I'll investigate his death."

"And the funeral?"

"Sure. Get me some wardrobe for the front. I'll go home and pack some bluejeans for the gumshoe work."

"One more thing," he said. "The dog doesn't go."

"Pity. He's never seen the lights of Detroit."

31

I CALLED ROSEY TO TELL HIM WHAT WAS HAPPENING AND HOW strange the world could be. One day we are fleeing for our lives because a man has hired someone to kill me. Another day in the same week, I am hired to find out who killed the man who was trying to kill me.

"I need some assistance."

"What do you need?"

"A weapon."

"Come get what you need."

"I'm flying with Craven to attend the funeral. Irony, huh?"

"Complete and pure. You want me to smuggle a gun on board the flight for you?"

"Not necessarily. I thought you might have some contacts in the Detroit area who could loan me something."

"You should have hidden those two weapons you acquired at Lake Nettie."

"Hindsight."

"Okay. I'll take care of it."

"Just like that?"

"Just like that."

"Mr. Wonderful strikes again."

"When do you leave?"

"Fly to Detroit tomorrow afternoon. The funeral is the next day. I'm pretending to be Malone's protégée."

"Keep an eye on his hands."

"Hey, this is a ninety year old man. I can easily outrun him."

"Not on a plane. I'll call you with the details for your request."

Rogers spent the morning researching the newspapers in the Detroit area on Joey Malone's killing. The press was brief and terse, their way of saying this maggot didn't matter. The obituary was more enlightening.

"The PR department of the magazine wrote the obit, for sure. Makes him sound like a lusty saint."

"All obituaries make people sound like saints. It's a genre of literature."

"No mention of wife or wives, nor children. Devout bachelor."

"Can't address that as to accuracy. I doubt his chastity."

"You suppose he had a thing for children?" Rogers asked.

"I don't want to know that. I already don't like him, and he's not even alive."

I was in the bedroom packing my suitcase. I had no idea how long I might stay. In fact, I was thinking I would just stay over and do some snooping around in Detroit to see if I could learn anything more than who killed Joey Malone. We detectives are supposed to be good at snooping. Sounds subversive.

"Says that he was a philanthropist. Honorary this, honorary that. I tell you, this guy had two lives. He made millions, but he also gave away millions. Hard to figure."

"Most people are schizophrenic. What else?"

"Hey, Miss Clancy, this is odd," Rogers continued. "Says

that flowers are accepted as a memorial, but that donations can be made to the American Cancer Society, Alcoholics Anonymous, and the Autumn Leaves Health Care Institute of North Carolina."

I stopped packing and walked into the living room to see if Rogers had anything displayed. Some beach in paradise was on the monitor.

"Show me what you found."

The screen changed and the obituary appeared in full view.

"Well, I must admit that the first two are rather ironic for an addicted smoker and an alcoholic."

"Who told you that?"

"Big Daddy Malone."

"Maybe junior had some regrets with his lifestyle."

"Incurable optimist are we?"

"Addicts can have regrets."

"Oh, I'm sure they do. But he doesn't fit the mold. At least according to what papa told me. Despite the strangeness of the AA and the cancer people, it's the last one that doesn't seem to fit at all. What are his connections to North Carolina? And where is this Autumn Leaves Institute?"

"Maybe that's why Big Daddy hired you, baby."

"And that's why I have you, Love. While I'm in Detroit grieving over this perverted merchant of trash, you see what you can learn about that place in North Carolina."

I finishing packing and took both dogs for a walk. Sam didn't require a leash, but Blackie preferred it. I think it made her feel upper class. I kept a brisk pace on these walks, and she loved to trot with her tail held high. Dignity personified. Sam would explore, but return every two minutes or so to check on us. Father Protector.

An hour later we returned. The dogs headed for the soft comfort of their favorite furniture and I took a shower.

I checked with Margie about taking care of the dogs for several days. She said she was glad to do it. While she never said it, I had the feeling that Margie could use the money I paid her for the dog sitting. It worked out well for both us most of the time.

After a quick salad and a glass of Piñot Grigio, Rogers was beckoning me with her report. Efficient and fast.

"Place used to be called Autumn Care Nursing Home. Changed its name a couple of decades back to the Autumn Leaves Health Institute. Came up with several million around that time and added some buildings as well as renovated existing facilities. Located in Mooresville, NC."

"Who owns it?"

"Nothing on that so far. Has a Board of Directors, but none of the names suggest anything. Lots of files and contracts to go through. I'll keep searching. Just thought you'd like to know that tidbit about the windfall and the name change."

"Check to see if anything happened to *Lusty* magazine around the same time that Autumn Leaves was improving."

"It could be that his estate just randomly selected this charity."

"Unlikely. I smell a clue."

"You super sleuths are all alike. You look for things we mortals only chalk up to coincidence."

"We mortals? When did you join the human race?"

"Hey, Bubbette, you created me. I have personality, style and a fine working brain. The body could use a nip and tuck here and there; but, you gotta admit, I have heart."

"Yes, ma'am. I admit that and the other. Think I should turn you into a robot so you could walk around and actually do things for me?"

"Watch that, Peaches. I do plenty for you."

"Yes, you do much for me. I am grateful. But the attitude …."

"Make you look good most of the time. Where would you be without me, Tootsie? Saved your bacon more than once. Hows about a little respect for the intelligent machine over here, Babes?"

"If I had a hat, I'd tip it."

"Darn right. Some people's kids. You'd be in a mess if I decided to go on strike. Then you'd dance a different tune."

"Okay, okay. Work out your aggression by finding out who owns that facility in Mooresville, North Carolina. Chase down anything that might lead you to *Lusty* or the late charmer, Joey Malone."

"Anything else, Massuh?"

"Yeah. Search all of the employees of *Lusty* and see what you come up with. Remember, we're working two cases here. I haven't given up on finding the connection between my father's death and Craven Malone Industries, Inc."

32

Rogers had found nothing of substance by the time I left for the airport to meet Craven and his entourage. It was mostly an uneventful flight to Detroit except that I did get to meet Malone's real traveling secretary, a hard-nosed woman by the name of J.C. Whitmore. She sat next to Malone the whole trip and took care of his every little whim. I had the privilege of sitting next to Pee Wee Lunden, baby brother to Reno Lunden. Since I had already had the delightful pleasure of meeting Reno, it was nice to sit next to his brother, Pee Wee, and discover that he had an equal amount of personality. In fact, Pee Wee may have been just a tad more obnoxious than his older brother. Reno seemed to be a quiet ogre. Pee Wee could make noises wide awake or asleep. He passed most of the trip snoring and whistling. He awakened in time to catch the food being served. He belched and complained during that interval.

By the time we arrived in Detroit, I felt like wrestling an alligator. Since I had no gun with me, I couldn't shoot anyone. Wrestling seemed more appropriate for my mood.

Whitmore and I were standing together while Malone

was on one of the airport phones. Pee Wee, Reno and Georgio were roaming around trying to keep an eye on their boss as well as us. They looked very much out of place. I decided that those three would have been out of place anywhere. I was out of place myself.

"Worked for Malone long?" I asked attempting to be polite.

"Twelve years."

"He travels a lot."

"What does that mean?"

"That means he takes a lot of trips and requires the assistance of a traveling secretary."

"I am not just a traveling secretary. I work when he doesn't travel."

"Good," I said trying to defuse her steamy disposition.

"I'm a trained nurse as well as a business associate."

"Really. Do much nursing?"

"Only for Mr. Malone."

When I remembered that Craven Malone was ninety years old, I decided it was a good thing that she was a trained nurse. A lull came in our stimulating conversation and I walked over to the shop selling magazines, books, and Detroit souvenirs. I was standing in the back corner of the shop when a stranger approached me. He was carrying a briefcase.

"Clancy?"

"Yes?"

"Mr. Washington said to give you this. Said you might need it here in Detroit." He handed me the briefcase.

"Here's the key. Locked for security."

I took both the case and the key. He was gone before I could even say thanks. I had no idea what I was supposed to do with this loaner when I was ready to leave Detroit. Maybe Rosey would call me and tell me. Or I could dump it in the water like I did the last weapons I had here in Michigan days earlier.

I returned to Whitmore who was now sitting down.

"Nice briefcase. Buy it in there?" her eyes glanced across the way to the shop.

"Naw. Ran into an old friend. Something I might need while here."

"Hope it doesn't set off some bells and whistles before we leave," she said.

"Me, too."

Malone finished his phone call and walked over toward us. He had a strange look in his eye as he approached.

"Something wrong," I said.

"Who are you?" he said.

"Beg your pardon?" I said, a little confused.

He looked at J.C. Whitmore and pointed to me.

"You know her?"

"She's with us, Mr. Malone. It's okay. You hired her. It's okay. Let's go get a cab and get to the hotel. I think you need to rest." Her tones were motherly. She hadn't spoken to me that way.

Malone, Whitmore and Reno got in the first cab. That left me, Pee Wee and Georgio to share the ride in the second one. Thrill a minute.

We were staying at the Hotel Pontchartrain on Washington Boulevard. Four star luxury. Beat most of the places I stayed. Malone had booked three adjoining suites for us. I had the outstanding pleasure of rooming with Whitmore, and we were in the suite next to Malone. I was happy to draw Whitmore out of that menagerie. It could have been a whole lot worse. The three ogres shared a suite. Malone shared his suite with no one.

I was watching Whitmore unpack. Georgio brought in two hang-up bags that I had failed to see before now.

"These clothes are for you," she said. She hung the bags on the right side of the closet. It was a large closet.

"I am to be his traveling secretary."

"I know. Think you can handle the charade?"

"I'll watch you closely and learn."

"You being smart?"

"No. Honest. Think I should watch Pee Wee?"

She finally smiled. Up till now, I wasn't sure she knew how.

"They're not too bad when you get used to them."

"You've had twelve years."

"Not really. Georgio has been around that long. Pee Wee and Reno are relatively new. They replaced a couple of guys who retired." She said *retired* in a funny sort of way.

"Euphemism?"

"You bet. Malone caught them stealing."

"Oh."

"He have those memory lapses often?"

"More and more frequently now. Probably early Alzheimer's."

"Could be just good old fashioned hardening of the arteries."

"That, too. Considering the fact that the man is over ninety, I think he's in remarkable shape."

"Granted. But the memory loss thing could become a serious problem. He have a will?"

"Of course."

"You the executrix?"

"No."

"What happens if the memory goes and does not return?"

There was a knock on our inter-suite door. Malone's side.

"Don't know, but I imagine it would be bad," she said as she walked over and opened the adjoining suite door.

"What would be bad?" Malone said as he entered the room without being invited. Memory lapses, but great ears.

She forced a smile at him but didn't answer his question. He looked around as if he owned the place.

"You like this, Clancy?" His attention moved elsewhere.

"Very nice."

"One of the best in Detroit. I like to stay here whenever I'm in town."

"You didn't stay with your son?" I said.

"Hell, no. I'd sleep in a tent by the river before I …" his voice trailed off without finishing the line. I got the idea.

"Thanks for the wardrobe," I said hoping to move away from the delicate subject I had invaded.

"You try them on yet?"

"Haven't had time."

"Well, do it. We're going out this evening. We can mourn for my slob of a son tomorrow. Tonight we party. Choose something… ah, on second thought, you help her, J.C. We're going to George and Harry's tonight. You'll love it."

He left the room. Places to go and people to see. One could only imagine what kind of CEO he had been in his early years. A shaker and a mover. No time for frivolities. Whatever he wanted, he got.

"George and Harry's?" I said when the door closed behind him.

"George & Harry's Blue Café. Great food and good music, if you like jazz."

"You like jazz?"

"I don't like music period. Jazz is especially distasteful. But I like the food there. Mr. Malone pays me well."

"For going with him?"

"For being seen with him. He says it keeps the gays away. Nothing between us except business. I wouldn't do that."

J.C. Whitmore was a stern talking, tough acting woman,

but she was attractive enough with some slight modifications. She wore her hair short, but not so you would mistake her gender. I was a few inches taller, but we appeared to be about the same size. I did notice that her hips were broader than mine, but that was probably due to sitting at the computer for Craven Malone and doing whatever business she did. She appeared to be in her early thirties. No lines under the eyes as yet.

"Nor I. So, what do you recommend I wear to the Blue Café?"

She opened both bags and began a rather serious selection process. It appeared that J.C. was all business all of the time. She handed me a short, white dress with a very low line in front. I am not what anyone would call chesty, so I smiled and declined the offer to reveal more than I had.

Without a word or a facial sign, she hung the white, plunging neck-line next to the bag and retrieved a short black dress that was more modest in my estimation. It fit and actually made me look halfway good. Personal opinion. Operative word being *halfway*.

"This one appears to fit," I said after changing into the black one. "What do you think?" Girl talk.

"It's a dress." Thank you, J.C. I needed that vote of confidence for this gig.

I should have known better than to expect a friendly exchange. Undaunted, I persevered to be Miss Personality with Miss Hard Nose.

"You have a guy back in Norfolk?"

"What? A boyfriend?" she sneered at me.

"Something like that. A regular, someone you date?"

"Date? Don't be absurd. Men know better than to bother me."

"How do they know that? You give off a scent?"

"I was married once. Didn't last long."

"Painful?"

"For him."

"You sound bitter."

"I am. I had to spend seven years in prison because of him."

"Sorry to hear that. He get you involved in something?"

"No. I killed the bastard after he raped me."

33

George & Harry's Blue Café was better than billed. I happened to like jazz, so the evening was enjoyable even with a ninety year old and Bad Ass Whitmore. Appropriately enough she spent the evening downing Whiskey Sours. She was drunk before ten, but it didn't help her disposition. I remained sober in order to stay alive.

Malone had Red Snapper Keywest, something the waiter recommended. It looked good, but I was in the mood for something a bit feistier. One of the house favorites was their Bayou Jambalaya, a Cajun stew of chicken, seafood and spicy sausage. The menu said it was simmered in Creole Sauce. The best part was that it was served over corn bread. Brought back fond memories of the corn bread I grew up on. It was just as good as my Mama's, but I would never tell her that.

Whitmore was well past sobriety when her Chicken Alfredo came. She played with it for twenty minutes while Malone and I enjoyed our meal. Our bodyguards sat at another table and they each ordered the 18 oz. Prime Rib. Carnivores supreme.

The jazz artist of the evening was a local talent who played the sax and sang some. I preferred the sax to his singing, but he was obviously a favorite among the other patrons. The background musicians – trumpeter, guitarist, and clarinetist saved us from listening to the soloist acappella. Whitmore even applauded, but that didn't count since she was past drunk. Malone seemed to be non-committal about the music of the night.

"You come here often?" I asked him during one of the softer tunes and no singing.

"Every visit. Know George and Harry personally. Good people. Was here the first night they opened. Have some vested interest in the place."

"Financial?"

"That, and I love good food."

"I take it you and your son didn't see eye to eye on many issues," I said, changing the subject.

"He wouldn't listen to me at all. Too damn independent. Headstrong. Figured he knew it all and could do no wrong. I offered him guidance, and he refused at every turn. He did do one smart thing."

"What was that?"

"Make Andy the editor of the magazine."

"But you don't like the magazine."

"Correct. But that doesn't mean I don't think it should be run efficiently so as to make money. Remember, it's one of the companies my corporation owns. I like making money."

"Even money made from sleaze?"

"You working for me for free or you plan to accept my money made from sleaze?"

"Not all your money is questionable."

"True enough. How will you know which dollar is and which isn't."

"I'll smell them."

He smiled and finished his glass of Bordeaux Blanc. He looked at his watch and gestured to the three pigs at the other table. I figured it was time to leave.

"Take care of J.C. She'll need you to tuck her in," he said to me.

I wanted to say something about charging him extra for this, but I decided against it. I was being paid handsomely for my charade here in Detroit, so the least I could do would be to help poor old soused J.C. back to our hotel suite. I was glad that it wasn't Pee Wee that was drunk next to me in the cab. J.C. sang Beach Boys' songs all the way back across town. By the time we reached the Pontchartrain, my estimation of the jazz singer of the evening was improving.

Georgio helped me carry J.C. to our suite. She was more like a feather for him than a person. I made a mental note not to cross Georgio unless I had a gun close by. Georgio dumped J.C. on one of the two queen-sized beds. She had stopped singing somewhere between the elevator and the suite. She was gone.

Georgio stood there for a moment looking at her, almost as if he expected me to tip him. I gave him my most fearsome stare and he left the room. Intimidation.

I undressed her and tucked her in. The funeral was after lunch tomorrow, so she had plenty of time to sleep it off. The silence in the room was good for a change. No small talk with a belligerent woman. Appealing.

I unlocked the briefcase to see what goodies Rosey had sent my way. The case had two handguns. The Smith & Wesson Model 360 was just like my gun except that it was a .357 instead of a .38. There was a slight difference in weight, still it had a nice balance. The other Smith & Wesson was Rosey's weapon of choice, the 9mm 952. He couldn't come, so he sent along his best friend. The 360 came with a shoulder holster and the 9mm had a waist holster. It was an easy call for me to take only one. I chose the shorter .357. Familiarity and comfort. I promised myself that I would avoid at all costs any kind of conflict that would require the carrying of two guns.

A limo was scheduled to pick us up at 12:30. Before the car arrived, J.C. and I had room service bring us a sampling of brunch around mid-morning. She was still craggy, but fiercely thirsty. After two or three glasses of water, she was starving, she said. I was hoping that the hangover would improve her disposition. I was wrong.

I was already dressed and resting in one of our many comfortable suite-chairs while Whitmore was running around the room in her slip, screaming obscenities because she couldn't find the right dress to wear. Malone had the good sense to buy me several suits for that business look. I selected a dark gray one with slacks for the funeral. Black would have said more than I wanted to say at Joey's passing. I thought that the gray was rather non-committal. I chose a light blue blouse with a French collar. Short, black pumps set off my stunning outfit for the graveyard affair.

The gray suit did two things for me. It gave me that business-look that Malone wanted and it permitted me to hide my .357 under my left arm. I hated the idea of carrying a weapon to a funeral. In fact, since my escapade with Rosey at his hideaway cabin in Virginia, I hated the idea of carrying a gun at all. Still, the reality was that I was in a dangerous business and now I was in a big city investigating a murder. I carried the gun. Survival conquered scruples.

We were all climbing inside the limo in the pouring rain when J.C. Whitmore came scurrying up looking pretty good for hard-nosed woman with a hangover. She was dressed in black from top to bottom. She was even wearing black hose. Professional mourner.

The funeral was a graveside service only. Craven Malone

was the only family Joey had. That meant that the entire family showed up for the service. There were maybe fifteen people gathered for the event, counting the six of us.

Some of us were standing around the grave under umbrellas while Craven and a few others were seated in chairs underneath a dark red canopy. I was half-heartedly listening to the priest languish on and on about the dearly departed, although I don't think he ever used that expression. His long and morose sermon fit the weather for the day, but not my personality. J.C. and I were among those standing under umbrellas. The three stooges were standing off to our left keeping an eye on the proceedings. They didn't have umbrellas. They looked out of place. I almost felt sorry for them.

"Which one is B.A. Dilworth?" I whispered to J.C.

"The one sitting to the right of Mr. Malone."

"She looks weathered."

"She's mean, too."

"You have business dealings with her?"

"Not if I can help it. Mr. Malone handles her okay, but generally he lets her run her show. That's best for all concerned. She's a bitch."

I wanted to say something like "you should know," but I refrained because the funeral was going along so morbidly well, and I so hate to ruin the ambience of any occasion.

We were drying out in a spacious room at the nearby Catholic church where Joey was a member. The priest mercifully terminated his message, and we sloshed our way to the vehicles that brought us to this place. I will admit that the good Catholic ladies of this diocese knew how to put out a spread. There were tables of food all around us and the somber tones of the priest's message were all but lost in the gaiety that erupted once we dried out. The three stooges were not quite as gay as the rest of us.

For an old man, Craven Malone got around exceptionally well. His was an outgoing personality, and he certainly knew how to network. I watched him for several minutes before I finally decided I might as well network myself. The funeral was over and now I had to find out who put Joey in the ground.

I found B.A. Dilworth sitting alone eating raw vegetables and fruit. She was close to my height, but weighed far less. She was thin. Her face was taut, but I noticed a few wrinkles under the eyes. Her hair was a shade of blonde. She probably had it colored every week or so. She was wearing a black dress with pearls. Elegantly mournful.

"Mind if I join you?" I said, approaching the bitch with caution.

"You're Craven's new protégée, correct?"

"That's me."

"And your name?"

We hadn't discussed changing my name, so I told her the truth.

"Where you from?" she asked.

"Virginia."

"Where'd you meet Craven?"

"Mutual friends."

"He's a hard worker. Relentless. More energy than I have."

"Were you close to Joey?"

Her eyes widened and she stared at me without answering. I wondered if I had actually said what I thought I had said. Maybe the words came out wrong. I wanted to repeat it, but I was afraid to say anything at the moment. I waited.

"Why do you ask that?" she said rather defensively.

"Oh, no reason. I had heard that you were business associates."

"Yes. Business associates. I don't know what else you have heard, but we were not close." She sounded firm and convinced, so I decided not to challenge her on that point. Besides, I was making mental notes and learning. I had truly heard nothing as to their relationship.

"I don't know many people here, except the ones I came with. Do most of these folks work in the office with you?"

"Honey, most of these folks work for me."

"And I bet they love it, too."

She stood abruptly, placed her plate hard on the seat she had just vacated, and walked off towards Craven Malone. Anger personified. Obviously my winning personality had captivated another individual.

34

"What in God's name did you say to Andy at the funeral?" Craven asked me as we were speeding along towards our hotel in the stretch limo.

"Just being my friendly self. Wanted to get acquainted with her."

"Well, she certainly did not take a liking to you, whatever you said. She called you several choice names and suggested rather strongly that I dismiss you as my protégée."

'Good thing you don't take orders from her," I said.

He coughed a few times in an unsuccessful attempt at clearing his throat. His color was a shade whiter than normal. He was struggling. J.C. leaped across the seat to assist him.

"Are you okay, Mr. Malone?" she asked.

"Fine, fine. Just lost my breath there for a moment. This old body is closing down quickly. I need some rest, that's all."

He coughed again and this time strained to clear his throat. Sounded the same to me. J.C. remained at his side the rest of the trip back.

I stayed in the lobby while the rest of our motley

entourage retired, presumably, to their suites. I had no real reason to remain in the lobby except that I wanted a break from my business associates and needed some privacy to call Rogers. Time to check in.

"How's life with the rich and famous?"

"Luxuriously boring."

"No handsome hunk waiting on the terrace anxious to sweep you off?"

"Rein in that wild imagination of yours. Tell me about that home in Mooresville."

"Not much to report."

"Pulling my leg?"

"Not this time. Apparently they were given an anonymous gift, and the donor insisted that no paper trail lead back to him or her. Everything seems to be above board as far as I can discern. I can find no misappropriations or even the hint of impropriety. Looks like you will have to travel to Mooresville and check them out in person if you are to find something."

"And I pay you so well to find things out. Now you fail me."

"My efforts have not been completely wasted, love."

"You have something with which I can actually work?"

"Guess who is the head of state at *Lusty*?"

"Now that Joey Malone is out of the picture?"

"Even before that."

"You mean it wasn't little Joey?"

"Joey was the boss on paper, but the files I hacked revealed a rather different pecking order."

"Enlighten me."

"Barbara Anderson Dilworth. Have you had the pleasure?"

"I've had something, thank you. Pleasure would not be my first choice of terms to describe the encounter. Generally speaking, she's a bitch, and that's a nice word for her. She's the editor, of course she runs things."

"She's been that since the late sixties. Can't find anything yet on how she got there, but she came in as Assistant Editor two years prior to her big advancement. Nothing like a quick trip up the corporate ladder. She's a cutthroat. Watch your backside. Dangerously smart. Anyhow, it's documented that Joey Malone liked her from the beginning. I found some non-public interoffice memos to that effect. I read a little between the lines and figured that maybe there was something more than professional respect between Dilworth and Malone."

"Believe me, I've met her and there is nothing alluring about this woman's appearance or charm. She goes by B.A. to everyone but Craven. You can easily figure out what that B.A. stands for behind her back, and it's not Barbara Anderson. You truly think she and Joey were an item."

"I found nothing that absolutely confirms it, but you know my female intuition. I sense something there. Subtle, well hidden from public scrutiny, except to an expert like me."

"Toot your horn, babes."

"Well somebody has to. Getting a compliment from you is like getting tea out of a milk pitcher."

"I adore your metaphors."

"Classy, huh? So, snoop around Editor Dilworth, but do be careful. She's actually fired more people than she has hired. Strange stat, but verifiable. And since her charm is closely linked to that of a piranha, you might keep both eyes open and on her around the clock."

"Noted."

"I'm just sayin'."

"Dogs good?"

"Margie is spoiling them rotten. Wait. Here comes Sam

now. Let me see if he wants to say something to you. I'll turn on the speaker phone and you two buddies can talk."

I heard a whine and then a short bark. Clear enough to me.

"Hey, buddy. You taking care of the place for me?"

A single bark response.

"Margie handling your every whim?"

One bark.

"When I get back, we'll travel to North Carolina together. I have a several-day trip down to the Tar Heel state. I'll need my partner on that one. You up for some investigative work?"

One bark.

"Rogers?"

"Yes, ma'am."

"See if you can find anything on Joey Malone's murder investigation. The Detroit police are bound to have a file on it already. Call me back tonight and give me some names to check. Ten or so."

The line went dead. She never really got phone etiquette.

"You got a partner?" Reno's burly voice interrupted my pondering on B.A. Dilworth just as Rogers disconnected us.

"I have lots of aides and contacts who help me from time to time," I said. I figured I could probably tell Reno the truth and it would be safe with him since his IQ matched his waist size. However, not wanting to risk exposure to him and his contacts, I decided against being openly truthful.

"Peoples on the inside?"

"You could say that."

"Like me. I sorta have some pull on the inside myself. I know some big-time folks who sets the mood, you know?"

"Sets the mood?" I said.

"Yeah. You know. In charge. Runs stuff. Tells peoples what to do and how to think."

"Oh, yeah. Those kind of folks. I bet you do."

I walked towards the elevator thinking we would part company and life would be grand. He followed me.

"You come looking for me?" I said as we both entered the elevator to go up.

"Yeah. Mrs. Dilworth said I should find you and see what you wuz up to?"

"I'm up to five feet and nine inches, Bubba," I said and put my right arm on top of head to help him understand my line. "Tell her that."

"Huh?" he said. It didn't help.

35

Craven Malone and B.A. Dilworth were having a private meeting in his suite. I didn't remember seeing her come in the hotel. Perhaps she had walked through the lobby and seen me on the phone. Reno was sent down to retrieve me. Apparently everyone, in addition to every thing, has its place.

"You think I should crash the little meeting next door?" I said to my roommate.

"What meeting?" Whitmore said.

"Craven and B.A. are in session."

"Mr. Malone and B.A. Dilworth?" she seemed genuinely surprised.

"That's what my watchdog told me."

"Your watchdog. What are you talking about?"

"Reno came down to the main lobby to entice me to come upstairs. Apparently B.A. was worried about me being alone downstairs."

"Makes no sense. Why would she be concerned about you … unless she suspects something."

I was surprised at her insight. I also happened to agree

with her. She must suspect that I am not just another protégée. Bad acting on my part. Too much wit to be a business associate.

"Think I blew my cover?"

She chuckled at me.

"What? Don't I act like a person under the employee of Mr. Craven Malone?"

"Not in a million years, lady. You're not subservient enough."

"You don't grovel so well yourself," I answered.

"Only when I have to. Around the boss, Mr. Craven, I grovel. He could fire and replace me in a breath. I make too much money to have to change my lifestyle at this point. I could never find a job making six figures."

I had assumed she was highly paid, but my number didn't have six digits before the decimal.

"Everyone has his price."

"Don't sound so damn uppity. You have a price, too."

"Everyone can be bought?"

"You betcha." Wow. She actually used some slang.

I dropped the subject since she obviously had her mind made up about people in general. She may have been right, but I would like to think that I could draw lines at some points along the way towards selling out. I still figured that there would be some things I would not do. Not that I could not do them, just that my scruples would stop me short of violating my own ethics. One hopes. The end does not always justify the means. However, I had to admit even to myself that my most recent squabble alongside of Rosey at this cabin retreat forced me to give pause. I killed three people.

"I think I'm going to go next door."

"You're crazy, you know. You're asking for trouble."

"Craven will be upset with me?"

She chuckled, but it was not the sound that comes from someone amused. More like an incredulous laugh. Derisive. To the point.

"Hardly. Mrs. B.A.D. is the serpent in this story," she said.

"I thought you could only crunch numbers and do health checks. I like that, Whitmore. Mrs. B.A.D."

"Wait till you taste her venom."

"Voice of experience?"

"No. Reader of data."

I checked my weapon under my left shoulder hidden by my jacket. Just in case Dilworth got ugly, I could always shoot her. I knocked on the door.

"Come in," Craven's voice rasped out from the other side.

I opened the door and found Malone and Dilworth sitting in the living room section of his suite. They were drinking something.

"Yes, Clancy? You need something?"

"Enlightened conversation," I said.

Dilworth gave me a strange look.

"Have a seat. Join us. We were just talking about the new subscription figures released for *Lusty* this quarter."

"Up or down?" I said.

"Up," Craven said with great enthusiasm. I figured he was acting since he had previously told he hated the magazine. Playing to the crowd.

"Why are we having this conversation with this peon?" Dilworth said.

"Oh, I'm sorry Andy. I should have told you earlier, just didn't have time. Listen, this is strictly hush, hush. Clancy here is a private investigator. She's working for me to find out who killed Joey."

"The Detroit police can do that. In fact, they are very good at what they do. I would trust them a whole lot more than some prowling private eye."

Her disdain for me was more than just as a peon business associate. True affections run deep. So do afflictions.

"Well, Clancy here will just make sure that things add up, that's all. She's not here to get in the way of the police work. You never know, she might find something they overlooked."

Dilworth rolled her eyes as she sipped whatever it was she was drinking.

"Would you like something from the bar?" Craven said to me.

"Martini. Shaken, not stirred."

"Well, well. A regular James Bond, we have here. Licensed to kill?"

"Yes, ma'am. Especially vermin."

If looks could kill, I'm already dead and someone is writing my eulogy. Dilworth was not like Reno. She was especially fast on the uptake. I would definitely have to watch my back with her.

Craven was at the bar shaking my Martini. Dilworth was giving me the evil eye.

"So this explains, I suppose, why you were asking those horrid questions of me at the reception."

"Suppose so."

"And all this time I just thought you were a rude and obnoxious underling."

"I am rude and obnoxious. Underling is a stretch."

I thought that deserved a smile, but she was a tough audience.

"Olive with this?" Craven called from the bar.

"Absolutely."

"So you heard that Joey Malone and I were close?"

"Not exactly. Sometimes you ask questions just to see what the person will say. You assume a bit here and there, and then you watch reactions. Clues."

"So you have heard nothing about Joey Malone and myself?"

"Nary a peep."

"What?"

"Not even a whisper. Your reputation is still intact."

She finished her drink in obvious displeasure. She set the glass down on the table beside her with such force, I knew that the glass would surely break into small pieces. No breakage. Sturdy glass.

"Craven, I must be going," she stood up when he handed me my drink. "Thank you so much for all you have done. It was a lovely funeral."

They embraced without touching. It was that high-society ethereal cheek to cheek sort of ritual that goes on among folks who love to pretend.

"Well, Andy, you did all the arranging from this end. Couldn't have done it without you. Let me know if you need anything. I mean that. Call me anytime."

"You're a dear. Thanks for the drink and the suggestions. I'll let you know if anything comes up."

He walked her to the door. They embraced once more without touching. Love that maneuver. Must get her to teach it to me sometime.

Craven walked back to the chairs and sat down. He let out a great breath and stared at me over the tops of his reading glasses.

"You really piss her off, don't you?" he said and laughed. It was a good, strong hearty laugh as if he really enjoyed what was happening.

36

We were riding in separate cabs heading towards The Rattlesnake Club for our nighttime meal and adventure. Craven and his associates were returning to Virginia Beach the next morning. Our last evening on the town together. Whoopie.

I was riding with Reno and Pee Wee. Georgio rode with Malone and Whitmore. Something was up. My keen detective skills were buzzing around inside my intuition. I could taste it, but I couldn't identify the label.

"Boss says you stayin' in De-troit," Reno said. We were friends by now. Intimate communication will do that.

"Found some work to do."

"Big cities can be dangerous."

"So can little villages," I said thinking of my hometown.

"Yeah, but there's more bad here than good. Watch your step."

I was touched. His tone sounded as if he genuinely meant it as a warning to be careful. It could have been a warning shot across my bow.

"Whatdaya know about De-troit?" Pee Wee said.

"I know plenty," Reno said with gusto.

"You know squat," his little brother answered.

"Know more than you do," Reno offered.

"Shut up. You talk too damn much."

Reno stopped talking. Pee Wee looked out the window. It had stopped raining, but the streets were shiny from the city lights. Maybe Reno did talk too much, but a heads-up to a world class detective never goes unheeded.

The Rattlesnake Club has a great view of the Detroit River. Their specialty is steak, thank God. They also offer a variety of seafood, so I was relieved to discover that I could dine with the crew once more and eat something I could name. I was also relieved that Craven was still picking up the tab.

Instead of separate tables, the hired guns dined with the rest of the family. I included myself in the hired gun category since everyone in our little group now knew who I really was and what I was supposed to do. I still wondered what I was supposed to do despite my having a rather strong sense of who I was.

Our host began his dining pleasure with an appetizer of Malpeque and Cape Ann Oysters with Lemon Vodka Mignonette and Spicy Shoestrings. They sounded exotic to me, but I somehow managed to pass. Whitmore chose the Yellow and White Peaches Entwined with Prosciutto, Arugula and Vidala Onions, accompanied by the Parmesan Crisp. I love the names of these dishes. Sounded truly uptown. All the way. I passed on the peaches and onions, despite the great looking crisp.

The three stooges and I had more in common than I realized. Without planned collusion, we each decided to watch the boss and Whitmore eat their *starters* while we sipped our way to the entrees of choice.

I was sure that Whitmore would actually voice some

displeasure when Malone insisted that everyone order some cut of steak, but all I saw in her was some mild disfavor reflected in a slightly raised eyebrow. I could tell that beef was not her first choice. J.C. and I chose the small Filet Mignon, while the burly boys and Craven indulged in the entire cow referred to as the Prime Porterhouse.

"I promise to stay sober tonight," Whitmore whispered in my ear.

"No jazz to swallow."

She actually smiled. I was making progress, but to what end. One never knows what information lurks inside the least suspected suspect. After all, she had already confessed to me that she was more than just capable of murder. I really did not consider her a serious suspect in this investigation, but she might know something that could help me. The probing detective is ever vigilant.

J.C. was sitting on one side of me and Craven, the other. That meant that I was privileged to enjoy watching the three heavy weights dine sumptuously on their cows of choice. Not a pretty sight.

When Craven had finished what he could of his Porterhouse, he pushed his plate away and took out a cigar. He didn't light it, but he puffed on it as if it were lit. I was grateful for his discretion. He moved his chair slightly in my direction.

"Where do you plan to start?"

"The police."

"Just waltz in and start asking questions?"

"Subtle, huh?"

"But they won't help you, will they?"

"Probably not."

"So then, what next?"

"Play it by ear."

I took my last bite of steak. I had to admit that it was

downright delicious, even if I didn't really prefer sneak. Sometimes forbidden foods have a delightfully sinful affect on me when I indulge.

"So you don't really have a game plan?"

"Yes and no."

"What does that mean?"

"I have a game, but not much of a plan."

"You're not going to tell me much, are you?" he said with a resigned tone.

"No."

"You'll call me when you have something." It was not a question, but he was searching for affirmation.

"You'll be the second to know."

"Who'll be the first?" he said quite indignantly.

"The killer."

My cell phone rang as we were walking out of the restaurant. I excused myself from out parade and entered the ladies room.

"Yes, ma'am?"

"I hear voices around you. Dining out?" Rogers said.

"Just finished. On the way out."

"Two things – the police detectives assigned to the Malone case there are Dennis Morland and Tony Scarletti. Morland is the senior of the two. They've been doing detective work for several years and the records show that they are good. They've been partnered for some five years and counting."

"Number two?"

"Found a kernel to chase on Dilworth. She was married for a short time to a guy named Dilworth. Imagine that. Reginald Oswald Dilworth, the 3rd. His grandfather and father were big in the newspaper industry in Chicago. But that's another story. Barbara Anderson Dilworth was actually Barbara Lily Anderson before she married into money and a career. And guess where she is from?"

"Norfolk."

"I love it when you are wrong. Makes me feel needed. No, ma'am. She's from ... ta-da ... Mooresville, North Carolina."

"Interesting," I said. Actually I already figured that somehow Mooresville would play a role in the life of one of the characters in this Detroit drama. I wasn't too surprised that it was her.

"Tis' rather, isn't it? I'll keep searching for more. I found all of that quite by accident, but with my ever-penetrating skills, voracious tenacity, and penchant for acquiring more and more data, it should come as no surprise to you that I always come through. I like back channels. Accidents are what I really go looking for."

"You're a jewel. Since I have some actual gumshoe work to do here in the city, I'll call you if I discover something else for you to chase down."

"Stay alive, sweetie."

37

When I awoke the next morning, J.C. Whitmore was dressed and packing. They had an early flight out of Detroit.

"Can't say it's been a pleasure," she said.

"Ditto, here," I said not fully awake.

"I do hope you find out who killed Joey Malone."

"You liked Craven's son?"

"Not a whit. But I like Craven Malone and he wants to know who did this. He didn't like Joey, but Joey was his son. You understand?"

"Sure."

"Blood's thicker than water, whatever the hell that means."

She took her bags and left. No goodbye. She did leave the radio on for me, even though I had not asked for such service. Country music was blasting away. When I finally forced myself to get up and turn off the misery, Bobby Bare's classic *Detroit City* came on and I was forced to pause and listen. After a few lines, I decided that it was too early in the morning for beer-drinking music, so I clicked it off.

A few of the lyrics stayed in my head: *I dreamed about my*

mama, dear old papa, sister and brother. I dreamed about those cotton fields, waiting for me there. I wanna go home.... Some of that was true. Life is crammed full of nostalgia, even when you don't try to conjure it.

Craven said I could stay on at the Pontchartrain as long as I was in Detroit. He would cover my tab. Sometimes he acted like a nice old man with lots of money. I thanked him, but was my usual non-committed self as to whether I would stay there. I would have to play this by ear until I could see what my future held in this great city.

I showered and had room service deliver a Continental breakfast before I hit the streets. I decided to continue wearing the business suits that Craven had bought for me. The jacket helped to hide my concealed .357 Smith & Wesson. I voted to be hot and prepared, rather than cool and vulnerable. The lyrics of Bobby Bare were gone by the time I left the room.

The main desk of the hotel provided me with a map of the city and a guide to the bus lines. Susie tourist, ready for the sites. After forty minutes on the bus, I had enjoyed as much of mass transient as I could stand. I found a car rental place on my tourist map, rode the bus another fifteen minutes to that location, and then rejoiced silently when I exited. I rented a dark green Ford Taurus. I wanted something that didn't look like a detective trailing two policemen. The Ford Taurus did it. Dark green color helped a lot.

I parked in front of the First Precinct Station on Beaubien. I gambled that my two police detectives worked in the First Precinct. I had nothing to go on. Just time. If I were wrong, then I move on to the Second Precinct. Efficiency at work. I could have asked some beat cop, but policemen tend to get suspicious of folks asking out-of-the-ordinary questions. I sat tight and waited. Fortunately, I did find a photo of Morland on page one of the local press. I figured that whoever was with him must be Scarletti. The powers of deduction.

I was dining on nabs and a Coke when I first spotted Morland with another man driving out of the precinct around 1:15 that afternoon. I followed them. My Taurus did an excellent job of keeping up with them in traffic. I may have to reconsider my long- standing opinion of dark green cars if it kept this up. While they made several long stops all over town, I had plenty of time to read while I waited on them to return to their car. I had a couple of newspapers that reported on the initial version of what had happened to Joey Malone. I knew that the police seldom give the press the entire story, but I had nothing else to go on. I needed to know what little I could while spending the afternoon following Morland and the one I assumed to be Scarletti.

Joey Malone was found dead by his maid on a Saturday morning. The initial article from the first paper said that it was probably a heart attack. However, the second paper said that the police had ruled out natural causes. Aha. Foul play. Great detectives keep up with stuff like that. The third article from this morning's edition provided a statement from the Medical Examiner who said that he was poisoned. Foul play, indeed.

There was no mention of the type of poison, nor any other gory detail that we public so enjoy when a wealthy celebrity who happens to be a sleaze-bag dies.

Morland and the other fellow were just leaving a small white frame house on the lower west side of the city when I decided to take my life in my hands and announce my presence. With my usual charm and sexy style, I approached the two detectives.

"Detective Morland, my name is Clancy Evans. May I speak with you for a moment?"

Dennis Morland was as refreshing as rain to a drowning

person. I expected him to be rough and uncooperative. He did not disappoint me one bit.

"I don't like to talk to reporters," he said without pausing in his walk towards his vehicle. The other man kept pace with Morland.

"I'm not a reporter."

He stopped.

"Whattaya want?"

"I have some questions about the Joey Malone murder case you're working on."

"Do you, now? Well, well. And what interest is the Joey Malone investigation to you, Clancy Evans?"

"I was hired by Joey's father to find out who killed his son."

"Good for you, Clancy Evans. Wish you all the luck in the world," he started moving towards his car again. "But if you think I am going to stand here in the hot sun exchanging pleasantries and case notes with a damn female gumshoe about a case I am working my tail off to finish, then lady, you're in for a rude awakening."

He and the other man continued to their car. I followed behind him.

"How about dinner? My treat."

Morland stopped moving after he opened his car door. The other man was already seated inside the car. Cops like food.

"Both of us?" Morland said.

"Of course."

"We name the place."

"Naturally."

"Follow us," he said.

I followed them to Mario's Italian Restaurant on 2nd Avenue. They gave us a private table in a corner after I asked politely and gave the hostess twenty dollars. I figured that

Craven Malone could afford my business expenses in search of the truth.

We each ordered the special dinner consisting of spaghetti, lasagna, and chicken cacciatore. Along with the fresh, homemade bread, spiced olive oil for dipping, salad and some very fine Chianti, it was more supper than I could handle. The men continued after I stopped to catch my breath.

"Great food, huh?" Morland said to me.

"Good Italian. Chef must be from Italy."

"Don't know," said Scarletti, who finally had introduced himself to me as we entered the restaurant. "He's good, that's all that matters."

"The taste is it," I said.

Morland put his fork and knife down and finished chewing some food. He took a large swallow of his Chianti and set his glass down empty. He looked across the table at me.

"Look, Evans, we don't like PI's coming around and bothering us while we're working a case. But since you're such a nice person and all, and since you bought us this delicious meal, we might be inclined to help you a little. Here's the deal – whatever we find, we let you know. Whatever you find, you let us know."

"Sounds fair."

"Hell, it ain't got nothing to do with fair. It's got everything to do with pride and the fact that we've been busting our balls over this case since day one. City Hall wants this one solved quickly. This man was a highly visible person in our city. Sure, he was sludge you wouldn't want on your feet, but he gave generously to all types of charities and fund raisers."

"And campaigns."

"Nobody said nothing about campaigns, Evans," Scarletti said.

"Implied," I said.

"Look," Morland continued, "it ain't in our best interest to help you. We don't like competition."

"I'm not looking to solve the case before you do. I don't even want credit for it. I just want a breadcrumb when you find something. I would even be glad to help you incognito."

"We don't need no dame helping us," Scarletti said.

"Didn't mean to imply you needed help, but it would seem that since you are receiving some pressure from downtown, you might like to have some secret help. No one would have to know but us."

"How do we know we can trust you?"

"You don't. I give you my word."

"Not good enough," Scarletti said.

"Wait a minute. Let's think this through, Tony. The Captain is on our butts to end this thing as soon as we can. We can keep her on a short leash and run her out of town if she is lying to us."

"But if the Captain finds out, he'll put us back working a beat."

"We'll say we never knew she was here."

"Well," I finally said, "I can see that you guys are really struggling here with your integrity. Let me see if I can help the situation."

I told them my case, the thirty-two year old unsolved murder of my father and the connection I had with Malone Industries. I also told them about Joey's contract on me, and then his untimely death before his father could even pull the plug on the contract.

"Well, it would appear that you do have a vested interest," Morland said.

"Distant from your interest. Still, no reason we can't join

forces and learn something together as we go. Maybe you'll find something that will help me, and I could find something to help you. Beats working against each other."

"Okay, here's the deal," Morland said finally. "We meet for food every other day, your treat. If we find something substantive, we'll call you and bring you along with us. In the meantime, we'll give you some items to check that won't get you too involved in the public so there won't be unnecessary questions asked. You have to keep a low profile. Very low."

"Lower than that," Scarletti said.

I agreed to his proviso, gave him my cell number and hotel room number. I also told him I had access to a very thorough computer source who could trace just about anything they might need traced.

"How could a female private detective have access to something like that?" Scarletti said.

"Craven Malone has deep pockets," I said.

38

It was raining when I awoke the next morning. I was suffering from a slight headache, probably from the third glass of Chianti I had during the Italian meal the previous evening. My suite had a small refrigerator for my leftovers from the bounty of Italy. I could smell them all the way across the room from my kitchen facilities.

My cell phone rang.

"You still sitting pretty up there on the top of the world?" Rogers' voice was simply too cheerful for my taste at this early morning hour. I looked over at the clock. It wasn't even eight.

"Why are you calling me so early?"

"Make hay while the sun shines. That's what I always say."

"You say nothing of the sort. I've never ever heard you say that. I hope you have something for me and it better be good."

"Do I fail thee, ever, fair damsel? My words are my treasure. My truth is my power. My relentless quest for justice is my reason for being."

"Brother. You sound like a Shakespearean intro to the old Superman television show. What have you got?"

"Two items of interest. One, I was meandering around in the database of the police there in Detroit city and accidentally came across a request for information on you, of all people. Imagine that."

"Yeah, imagine that. Who from?"

"Someone in the Detroit Metropolitan Police System."

"I would very much like to know who."

"Thought so. I'll sit on it until I discover who made the inquiry. Would you like me to send a reply of only the good stuff?"

"Not until you find out exactly where it is going. I don't even want good stuff about me going to just anybody."

"Any particular reason that the Detroit police would be investigating you? I know you have been in town long enough to cause mayhem and chaos, but, really, even for you, this is fast."

"You're so good for my self-imagine. The answer is … yes and no. There are two guys, detectives, those names you gave me at your last report. I can imagine it is one of them, if not both. The only problem with those two is that they would not go through police channels to find out about me. Too dangerous for them since we have agreed privately to work this case together. Sort of."

"I have some questions about that, but, I shall wait on asking. I'll find the answer for you quickly. Anything else you need?" Rogers said.

"You said you had two items. What's the other?"

"Oh, yes. Seems that Craven Malone and B.A. Dilworth got together at his Virginia Beach resort home."

"Craven just left from here this morning."

"He and B.A. arrived in Norfolk today. Shared a flight, it seems. They're together as we speak now."

"Together, together?"

"Well, I wouldn't know that and I certainly wouldn't want to speculate."

"Sure you would. What do you think?"

"I think he could afford better. But I don't think they're in bed, together to together, if that's what's lurking in that gutter mind of yours. I think that whatever they are doing *together* is all business."

"How did you find this out?"

"Really now. You want to ask me that kind of question, after all this time we've shared together?"

"Never mind. I forget you have far-reaching tentacles."

"I can reach around the world, Mama, in seconds. The entire globe is my backyard."

"Stay in touch about that police check on me. I need names."

"Your wish is my command."

She disconnected us. I lay there wondering what Craven was up to, or for that matter what B.A. Dilworth was up to. I wondered if Morland and Scarletti had checked on me. I wondered why they would risk divulging my presence by such checking. I also wondered how Morland and Scarletti could check on me during the night. Trust is a narrow, crooked street.

After my shower, I dressed and added my Detroit .357 just in case I had trouble with the waitress at breakfast. I had decided to enjoy some food downstairs in the lounge. It was one of those all-you-can-eat buffets that seem to be so popular among overweight Americans. Go figure. I had a bagel and fat-free cream cheese with orange juice and black coffee. Nourishment.

On my way to the elevator to return to my lavish suite, I spotted a man in a black and white checkered coat watching me from behind his newspaper. It was easy to see that he had his mind on something other than reading. The sports section was upside down. Clever detectives spot these things immediately.

I took the elevator to the floor above my suite and used the stairs to get down to my room level. I waited by the door to the stairs to see if Mr. Ace Tail would go to my floor. Cat and mouse. I was playing the cat this time.

Bingo. Ace got off the elevator on my floor and walked directly to my room door. He put his ear against the door. He turned and looked up and down the hallway. I was neatly hidden in the shadows. He appeared confused, and well he should have been. I have been eluding men rather expertly for years. This one was absolutely no challenge.

I waited for him to get back on the elevator. It never occurred to him that there might be stairs in this place. I followed him using another elevator. We were heading to the lobby.

The elevator doors opened and I eased out just in case he had developed some sense going down. I hated to give up my advantage so early in the game.

I should not have worried. Ace was walking out the front door of the Pontchartrain. I decided to tail him. I hadn't anything else to do since Morland and Scarletti wanted me to lay low, like B'rer Rabbit. This could be fun.

It was easy staying behind him and not being seen. He never turned around to look. We walked a brisk pace for several blocks, then he turned the corner at 6th Street. I eased to the corner and craftily peeked around the corner. He was talking to Scarletti who was seated in a car. Ah, the bond of trust. 'Tis so fragile.

After several minutes of meaningless dialogue, Ace got into the car and the two super detectives drove away. I'm guessing it was meaningless since Ace had nothing to report except his inability to stay with me. I'm sure that was wonderfully exciting news for Detective Scarletti.

I returned to my suite after I watched Scarletti and Ace drive away. My door was open, so I figured that the maid must be inside cleaning.

The room had my personal items thrown all over it. Everything was either on the floor or on my bed. Two men were standing close together at my bed looking in the briefcase that had brought me my Detroit weapons. They were admiring the 9mm that I had left.

My .357 was drawn and on them before they realized that I was in the room.

"We can do this easy or hard. Your call, boys. I prefer easy."

They were stunned and speechless.

"Place the 9mm gently back in the case and move away from the bed."

They didn't move. Both were average height and wearing sport coats and khaki pants. One had a red, white and blue stripped coat. Patriotic. The other had something green with squares in it. Low budget shopping will do that for you.

I pulled the hammer back on the .357.

"So, you choose hard. This is certainly going to make a mess for the maid to clean up."

"Wait a minute," Mr. Green Squares said with a hint of anxiety. "Sammy, put the gun down."

Mr. Patriotic awoke and placed the 9mm back inside the briefcase. They both stepped back away from the bed.

"Put your hands together behind your heads and face the other direction."

They slowly obliged.

"If you move to scratch anything, I will shoot you. I'm sort of nervous having two men uninvited in my bedroom here. You'll have to forgive me when I shoot you and I miss the spot I'm aiming at and kill you. Nerves."

I walked up behind Mr. Patriotic and put the muzzle of my .357 against his left temple. Using my left hand, I found a .38 holstered on the left side of his waist under his July 4th coat. I tossed it onto the bed. I moved carefully to the far side of Mr. Green Squares. I placed my .357 against his right temple and found a .45 in the same spot where Patriotic had his. I backed away from them and tossed his weapon onto the bed.

"Now, guys, let's talk about this."

"Nothing to say," Mr. Patriotic said.

"Not a good beginning."

"We got nothing to say," Green Squares added.

I immediately decided that the brains of this duo was Mr. Patriotic and that Green Squares was the weakest link here. I picked up the .45 and using the butt, I hit Patriotic across the bad of the head hard enough for him to groan. He crumpled to the floor, slightly out of it.

"What the hell are you doing, lady?" Mr. Green Squares said.

"I want to talk. Will you talk with me?"

"I ain't got nothin' to say."

"I hope you have lots of aspirin."

"Wait, wait. What do you want to know?"

This was going to be easier than I had imagined.

"Who sent you?"

"Tony Scarletti."

39

After I discovered that the two clowns were looking for anything that their employer, Tony Scarletti, might use against me, I let Mr. Green Squares drag his semi-conscious partner out of my room. I then called the hotel manager to complain and he sent the hotel security to my room to check on me. I put the briefcase containing my 9mm out of sight before the security man arrived. I also placed the two guns I had acquired from the poorly dressed criminals inside the briefcase. I concluded that Michigan was a good place to acquire guns. So far so good.

The security man assured me that this sort of thing did not happen to their guests normally, and that it would not happen again. I smiled and thanked him.

I then called Rogers.

"Dig for information on Tony Scarletti. Either he doesn't trust me, or he has something to hide. Anything yet on who is investigating me at the Detroit police department?"

"Scarletti. I found the original document, the request. Name at the bottom. Signed."

"Did this info request come through the proper channels?"

"Don't think so. It was a fax sent to a specific detective here in Norfolk. Someone named Tom Smith."

"Must be a friend of Scarletti's. So what did you tell Tom Smith about me?"

"You know me so well. Yes, Tom Smith found the document I managed to make available for his search and it was all good stuff. Nothing dubious whatsoever. You can relax. I mostly lied to your credit."

"The Norfolk Police had some incriminating data on me?"

"Not really. They did have some personal info that I either deleted or altered. I hid the stuff that would allow them to know more than I thought they should know about you."

"And the actual Norfolk file on me?"

"It's still on their computers, just harder to find. They have computer gurus who will discover it when they really need it."

"This Smith guy in Norfolk, he say anything in his fax to Scarletti that might be helpful to us?"

"Maybe. There was a personal note scribbled at the end of it that said, 'give my love to my sister.'"

"Family all around. Okay, I need some info on Scarletti. Anything that you think might show that he is dirty. Even some hints of impropriety. Dig everywhere. I want to know everything I can about him. He sent some goons to my hotel room and they rummaged through my wardrobe. I don't care for that. Find what you can. If he's a dirty cop, then he'll stop this charade. If he's just being nosey, he'll stop as well. I have four guns now."

"Information is power, huh?"

"Bank on it."

"I should get back to you this evening."

I spent the afternoon cleaning my Detroit guns, dozing, and wondering. I toyed with the idea of ordering some exotic drink from the bar downstairs, but I never liked mixing work with alcohol. Dulls the senses.

I must have finally fallen asleep because it was after five when I regained my awareness of time passing. I had been resting my eyes for over two hours by that point. I remember some stupid dream about being chased by timber wolves in downtown D.C., but weird dreams were a usual fare for me.

The phone rang. I figured it was a bit early for Rogers to be calling.

"Clancy, Morland here. We need to meet."

"Supper?"

"Not this time. And we need to meet in some out of the way place."

"Name the spot."

"Lobby of Hotel Baronette. It's out near the Twelve Oaks Mall. Just catch a cab and it'll take you to the front door. Around ten o'clock."

"Just you and me?"

"Two to tango."

He hung up. No one liked to say good-bye on the phone anymore. Perhaps it was one of those cultural shifts, like the usage of *thank you* and *please*. Wasn't too sure I enjoyed these cultural shifts.

I had plenty of time to eat before my clandestine meeting with Morland, but not much time before Rogers would ring. Having some ravenous craving for meat, I called room service and had them bring me a large hamburger with everything, including some fattening French fries. I also indulged in a chocolate milkshake. Might as well go full-bodied all the way.

Rogers called close to 7:15 and I was still munching on

fries and savoring my last swallows of milkshake. I was falling in love with room service here at the Pontchartrain.

"Scarletti has been on the Detroit force for twenty-four years, two years longer than Morland. Yet, as you know, Morland is the senior man. Rank. Sounds to me like Mr. Scarletti hasn't played the game squarely during his tenure."

"Hmmm," I said.

"Does that mean *yes* or that you don't understand?"

"Probably means that something is amuck."

"Seems that Morland was paired with Scarletti about five years ago, the result of some misbehavior on the part of Scarletti. Still, this is conjecture on my part. But, I'd say that I'm not far from the truth. Something happened when Scarletti was with his then partner, Tim Runyon. He and Runyon had been together for close to three years when Runyon was killed in the line of duty. I couldn't find anything directly linking Scarletti to the shooting. At the time Runyon was killed, Scarletti was up for a promotion. He didn't get the promotion."

"So he was assigned to Morland following that."

"One way or the other, Morland and Scarletti were paired."

"Anything else in his file?"

"Nada."

"Check Internal Affairs. Maybe they have something."

"I'll call when and if."

"Call me late. I have an appointment at ten."

"Young ladies should be in their rooms preparing for bed by that hour."

"Go do your work and mind your own business."

"Tsk, tsk."

Maybe her attitude was a glitch in the system. Maybe it was a programming error. One of these days I will have to look into that and repair her dialogue chip. Or remove it.

40

CABBIE MARSHA DEWINTER DROPPED ME AT THE FRONT DOOR of the Hotel Baronette. She was the kind of driver who gave away a mountain of Detroit trivia but seldom asked any questions. I learned more than I cared to know, but it was not an altogether unpleasant ride.

Morland was sitting in a chair by a lamp in the lobby strategically situated so that he could view the front door as well as the elevators and the front desk. I sat down on the sofa on the other side of the table and lamp where he was pretending to read the newspaper.

"Where's your partner?" I said.

"Can't say, but he's the reason I'm here."

"He send you or you two working some angle on me?"

"Whattaya mean?"

"Have you had any contact with him since we had supper last night?" I said.

"We worked today. Haven't seen him since about eight or so. Why?"

"Scarletti's been a busy man," I said.

"Whattaya driving at?"

"He sent some goof-ball to spy on me, like I was some third grade investigator, and then he sent Mutt and Jeff to my room while I was trailing Mr. Goof-ball back to Scarletti himself. I spotted Goofy and Scarletti together, but they didn't know I was there. He's not too swift with subterfuge."

"He's contacted his brother-in-law on the Norfolk Police force to check into you."

"Tom Smith. I know."

"How could you possible know that?"

"I'm a shrewd investigator. I have my sources."

"But he was using the precinct computer and there was no way this information was made public. We have our own server."

"True, but you should know that nothing is safe on computers these days."

"You hacked into the police records?"

"Moí? Never. But I know someone who did. I am, hopefully, one step ahead of Tony. What's he after?"

"He didn't want to do this thing with you. Said you'd just get in the way. Was adamant, even after we left last night. Says he doesn't trust you."

"Well, after sending those goons around to search my room, I can say that feeling is mutual. If he wants to know something, why doesn't he just ask?"

"He wouldn't believe you. He's not used to people talking straight. Tony's a good guy with some weaknesses. I think –," he stopped and looked around the lobby.

I waited for him to continue. He studied the front desk and then the pathway to the elevators. Nothing seemed to be suspicious to him, or at least he showed no signs of alarm.

"Why are we meeting alone?" I said finally.

"I think Tony's on the take. I think he's on Big Bob LeFoy's payroll."

"Big Bob?"

"Hokie, I know, but that's what he goes by. Has gambling interests, prostitution, and drugs. Rumored that he has some cops working for him, but IA's been on this for years with no success. Big Bob is squeaky clean, at least by provable facts. Suspicions won't get an indictment. So, tell me, is there anything he can find out about you that would force me to terminate our little arrangement?"

"Am I dirty?" I said with mock disdain.

"Something like that."

"Unlikely. I know exactly what was sent to him, so unless he digs up my past and discovers that I used to lie to my mother, he's got nothing but dead ends."

"All the cops in Norfolk love you?"

"Didn't say that exactly. If he gets his brother-in-law, Tom Smith, to do some leg work, he might find some bitterness here and there. I've irritated some administrators and some of my superiors, but I did good work as a cop. I still do good work."

"Yeah," he said and looked away to study the front door, then the elevators.

"You think Scarletti is suspicious of you?"

"Can't take any chances. I think Tony had something to do with the death of Tim Runyon. Nothing provable. Still, I have a strong sense that he either set him up, or he pulled the trigger. I can't take chances. I don't want my death benefit to start prematurely for my family."

"Better safe than dead."

"Got that right."

"How do we play this?"

"For starters, let's do the basics. Let's keep this between us. No confrontation with Scarletti about the man following you or the goons he sent to your room. By the way, they didn't find anything, did they?"

"The butt of a borrowed .45 up against the head of the one wearing the patriotic coat."

"I see you're a wild woman when duty calls."

"Not really my style, but sometimes situations dictate erratic behavior."

"My hunch is that you are a straight shooter. It appears this is a situation for you to display that erratic behavior, and not say anything to Scarletti. Let's see how this plays out."

"Not a problem. We'll play your rules until the game turns south."

"Supper, tomorrow night?"

"Mario's again?"

"Naw. This time let's let Mr. Malone take us to the Rattlesnake Club."

"Is that as dubious a place as it sounds?" I said.

"Naw. It's an upscale dining spot with high priced steaks and lots of big shots playing the game of pretend."

"Sounds like fun," I said.

41

THE DAYS WERE BEGINNING TO RUN TOGETHER FOR ME. TOO much of the same routine and not enough excitement. I was not making any progress on either case, so I decided it was time to take action and stop all of this waiting around.

It was 12:02 when my phone rang.

"Didn't catch you napping or in harm's way, did I?" Rogers began.

"Neither. Just sitting here making resolutions for tomorrow. Nothing is really happening, so I think I shall go rattle some cages or rustle some bushes."

"You humans have some strange metaphors," she said.

"Yeah, we do. But you get my gist."

"I've worked with you long enough to say yes, I do. Maybe I can help you rattle or rustle something."

"Give me something good."

"Tim Runyon sent a note to Internal Affairs saying that he suspected something major coming down with Big Bob LeFoy. Heard that name yet?"

"Believe or not, it has surfaced."

"Runyon thought his partner was in on it, or had something to do with it, but he had no proof. The note said he hopefully would have some proof in a day or two. That note was sent the day before he was shot."

"Doesn't make any sense to me. Why would Runyon be working with IA? Cops don't help IA investigate cops generally."

"You think it doesn't ring true?"

"Let's just say I am suspicious."

"Maybe this Runyon guy was undercover, you know, someone that IA brought in to investigate some dubious police activity."

"But he and Scarletti had been working together for three years at the time he was killed."

"Perhaps it was a long-term investigation. Maybe this Big Bob character was worth the added expense and time of planting someone close to Scarletti in order to get close to Big's organization."

"To whom did Runyon send that note?"

"Fellow named Smith."

"There's my lead. I need to find this Smith guy and talk with him. Smith in Internal Affairs?"

"That's all it said on the note I copied."

"Five years ago?"

"Yep."

"Keep digging."

Before I could add a quick *bye,* she was offline and on to something else. Efficient to a fault.

I slept until seven, showered, and had a quick muffin and orange juice from room service. I had the main desk bring me a large metropolitan phone book. I planned to rattle some chains via the telephone.

I called Internal Affairs.

"May I speak with Detective Smith, please?"

"Which one?"

This was going to be more difficult to rattle than I thought.

"Oh, dear," I began in my best desperate-female voice. "I work for the Police Gazette and we're doing a follow-up on the death of Detective Tim Runyon a few years back. I came across the name of Detective Smith on a document, but we have no first name. I just wanted to talk with him regarding the death of Mr. Runyon."

"Hold on," the voice, now full of authority, said to me.

I held tight. My scheme was not working very well, and I certainly did not like my Police Gazette angle. It was all my feeble brain could conjure. I should have had a contingency plan.

"This is Captain Walt Arnold. May I ask who is calling in regards to Tim Runyon's death?"

"I work for the Police Gazette and we're doing a follow-up story about the death of Tim Runyon."

"I got all of that from the Desk Sergeant. I want to know who you are."

"Oh, I'm a reporter for the Police Gazette."

"Good for you, young lady. What's your name?"

"Sally Markam."

"Well, Miss Markam, I can't give out any information regarding that case."

"I certainly understand the need for discretion, Mr. Arnold."

"Captain Arnold."

"Sorry, Captain. I was saying, I do understand discretion. But if I could just speak with Detective Smith about this, it would only take a minute or so."

"There is no Detective Smith here, Miss Markam. Your information must be incorrect. How did you get the name Smith?"

"Well, I inherited the notes of the reporter who did this

story five years ago. I found the name Smith scribbled on his pad. It said only that Smith worked for IA and that he had some information about Detective Runyon's death. Nothing more. I wish I had something else to go on. You sure there is no Detective Smith who might know about this?"

"I'm sure. But even if there was someone here by that name, I wouldn't let you talk with him. It's against police policy. We don't like the lives and deaths of our policemen spread over the media with unsupported allegations."

"Oh, me either, sir. That's not what this story is about. This is a tribute to the life of Detective Runyon. I was hoping that Mr. Smith could provide some light on why he was killed and what he was investigating at the time."

"Can't help you, Miss ...," he paused when he couldn't recall my name.

"Markam," I said quickly.

"Markam, yes. Wish I could provide some help for you. Thank you for calling. You might check your sources again. I think you have a wrong name."

I hung up and wondered if I had just gathered a clue, or been brushed off. Maybe both. I could figure that either Captain Arnold was misleading me intentionally, or he was telling me the truth, that there was no one there by that name. I could work either direction. Or both. I started with the assumption that there was no one there by that name. Maybe there used to be.

I called Rogers.

"Get me a roster of all the men and women who worked at Internal Affairs when Runyon was killed. Then get me a roster of all the men and women who work there now."

"Hold while I search."

"You can do that now, while I wait?"

"Faster than a speeding bullet."

"I'll hold."

I walked to the window of my suite and looked out on the Detroit skyline. Overcast. Smog and clouds mixed for great breathing. No rain, just dismal looking. Great place to dream about cotton fields back home. Except that we didn't have cotton fields in Pitt County, nor in Norfolk for that matter.

"Okay, you have a precise name you want?"

"Some guy named Smith who was there at the time of Runyon's death and who is not there now."

"Smith … Smith … okay, here's Jennifer Smith, Allen Smith … Margaret Ann Smith … oh, goodie, here's a Tom Smith."

"Bingo. Tom Smith."

"I detect a note of familiarity."

"You should. That's the name of Tony Scarletti's brother-in-law in Norfolk. You gave it to me earlier."

"I was simply testing your memory skills," she said.

"Do some background on Tom Smith. How long in Norfolk? Where did he come from? Whatever you can uncover. Thorough, please."

"Can you wait while I do that?"

"I can."

I walked to my little refrigerator hoping for some leftovers to munch. Leftover Italian food from two nights ago was waiting on the bottom shelf. Cold lasagna didn't do it for me. My stomach growled.

"You still there?" Rogers asked.

"Listening to your every word."

"He's been there since Runyon was killed. A few months after the shooting, Smith put in for a transfer to Virginia. He cited personal reasons on his transfer application form."

"And he moved to Norfolk from Detroit."

"Clever girl. Sometimes you actually amaze me," Rogers said.

42

I WALKED INTO THE LOBBY OF *LUSTY* MAGAZINE'S BUILDING ON McComb Street, just around the corner from the Detroit Police Station. Location, location, location. Prime real estate. It gave the appearance of a first-rate business, not the sleaze I was expecting. A woman was seated behind a large oaken counter with an even larger oaken backdrop behind her. The backdrop had plastic flowers growing out of the top. There was a painting of some child playing in a field of lilies. Tasteful, but considering what I knew of them, a bit dubious.

The woman was wearing a bright red dress that fit her like it appreciated the opportunity, a white pearl necklace, and bright red eyeglasses attached to her face by white straps that ran around her head and dropped indelicately down her back. Her hair was pitch black with a streak of silver running along the left side. Color. Flair.

I was carrying a folder with embossed writing – Waynright & Sons Funeral Home. It was left over from Joey's sending-off party. I collect souvenirs. Sometimes such souvenirs can be helpful.

"Good morning," I said.

"Good morning," Miss Flair returned to me. "May I help you?"

"B.A. Dilworth, please."

"Let me check…oh, she's out for the week. Would you care to talk with someone else?"

"I'm from the funeral home that handled Mr. Malone's arrangements. We discovered some …. ah…. items. Tell you what, maybe I need to talk with someone who helped to handle his affairs."

"That would be Cyler Conroy, Mr. Malone's Personal Assistant. He worked closely with Mr. Malone's father in regards to the funeral. Such a lovely affair, too."

"I don't recall seeing you there."

"Oh, I was working. Cyler took photographs. We plan to do a spread in an upcoming issue. Sort of a final farewell, you know. Send off for a great guy."

I forced a smile.

"I understand," I said. First class organization. Probably will run Joey's spread next to some article about children running naked with adults. Quality stuff.

She smiled at me as if it were my cue to say something more. I returned her smile and waited for the light to go on. Desperate moments passed between us in elongated silence. I gave up on the light going on.

"May I see Cyler Conroy?"

"Just a moment. I'll check to see if he is available. Your name, please?"

"Clancy Evans." I gambled that Craven Malone had not divulged my identity with anyone but B.A.

"He'll be right out," she said after a few moments.

The lobby was small, just large enough for Miss Flair, her desk-counter, the artificial flowers, and a painting of a small blond girl sitting in a field of daisies. The artist depicted the child with a handful of flowers held up to her nose. She was smiling. For my taste, it was a rather oddly placed painting of innocence on the wall behind the desk of Miss Flair in the lobby of *Lusty* magazine.

There was a door leading off to parts unknown to her right. I assumed that was the door that Cyler Conroy would come through any moment now and be nice to me until he found out who I really was.

I was still staring at the door when it suddenly opened. Out came a short, slim man walking quickly in my direction. He appeared to be leaving the building as if just passing through on his way to catch a bus or cab or subway. He stopped abruptly in front of me and gave me his hand in an awkward fashion. The fingers of his right hand were aiming slightly downward rather than extended straight out in front of him. His thumb was pointing toward my heart. I grabbed what I could of his hand and allowed him to do the shaking. It was a rather strange greeting ritual, to say the least.

He was relatively young, but had prematurely gray hair, short and curly. The curls were more the result of a permanent than natural. His hair was compact, tightly woven and he had receding hair lines on both sides of his forehead. The widow's peak. His eyebrows were black as coal. There were three diamond ear rings all in a vertical line in his right ear lobe. He smiled slightly, showing a few teeth.

"Miss Evans, so good of you to come by. I do hope it is not an inconvenience for you and the funeral home. You folks did such a lovely, lovely job with the service for our boss. What a man! What a man! Let's go into my office where we can talk privately," he cut his eyes towards Miss Flair without moving his head so as not to give her any clue she was being downgraded.

I would have responded to him, but he gave me no opportunity and there was no reason to say anything. I followed him through the door into the world of publishing sleaze. I suppose I expected to see surly looking people in dark clothing all sporting oversized mustaches working with evil laughter being played in the background. It wasn't quite like that. It looked like a modern magazine or newspaper room, neatly divided into tiny cubicles with some openings now and then for gatherings of the workforce around the coffee maker and soft drink machines. Typical, if anything.

Cyler Conroy's office was first class. Wall to wall oak paneling, plush purple carpet with matching purple drapes that had tiny yellow flowers dispersed throughout greeted me. The room was spacious enough for an executive sized oak desk, matching credenza along the back wall next to the windows, leather couch with two matching chairs, and a bar to the left of the entrance.

If this was the way the personal assistant lived, I could only imagine what B.A. and Malone had to offer in their world of business management.

"Oh do be seated, Miss Evans," he gestured with the fingers of his right hand pointing in that downward position similar to our earlier handshake. He was pointing to the leather couch. He leaned against his desk and crossed his legs.

"Thank you," I finally managed to get out my first words to him.

"Angel said you had some items of Mr. Malone's?" he said.

I was processing whether to avoid telling him the truth or confess my sins and get straight to the reason I had come. I chose to stall on truth telling. Ever the sleuth.

"I love your office," I said.

"Oh, my, isn't it lovely?" he jumped from his cross-legged position and began to prance around the room as if conducting a guided tour. "The drapes are from Jasmine's, across the water, very exclusive. You know what I mean, honey. Pricey? Don't talk about it. And getting them to match this carpet, well, I thought it would take forever to get them to see the difference between dark pink and purple. Lovely shade, don't you think? Look how it goes with the oak furnishings and the leather. Heaven, don't you just love it?"

"Captivating," I managed to get out.

"Oh, thank you. I do all of my own decorating. In fact, I did Miss Dilworth's office and Joey's … I mean Mr. Malone's. Would you like to see their world of luxury?"

"Lead the way."

"Oh, you'll just love this," he pranced out ahead of me and continued his non-stop dialogue. "I just don't know what we're going to do around here without Mr. Malone, not that he ever did anything on the business end. But he was always here, always here. Sort of a fixture, know what I mean? B.A. Dilworth does all of the work, the publishing work. She runs this magazine. She's the real boss and everyone here knows that, Baby. Can I tell you stories about her! Make your hair stand on end. But she is really good at this, maybe the best in the business."

I followed along doing my best to dodge some of his words so as not to saturate myself with his verbiage. Cyler could talk and did. Frequently. Well, that's a little misleading. Nonstop would be a closer approximation to his style. We didn't have to go far before we reached B.A. Dilworth's office. Her name was on the door in large letters. Larger than I thought necessary, but maybe she was making a statement.

He swung the door open like Loretta Young used to do when she entered the room on her television show I watched some as a kid. Hated that entrance, but loved her stories. The gesture some how fit Cyler.

"Voilá! Isn't this marvelous?" he spread his arms out, this time gesturing with both hands and fingers turned downward.

The room was blue and gray. Mostly blue. The desk was mahogany with an executive highback chair. She had matching wooden file cabinets along one wall and only two chairs in front of her desk. Apparently she had no time to entertain like Cyler. The wall behind her desk was full of bookshelves. There were few books, but plenty of items displayed – silk flowers, pottery, photographs, one or two trophies, empty vases, and some exotic statues of naked people. The bookshelves were painted blue to match the blue carpet and the blue drapes. The yellow flowers dispersed throughout her drapes offered a striking contrast to the blues of the room. There was a blue shade on the lamp on the desk and another blue shade on the tall floor lamp in one corner. Her office appeared to be a little smaller than Cyler's and obviously bluer.

I started to pickup a photograph on one of the shelves to get a closer look and Cyler gasped loudly.

"Oh, Miss Evans, we mustn't touch anything in here. Oh, my god, no, no, no. She will have a conniption. The woman is absolutely obsessive-compulsive when it comes to her things," he emphasized *her things* with emphatic feeling. "I am taking a risk just showing you this room. We cannot for the life of the world touch anything in here," he had his right hand covering his heart and patting it as he spoke. He looked desperate. Lucky for me, I suppose. I didn't touch the photograph.

"Okay if I move my face closer to see the picture?" I said.

"That would be fine, just don't breathe on it too much."

I cut my eyes at him to see if he were joking with me. His face was as serious as death. B.A. must be the Wicked Witch of the East.

The photograph was of B.A. standing over an elderly woman sitting in a wheelchair. The woman was bent over unable to look at the camera. There was a man in a suit standing to the left of B.A. He was grinning from ear to ear. B.A. managed a smile, but nothing extraordinary. The background of the photo showed some type of institutional building, like a nursing home. There was a sign to the right of B.A. and the woman, but the sign was only partially visible in the photograph. I could only make out the last few letters of two lines. One line had the letters W-O-R-T-H and the next line down had the letters D-I-N-G. It was probably the name of the building. The Dilworth Building perhaps.

"Should we tiptoe out?" I asked.

"They'll vacuum in here later, so we're okay with that," Cyler said seriously. "We have to take the elevator to Mr. Malone's suite of offices. His is to die for."

Cyler curled his right index finger in my direction to encourage me to follow him to the elevator. What a guy.

43

Joey Malone's world of luxury knew no bounds. Where his father, Craven, had some taste and style, Joey's suite was wildly extravagant, even for a man with lots of money. The word excessive kept coming to mind as Cyler gave me the grand tour of his five rooms.

The center room was his main office. Cyler said he called it his inner sanctum. Around this center room of plush carpeting and gold-trimmed, white lacey curtains, was a desk the size of Texas built in a semi-circular style. The carpet was thick and white. Cyler insisted that we take off our shoes at the door.

"Don't you just adore this room? I mean where have you ever seen anything like this? The living end, I tell you. I just dreamed all of this up for him one night. He gave me some ideas and then said do it, so I did it. Lovely, huh?"

"Memorable," I said.

"Only very few people get to see this, Miss Evans. Oh, Joey had friends up here, but not many. This was a very special, special place for us… ahem…. him. It was special to me, of course, since I decorated it and picked out the fabric and the color schemes. I mean, you can't give yourself fully to some major, major project like this and not absolutely fall in love with it. Adorable, isn't it?"

Joey was beside himself with ecstasy for this room.

"So what is to happen to this room?" I said.

"Happen?" he looked surprised at my question.

"Well, I mean, since Mr. Malone is no longer with you. Do you have plans for this space?"

"You suggest that we change it?"

"No, not necessarily. Who gets it?" I finally asked bluntly.

"Oh," the light bulb went on for him. "Well, that would be up to.... let me see, I don't believe we've talked about that. I have no idea who would make that decision. I suppose whoever inherits the bulk of his worth," he answered in a sort of dream-like state, as if he were imagining himself inheriting the estate.

He then took me to the rest of the rooms. One was a complete bath with sauna, hot tub, a bank of showers, and a regular tub the size of Chicago, a little smaller than Texas. It was all done in a variety of soft pastels, mostly pinks, light reds and some blues and greens thrown in for imagination. The walls and floor were tiled. It was immaculate.

There were two bedrooms, each as opulent as the other. The only difference I could see was that one was red and the other was yellow. Choose the color of your mood. The furnishings were nearly the same, although I didn't really have time to note any small differences that Malone and Cyler might have concocted. Each of the four rooms around the center office were connected by a door. In fact, there were five doors in the center office, one to the hallway and the elevator, and the other four to the separate rooms. Convenience.

I walked over to the next door thinking that Cyler was

going to take me into the last room for one more extravagant show and tell. I stopped at the closed door.

"And what's in here?" I said.

"Off limits," he said flatly. There was no bounce in his voice or body. "Can't show you that room. Personal. Very, very private, you know? Mr. Malone had his secrets, and even though, God help us, he is gone, we must protect the dignity of his passing."

I was sick at my stomach, but I knew that I wanted to get inside that last room. It wasn't going to happen on my first visit.

We got on the elevator and started down to the main floor.

"You can leave whatever items you have with me. I will guard them with my life," Cyler said with that hand over his heart gesture he loved so much. Cyler the saint.

It was time for me to break my ruse and tell Cyler the truth. I hit the emergency button on the elevator to stop it. I could hear an alarm sound off in the distance. I figured we might not have forever, so I spoke quickly and to the point for Cyler.

"Cyler, I don't work for the funeral home that handled Joey Malone's services. I'm a private investigator working for Craven Malone to find out who killed his son. I need you to answer some questions for me so I can get on with my work of solving this murder. Are we communicating?"

Cyler's expression was priceless. His mouth was open a little too wide to be normal. His eyes showed some degree of shock. It was hard to tell what impression all of this had made on him. He didn't answer right away. No doubt my personality had mesmerized him.

I hit the button that made the elevator continue down and the alarm stopped ringing off in the distance. When the doors opened on the main floor, there was an army of people waiting to see if we were okay.

Two or three women fussed over Cyler as if he had just survived the collapse of the Twin Towers of the World Trade Center. One man stood aloof and asked me if I was all right. I smiled and nodded at him. Cyler allowed the women to practically carry him to his office and put him on the sofa. I followed along since I felt responsible for his dramatic behavior. The one he kept calling Babe retrieved him a glass of water from the bar. When they finally could see that he was probably going to live, they left the room. Babe shut the door behind her.

He held his right hand over his eyes and forehead for a moment after Babe had left.

"Talk to me, Cyler. I need to know some things."

He sat up quickly.

"You could have told me the truth earlier and not scared the bejeebers out of me. I'm petrified of enclosed spaces, like elevators. Especially when they stop in mid-movement! I'm not a well man, I tell you. That was so frightening."

I thought that Cyler should spend some time on the job with me.

"If Joey Malone had such a setup here at the office, why did he also have a hotel suite away from here?"

"I don't know," his tone changed. He walked to the bar and made himself a Whiskey Sour without asking me if I wanted anything. He took a quick sip before returning to the couch. Then he downed the whole drink with one gulp.

"Mr. Malone never confided his reasons for having so many places to sleep. I figured it must have been to entertain."

"He did a lot of that?"

"Entertaining? O, my yes, Dearie. Oodles of that. All the

time. Sometimes all day and all night. I made the arrangements."

"He didn't make his own arrangements?"

"I am the personal assistant, Miss Evans, Private Detective. I do everything.... well, ... *did* .... everything for Joey Malone. Everything."

He went back to the bar. This time he poured a double scotch. No rocks. He came back to the couch, sat down, and then gulped down the double. One gulp again.

"Excitement like this causes me to drink a little too much. Forgive me. It helps to steady my nerves."

"So you keep records of all the women he slept with?"

"Women?" he said and surprise was all over his face. "Women, you say. Oh, my, Dearie, you didn't know Joey Malone at all did you? He was as queer as a three dollar bill, Lovey. Just like me. Two birds of a feather. Made for each other. Except for one thing."

He waddled to the bar once more. Fixed another double scotch. Sipped a little and waddled back to the couch.

"What one thing, Cyler?"

"Oh," he held his drink high above his head as if to toast the dearly departed, "he liked little boys."

44

THERE WAS MORE TO TALK OVER WITH CYLER, BUT I HAD A dinner meeting with Morland and Scarletti at the Rattlesnake Club near the river. Cyler invited me to his place for drinks around ten. He finally got around to offering me a drink. Well, the promise of one anyway. Later, at his place.

Scarletti and I were sitting at a table waiting for Morland to arrive. He was drinking a club soda and I was staring at my very dry Martini. I ate the olive.

"You and Tom Smith close?"

"Tom Smith?" he said.

"Yeah, your brother-in-law who works for the Norfolk Police Department and gave you the report on me. That Tom Smith."

I was tired of dancing around these guys and letting them think that they were so smart and I was so inferior. It was enough to gall a woman. I was sufficiently galled.

"Well, you've been busy."

"It's what I do."

"Yeah, we're sort of close. So what else do you know?"

"More than you wish I knew."

"You been talking to Morland?"

"If Morland knows anything about Tom Smith, he's said nothing to me."

"What's Tom got to do with this case anyway?"

"You tell me. Why would a police veteran working with Internal Affairs up and transfer to a smaller police unit in another state with a lower salary?"

Before Tony Scarletti could figure out how to answer my question, Morland arrived.

"You two discussing the finer points of law enforcement?" he said.

Scarletti ordered another club soda and grunted something as Morland sat down.

"You got anything for me?" I said to Morland.

"Yeah, but let's order first. I'm starved."

They both ordered sixteen-ounce monster steaks and I opted for the petite filet minón, barely six ounces. With all the sides that come with a meal, I couldn't finish the smaller steak. Finally I stopped and watched Morland and Scarletti finish off their whoppers. They ate all of their sides as well.

"Wow," Morland began, "that was great. Can't beat the steaks at this place. Good meat. Now, some good news, Clancy Evans. You can go home and tell Mr. Malone that the Detroit Police have solved another grisly murder, and that tonight all is right with the world."

"Really. And who is the culprit this time?"

"We got a tip about this prostitute, a long time pro, and when we called on her we found Joey Malone's wallet in her apartment."

Malone gulped down his beer and caught the waitress' eye to bring him another one. Scarletti was still nursing his first beer. He seemed to be enjoying the conversation.

"So she lifted the wallet from him. Probably not the first wallet she's taken. Doesn't prove she killed him."

"Probably right about that. Some pros out there aren't satisfied with the easy money they make, they have to steal more," Morland said.

I let that one slide since I wasn't generally in the business of defending hookers. The easy money line was a tad sexist.

"That wasn't the thing," Scarletti finally spoke.

"What was?"

"The bottle of Percocet we found in her apartment," Morland said. "We also found Dilantin in her medicine cabinet as well. The Medical Examiner said that there was an excessive amount of Percocet in Joey Malone's body. Said it caused some kind of heart failure, and that killed him. Also found a small amount of Dilantin in him. The doc said that Dilantin helps the Percocet to work faster."

"How'd she get him to take so much Percocet? Make him think he was taking something to stimulate his libido?" I said.

"Something like that," Morland. "There's this wonderful stuff on the market called Gerilive Formula 12 that is supposed to slow down the aging process."

"Snake oil," Scarletti said.

"Yeah," Morland agreed. "But instead of finding Gerilive tablets in the bottle in Malone's penthouse, we found Percocet pills. The hooker, Bimbi Love, was the last one to see him alive. Plus we found her fingerprints everywhere in that suite of his. So we got a search warrant to check her place and bingo, we got lucky."

"Lucky, hell. We're good detectives, Morland. Don't discount that," Scarletti said.

"And her motive?"

"Robbery-homicide," Scarletti said. "Likely she was on something and maybe did it for meanness. Who knows? The D.A. will figure it out. Our job is done here."

"Case closed," I said.

"Yes, ma'am. Shut tight. When you find the smoking gun, you smile and go eat steaks on the smuck who hired some fancy detective to solve a routine murder committed by a prostitute. Sometimes I love this work," Scarletti was riding high this evening.

"Looks like all the pieces fit, Miss Evans," Morland said.

"Looks that way," I said. My head was swimming in questions to ask, but I decided against asking anything.

It was close to 8:30 by the time Morland and Scarletti left the restaurant. I took a cab back to the Pontchartrain. I had time to talk with Rogers before my late evening event with Cyler. The fancy detective had some work to do.

"What's cooking, sweetheart?" Rogers said.

"The police detectives believe the case on Joey Malone is solved. They have arrested a prostitute named Bimbi Love. She supposedly got Malone to take excessive amounts of Percocet and Dilantin. They say she put the pills in his anti-aging medicine and he simply took too many over a short period. Plausible, but I don't think all the dots connect for me."

"So you want me to check on one Bimbi Love as well as report to you on the meds she used to do him in."

"Supposedly used, sweets," I said. "And, I love it when you are a step ahead of me."

"Tsk, tsk, precious. I'm always a step ahead of you. Give me an hour and I'll get back to you on Bimbi and the meds."

I let her *step ahead* remark slide.

"I'll be having drinks with Cyler Conroy this evening. Cyler told me earlier today that Joey Malone was gay and that he preferred little boys. Not what I'd call the surprise of the century, but it does make me wonder why he had a prostitute in his penthouse apartment."

"It could be that he liked to swing both ways."

"Possible. That means I need you to do some background work on Cyler Conroy."

"Do you know that old adage … something about *all work and no play*?"

"Does not apply to computers."

45

CYLER CONROY'S PLACE WAS AS LAVISHLY DECORATED AS I HAD imagined. His colors were wild and bright, if I wanted to understate the obvious. It was easy to see that lavenders and pinks were the ones that lit his fire. His large living area had low-level lighting and that helped to hold the screaming colors down for me. His furniture was all white leather with lots of colorful cushions thrown around. Easy to recline. Relaxing for me was out of the question.

His condo was in an upscale neighborhood about five miles from his downtown office. He was paid well for his personal assisting.

I was on the sofa surrounded by a crowd of pillows.

"Well?" he said.

"Well?"

"What do you think of my place, Honey Buns?"

Apparently he had known me long enough to use terms of endearment.

"Lively, Cyler. Wild and imaginative."

"I know, I know. Don't you just love the mood these colors put you in?"

"Quite the mood."

"What can I get you to drink, Clancy?" He was standing behind the bar.

"You have any white wine?"

"Let me see. I think I have …" he disappeared behind the bar counter for a few moments. "No," he emerged once again, "but … oh, good. What about a light, dry White Zinfandel?"

"Sounds manageable."

He poured my wine. He was drinking a Whiskey Sour. He reclined in a white leather easy chair close to the sofa.

"So, I imagine you want to know all about my boss Joey Malone and his escapades with little boys."

"Not really, as delightful a discussion as that would be. I'll pass on the details. Did Joey Malone swing both ways?"

"Wow, for a classy female detective, you sure can talk dirty when you want to."

Probably a compliment coming from Cyler, but I let it pass.

"Only for show. He was a closet Homo, but I spotted him during our interview some twenty years ago. I have this inner-radar thing that just sort of lights up when I get close to my kind of people."

"I'll bet you do. So he did entertain female prostitutes in his apartment?"

"Like I said, only for show. He would have them come up and drink with him, but he never had sex with them or anything like that. Little boys were his thing."

"So you and Joey Malone were not lovers?"

"Never, Honey Buns. Business relationship all the way."

"Then how did you know of his preference for little boys?"

"I made all the arrangements for him, Sister. Personal Assistant means what it says."

"So you arranged for Bimbi Love to be at his apartment the night he was killed?"

"Yes and no, on that one. I introduced him to Bimbi some years ago, you know. Sort of set them up the first time. He probably called her this last time. They had some type of special arrangement. I don't recall making the call to get her over there. But she was a regular, you know. Don't really know what he saw in her. Honest I don't. Not a looker at all. You know some female hookers are dynamite. Great dressers and all. Style, real style. But not Bimbi. Must have been some chemistry between them."

"So why would she kill him? He paid her well, right?"

"I paid her well. I took care of all his finances. And you bet your sweet little butt he paid her well. Gave her a thousand dollars a night to keep him company."

He sipped his Whiskey Sour. My White Zinfandel was not quite cold enough to suit my taste.

"So why would she kill her Sugar Daddy?"

"I don't begin to know the inner-workings of a female, Sweetheart. Maybe he pissed her off about something. Who knows? But the police have all that stuff that ties her to the murder. Isn't it just awful? I mean, well, I suppose it was a peaceful way to go and all. He probably just went to sleep, right?"

"Not before he had a cardiac arrest. I'd say the last few seconds could have been horrible for him, unless the Dilantin had caused him to fall asleep. Then, as you say, it could have been almost peaceful. Better than a gun to the head."

"Oh my God, don't talk like that. What a wretched thought. Ohhh …." Cyler returned to the bar and made himself another drink.

"More wine?"

"No, thanks. I've had my limit. Tell me where you found the boys you arranged for Malone."

"Honey, I would love to do that. But you and I both know that I could get into big trouble with that. I mean B-I-G trouble. I don't even want to go there. Let's just say I have my sources and I did a good job of keeping the lid on that side of Joey Malone. I was paid well for my discretion."

We finished the evening talking about furniture and colors and clothes. For Cyler it was a lively discussion. For me it was killing time. I finally excused myself and left for the hotel.

I entered the elevator at the Pontchartrain and Scarletti came up behind me gently pushing me in the back. I could feel the hardness of something in the small of my back. I decided to assume that he had a small gun on me and that I might want to do what he said.

We exited the elevator and headed towards my suite.

"Have a nice meeting with Cyler Conroy?"

"Enlightening."

"I'll bet. Let's go inside your room and you can tell me all about it."

As soon as I had opened the door, Scarletti shoved me hard in the back and caused me to stumble across the room. I caught myself on one of the chairs in the sitting area. Scarletti approached me quickly and slapped me across the back of my head with his fist. It hurt. Would've been worst pain if he had used the gun.

"Turn around," he said.

I did what he told me. He took my .357 from the holster using his left hand. He put the gun on the bar.

"Sit in that chair and tell me everything you and Cyler discussed."

I sat down in the chair he had pointed to and began

talking about the furniture and colors of Cyler's condo. Scarletti slapped me again, a little harder this time. In the face.

"Listen, bitch, we can dance like this all night and your face will become raw meat soon enough. What did you learn from that fag Conroy?"

"Nothing you don't already know."

"Maybe after we've gone to bed for a few hours you'll feel like talkin'," he said and grabbed me by my hair. He dragged me into the sleeping area of the suite. He threw me onto the large bed and was on top of me before I could even think of some counter plan to protect myself. Scarletti was stronger than he looked.

He ripped my blouse and began kissing me hard when my cell phone rang. The unexpected sound distracted him just long enough for me to knee him in the groin. I put as much force as I could into my primary attack, hoping that it would hurt. He grimaced and moaned. It must have hurt. I felt better. He rolled off of me and I ran towards the bar to get my handgun. My phone was still ringing.

I took the gun off of the bar counter and sat down on the floor in the corner behind the bar. My head was reeling from his quick and fierce attack. I was not thinking straight and I needed to calm down. Collect myself. I tried to button my blouse, but the louse had ripped off too many buttons to do that. I was mad now. It was one of my new Malone blouses.

My seat on the floor gave me a good view of anyone coming out of the bedroom into the sitting area. He would have to pass in front of me at the entrance to the bar. I figured I could hold him off at my present location. I waited.

He was still moaning a little after several minutes.

"I was trying to give you a little pleasure before I killed you," his voice seemed to be getting closer to my position. I held my breath now and then to control my breathing and calm down some more. My gun was cocked and ready to unload on him the minute he came into view.

There was a loud knock on the entrance door.

"Open up. This is hotel security. Open the door!" the voice was shouting. The loud knocking continued.

I stayed on the floor behind the bar in my ready-to-shoot position.

Scarletti emerged from the bedroom and walked past the bar. He didn't see me hiding on the floor behind the bar. I stood up slowly and watched him walk to the door. He was not carrying his gun and had straightened his clothing to look normal.

He opened the door. I was right behind him at this point and hit him hard with the butt of my .357. He collapsed in a pile between the security man and me.

"Ouch," the security man said. "I'll bet that hurt."

"I hope so."

46

"I GUESS HE FOLLOWED ME TO CONROY'S PLACE AND THEN back to my hotel," I said to Dennis Morland as we sat in his office on Beaubien.

"You wanna press charges?"

"You bet your life. He tried to rape me."

"Attempted rape won't keep him for long."

"It'll slow him down and get him suspended."

"True, but he'll fight it."

"He'll lose."

"Maybe, but if he can eliminate you, then he wins."

"I'll keep my eyes open. Let's talk about Bimbi Love and the case against her."

"Solid case. All evidence points to her."

"What's her story?"

"Says she found him dead the next morning. Next to her in bed. She ran out of the room to get help and met the maid in the lobby. The maid came into the suite and called security and they called the police. The maid said she left before security arrived on the scene."

"Why did she take the wallet?"

"Keepsake or some such nonsense. Too much of a stretch for me. Anyhow, we had the pills from that bottle of anti-aging junk checked out by our labs and they were Percocet. When we found the Percocet in her apartment, two plus two made for a good case. Then as an added bonus we found the Dilantin in her place. The Medical Examiner found Dilantin in his blood stream. Too much of a coincidence, don't you think?"

"Where is she?"

"Where we keep all murder suspects."

"May I talk with her?"

"Sure. I'll take you over."

Morland led the way from his office to the holding cells. I followed.

"Thanks for calling the cops for me last night," I said.

"Least I could do. Scarletti overplayed his hand."

"Didn't have much of a hand in the first place."

"Some players always think they can draw to that illusive inside straight," he said.

"Fools try."

Rogers and I had talked late last night after my rendezvous with Tony Scarletti and my interview with the police officers who answered the call. As usual Rogers enlightened me on several fronts. Bimbi Love turned out to be a Darlene Sledge from Minnesota. She had a daughter seventeen named Gretchen Sledge who lived with her some of the time. She found some medical records on Gretchen that listed her as being epileptic. She was taking Dilantin for it.

Bimbi was dressed in a sweatshirt and jeans. Her dirty blond hair needed to be combed and she could have used a little makeup. They must have arrested her on her day off.

"I ain't talkin' with him around," she gestured with her chin like Rosey did.

I looked at Morland and he shrugged.

"I'll be back in a few minutes."

We both watched him leave us. I was on the outside of the cell looking at this poor, unkempt woman of about fifty. I was being kind. She looked more like an old sixty.

"I didn't do it."

"Who did?"

"I don't know. But I would never kill Joey."

"How long had you known him?"

"About twenty years."

"Long time."

"We were lovers."

"I was told Joey Malone was gay and preferred little boys."

"It's a lie!" she yelled at me.

"Only what I was told."

"Our relationship was a secret."

"What relationship?"

"My daughter is his child. Look, I don't know who you are, but I need some help here."

"I'm trying to help you."

"Naw, I mean I need something for this damn headache. It's killin' me."

"They'll bring you some aspirin."

"Won't do no good. I've had these headaches all of my life. I need something strong."

"Migraines?"

"Hell, I don't know what to call them. But I take that stuff called Percocet."

"Prescription?"

"Doctor in Mexico. Joey and I met a doctor there years ago and he sends us some pills every few months. Joey took care of it. Can't get a doctor around here to give you any."

"Did you give Joey some of your medicine?"

"No. I wouldn't do that. Joey didn't need it. He took that

vitamin junk or whatever it was called. It seemed to help him. He took several pills a day."

"How many?"

"Oh, I don't know. Maybe one or two every four hours. It didn't bother me none and it seemed to help him. Besides, I knew it was safe. Nothing much in that stuff. But he swore by it."

"So that night he died, you gave him some of those pills?"

"Yeah. Joey didn't drink all that much. I did the drinking. Anyhow, he wanted to go to bed early, so I kept waiting on him, getting up and getting his pills with water."

"You wait on him a lot?"

"Sure. I loved him. He took care of me and my little girl. So whatever he wanted, I did it."

"You give him any Dilantin?"

"Yeah, after we had sex for a while, he couldn't sleep. Said he was too excited. So, I had some of my daughter's medicine with me. I carry it around just in case she needs it. You never know when she will have an attack. And you can use that stuff for sleeping, too."

"You found Joey the next morning?"

"I got up early to go pee and when I came back I noticed he wasn't breathing like he usually did. He snored all the time. But he was quiet that mornin'. I shook him ..." she started crying softly.

I felt sorry for her. I was a sucker for a good story, and hers was plausible.

"Tell me about Gretchen. Where is she now?"

"You leave her alone. She don't need to be drug into this mess. Say, how'd you know her name? I didn't tell you her name."

"I'm an investigator."

"Police?"

"Private."

"I don't want to drag my daughter into this."

"I need to talk with her. She might be able to help you. So tell me where I can find her?"

Bimbi thought a good while before she spoke. I could tell that she was reluctant to tell me. I waited. Vigilance finally paid off.

"Check the soup kitchen downtown on Madison. If she's not there, then go a few blocks down the street to the homeless shelter. She works at both places. She likes to help people."

"Good. Maybe she can help you."

"Listen, lady, you be kind to her. She's a sweet kid, but she's different."

"What do you mean?"

"She's retarded a bit, but she's got a good heart."

"I'll be kind," I said and turned to leave. I remembered something, so I stopped. "Why did you take Joey's wallet from his room?"

"Keepsake. Had some baby pictures of Gretchen hidden in it. I don't know, I guess I'm just sentimental. I loved the man. He was kind to us. What can I say? I wanted something to remember him by."

"And not for the money?"

"What money?" she said.

"Money and, say, credit cards."

"You mean in the wallet?"

"Bingo."

"Joey never carried money or plastic. Didn't need to. Had that personal assistant that took care of everything."

"Enough said."

"Don't forget to get me something for my headache."

47

Morland failed to return by the time I was ready to leave Bimbi, so I took a cab to the soup kitchen downtown. It was a nice enough place right in the heart of the city. It was not quite eleven when I arrived, but the place was full of clients. Some were eating and some were still standing in line being served. I looked for someone who might be in charge. No one seemed to fit the bill, so I walked back into the kitchen area to seek help from one of the cooks.

A tough looking but friendly African American lady pointed Gretchen Sledge out to me. The teenage girl was serving the plates of the people passing by the window. She was smiling and greeting each of them as if she knew them.

"I need to talk with her for a few minutes. Could you get someone to take her place?" I said to the short, stocky woman who had pointed Gretchen out to me.

"I'll takes her place, Child. You jest go on and get her. You two cans talk in the pantry," she pointed to the small closet with a single curtain hanging in front as a door.

I told Gretchen I needed to talk with her privately about her mother, so she followed me willingly into the pantry.

"Is Mama okay?"

"Except for the headaches, she's fine."

"Yeah, she gets lots and lots of headaches. I wish there was something we could do for her."

"You live with your mother?"

"Yes, but sometimes I stay downtown in the shelter to help out. These homeless people need lots of attention sometimes. It's my job to help all I can. I work here every day but Sunday."

"Important work."

"Yes, it is, isn't it? I think helping people is the best thing in the world to do. What do you do for work?"

"I help people."

She smiled and seemed thrilled to be talking with someone like herself.

"Are you helping my mama?"

"I'm trying to help her. But I need you to tell me some things."

"What things?"

"Do you take medicine for your epilepsy?"

"Yes. I don't know the name of it, but Mama keeps it on hand. I have some in my purse in the other room. Would you like to see it?"

"Yes, I would."

She hurried out of the pantry and quickly retrieved her purse. She waited until she was back in the confines of our little space before she opened her purse and took out the bottle of medicine. It was a prescription bottle for Dilantin.

"What does your mother take for her headaches?"

"I don't know the name of it, but she gets it from some doctor in Mexico. We went down there some years ago, when I was a little girl, and this doctor mails it to us every few months. Mama told me that it is hard to get it in the United States of America. Is that true?"

"True. Do you know who your father is?"

"Yeah, but it's a secret and I'm not supposed to talk about it with anyone."

"Okay. I understand that. How about if I say a name and you nod your head if the name I say is your father? Would you do that for me?"

"That would be okay. That way we're not talkin' about it."

"Right. Joey Malone," I said.

"She smiled and nodded vigorously as if she was very proud.

"I'm sorry he is dead. You must miss him a lot."

"Yes, ma'am. I do miss him. He was very nice to me. Always nice. He bought me lots of things and took care of me and Mama. I loved him, even though I didn't get to show him off to anyone I know. We would go away on trips to Mexico and other places, and there we got to act like real families. You know? That was the best time of all."

"I guess so. Your mother and Joey ever fight?"

"You mean hit each other?"

"Or fuss? Loud talk."

"If you mean disagree, then yes. They didn't always see eye to eye. But if you mean yell and scream at each other, never. Never. I never heard them talk ugly to each other. They loved each other. We all three loved each other. I didn't get to see a whole lot of my daddy, but I knew he loved me. I also know that my mama loved him a lot. A whole lot."

"Do you know what your mother does for a living?"

"Yes, ma'am."

"Why would she do that if she loved your daddy?"

"What are you talkin' about?"

"She works the streets, doesn't she?"

"Oh, no ma'am. She quit that a long time ago. She goes out some and stands around talkin' with some of the women, but she never does tricks. She doesn't need to. Daddy took care of everything we needed. She's friends with lots of the ladies who work the streets, but she doesn't do that kind of work no more. She told me I mustn't ever do that kind of work. She says it's not good for you."

"Your mother is right. I'm glad you work here helping people."

"Have I helped my mama?"

"I hope so. Now I have to find the person who really killed your father."

"Maybe I could help you with that."

"How's that, Gretchen?"

"I have to go back to work now. Why don't you come back to see me and we can talk some more. I'll be home tonight. You know where we live?"

"I do."

"Then why don't you come around and we can talk some more. I like you. You seem like a nice person."

"I'll see what I can do. Thanks for your help."

She left quickly and was back in line serving plates when I exited the pantry. Good to see people working in jobs that they enjoyed.

"How long has she been working here?" I asked the African American woman who had helped me earlier.

"Oh, 'bout three years now, I reckon. Good worker, too."

"She acts as if she knows each person."

"She does. Knows 'em all, by name. Best medicine in the world is to come in here and be greeted by Gretchen. She's as good for them as that food we fix. Don't know what we'd do without her."

"She get paid for this?"

"A little, but not much. She don't do it for the money, Honey. She's got love inside of here," she pointed to her heart.

I returned to the hotel and called Rogers.

"You come up with anything to help me?" I said.

"Verification of what I have already told you. Found some old cancelled checks on Joey Malone. Marvelous what some banks do these days. Helps me a bundle. Anyhow, found some cancelled checks to a Carlos Cabrera in Mexico. I figured that must be the medicine that Malone bought for Bimbi."

"Let me tell you what I have learned. Factor this into your processors and then let me know what you think."

I told her everything I could recall from my conversations with Bimbi, Gretchen and Conroy. I also told her my brief exchanges with Scarletti, but I didn't think that they were noteworthy since he said little during our brief time together. His mind was preoccupied.

"Probably nothing more than what you have already determined. Someone is framing Bimbi Love. Sounds as if she and the daughter are on the level about Joey. And, it sounds as if Joey was not as much of a sleaze ball as you thought."

"I have been known to be mistaken now and then."

"Uh-huh. Now and then. I hear you. That be a confession?"

"You sound like Rosey."

"I think it's cool to use English that way."

"Cool?"

"Yeah, way cool. So cool. Like so smokin' to dialogue this way with my originator."

"I prefer that we use the English I programmed into you. Okay?"

"Okay. But variety is the spice of life, you know. What's your next move, Ace?"

"Dilworth still in Virginia Beach with Craven?"

"Headed your way today. Probably as we speak."

"You have any clues about what's going on there between those two?"

"Some call it love."

"You're kiddin'. The man could easily be her father. I don't buy the romance bit. Has to be something else."

"Something kinky?"

"Not necessarily, but it could be something to do with business. Craven likes B.A., although I cannot imagine why."

"Maybe she's a sweetheart underneath the veneer of a wretch."

"Ducks to swans?"

"Naw. Sorry. I think she's pretty obvious. But, she may not be all bad. Just mostly bad."

"Think she'd kill Joey or have it done?"

"Are you asking if my data about her would suggest that she is capable of murder, of this murder? If so, then the answer is of course. Absolutely. But if you are asking me if my data would suggest her to be a viable suspect, then the answer is no. But my data only goes so far. Limited on her at this point, you might say."

"Remedy that. Dig deeper. And do some more searching on Cyler Conroy. Oh, by the way. I meant to ask you to research Dennis Morland. You checked on Tony, but not Dennis."

"Grounds for this?"

"My thoroughness as an investigator."

"Yikes," Rogers said before she clicked off.

48

"I hope you like Chinese food," I said to Gretchen when she opened the door. I held up a sack full of choices. There were a few grease spots showing on the large bag.

"I love Chinese food! Wow! What a great surprise! How did you know?"

"Took a wild guess. Hungry?"

"Yes."

She cleaned off the table and we sat down and enjoyed our oriental feast. Gretchen made us some tea and we dined in style. Two girls devouring delicious food. I finished first and watched her continue. I don't think I was as hungry as she was.

"You know anything to help me with your daddy's death?"

"I know what I saw."

"Enlighten me."

"You asked about Mama and Daddy fighting. They didn't fight at all. But Daddy did fight with some others."

She devoured the last egg roll and then spooned out some more sweet and sour chicken to go with her fried rice.

"Who?"

She took a bite of the chicken and rice. I watched her chew with delight, then swallow. She sipped her tea. I was being patient. She was enjoying herself a whole lot.

"Mrs. Dilworth. She's the editor, right?"

"I think so. Where did you see them fighting?"

"Well," she said, and then took another small bite of chicken. She chewed and swallowed once more. "Mama and I were at Daddy's place one evening a few weeks ago, we were celebrating my birthday. It is always a special occasion when I get to go to his big house."

"You mean the apartment where he lived?"

"Yes, ma'am. It's so big, it should be called a house. Don't you think?"

"Big."

"Anyway, Mama and I were there when Mrs. Dilworth showed up. We hid in the back bathroom. We could hear everything they said."

I watched Gretchen finish her chicken and rice.

"Why did you hide?"

"Daddy didn't want anyone to see us there."

"What did they argue about?"

"Argue?" she seemed a bit confused.

"You know, fuss and fight."

"Oh. Okay. Well, they ar-gued about the magazine. Daddy wanted to sell it, but she did not want to sell it. She said some mean and hateful things to him. Told him, let's see, that it was stupid to sell something that made so much money. Yes, I think that's what she said first. Then," she paused to think, "... well, she talked like it was her magazine and not his."

"She said that?"

"Not those words, but Mama and I got the idea that she was being a little crazy. I think she lost her cool, if you know what I mean. I opened the door of the bathroom just a little to see what was going on, and she was acting crazy. Walking around the room, waving her arms, and shaking her fists at him. I was scared for him."

"I can imagine."

"She kept sayin' that he owed her … 'you owe me,' she yelled, really loud a few times. You owe me! You owe me!" she was imitating B.A. Dilworth and doing a credible job.

"What do you think she meant by that?"

"Don't know. I just know that Mama used to say that she hated that woman even though she was good at what she did."

"Being an editor."

"Yeah, I guess that's what she was talkin' about."

"Anything else?"

"You mean the fight we heard and saw a little?"

"Yes."

"I think she finally got tired of screaming at him. Then she told him he'd pay or something like that. He'd pay if he sold it to anybody but her."

"Did Joey ever say who the buyer was?"

"Some big shot here in the city. He called him Big Bob, but didn't talk about him very much. Said it was business and that we didn't need to know about the business. 'Don't trouble yourselves,' he used to say to us all the time. Don't trouble yourselves. Don't trouble yourselves. Hey, did you open your fortune cookie? That's the best part. I always like to read my fortune."

She handed me the little piece of paper that had come out of her fortune cookie. It read: Your smile and charm will take you far.

They probably got that one right.

"Here, open this. See what it says for you," she said as she handed me a cookie wrapped in plastic.

Mine read: Danger could be around the next corner.

"What does it say?" she said.

I told her.

"That's awful, Miss Evans. Maybe you had better stay here with me tonight. I don't want anything to happen to you."

"Me either."

"Could you stay here tonight?" She sounded lonely.

"Tell you what, let me use the little girl's room and I'll think about it."

She took me through the narrow hallway back to the bathroom.

"Sorry about the mess," she said.

"I'm used to worse," I said and closed the door.

My cell phone rang. It was Rogers.

"Interrupting something?"

"What you got?"

"I was nosing around the Detroit police files again and a bulletin just came up that said Tony Scarletti was out on bail pending a hearing set for September 21. Thought you might want to know that."

"Good to know. I'll keep my eyes open."

"And your gun close."

"That too. Say, tell me how much money is B.A. Dilworth worth?"

"Got a few minutes to wait?"

"Yeah. I'll stay on the line," I put the phone in my pocket while I finished up in the bathroom.

I could hear loud shouting in the other part of the apartment. Gretchen was talking to someone who was yelling at her. Sounded like a man's voice.

I turned out the light and cracked the door of the bathroom. I could see down the hall, but not into the living room/kitchen area where we had eaten. I eased out into the hall with my gun drawn.

"You alone?" the man's voice shouted. Sounded like Scarletti.

"Who are you?" Gretchen said.

"Never mind, just tell me if anyone is here with you."

"I live alone. You're scaring me. I think you'd better leave, or I'll call the police."

"I am the police, you twit. Sit over there."

I was at the edge of the hallway where it turns into the living room. Scarletti was walking toward my position. I quickly moved into the light, gun drawn and surprised him.

Gretchen screamed. It must have been my gun.

"Get your hands up," I said to Scarletti. He didn't move.

"Well, bitch. Looks like we get to finish what we started last night. You should know I have lots of connections. Here I am, free as a bird."

"One more time, Tony. Hands high, above your head. Any other movement, and it'll be your last."

I tried to remain calm considering my recent history with the scumbag. So far, so good. Miss Calm.

Tony then did a very stupid thing. He turned his back on me, and as he did, he drew his gun. No doubt he was thinking that I would be fooled by his movement. Or he thought that he could draw his gun, turn around quickly, and shoot me faster than I could pull the trigger on my cocked .357. Same as drawing to an inside straight. Odds are against you.

He was wrong.

Gretchen screamed and began crying as soon as the sound of the gun went off. Tony was knocked back several feet. Gretchen had been out of the way, to the left of the bullet's path. Tony was almost dead.

I kicked the gun out of his hand and then kept a safe distance from him. I was taking no chances with this guy.

"Good shot, detective," he said in a rough voice. "I didn't

think you had the balls to do that. That's funny, isn't it? Joking here at the end. Way to go, Tony."

"You working for Big Bob LeFoy?" I said.

He shook his head and then closed his eyes. He was gone.

Gretchen hugged me and was shaking all over. I calmed her down and then called the police. I asked for Morland and told him what had happened. I left out the part about him shaking his head when I asked if he worked for Big Bob.

Morland arrived in about fifteen minutes with a couple of uniforms. He took my gun and then my statement. He talked with Gretchen and her story matched mine mostly. He told me to come in to the police station the next day and then left. The two uniforms stayed until the crime scene unit finished their work.

I took Gretchen to my hotel suite and we talked about life for a few hours and we girls went to sleep.

49

I DON'T TRUST DEATH-BED CONFESSIONS MUCH, BUT I DID wonder at Tony's head shake at my question about Big Bob. He could have been trying to throw me off, or he could have been telling the truth. I would file it for the time being. It might help, then again, it might not. Such was detective work. I was filing a lot of things these days.

While Gretchen was still sleeping, I called Rogers.

"You okay?"

"Yeah. Just tired. Need to stop this crazy job for a few weeks," I said.

"Need to stop killing people."

"That, too. So tell me what you found out about B.A.'s net worth."

"Sixteen million, give or take a few thousand here and there."

"Wow."

"Inherited mostly. But she's a frugal wag. Doesn't live too extravagantly, at least not by her credit card records. Most of it is invested, of course, but she does keep close to $200,000 in a money market at her bank. Plus she has a checking account of about $98,000 and some change. That enough?"

"Well, it tells me she has money. How much do you figure the magazine is worth?"

"I knew you were going to ask me that, so I checked it out. Somewhere around $30 million. Market value. Could be sold a bit higher or a bit lower, but that's size of the ballpark we're dealing with here."

"So, she really didn't have enough to buy the magazine."

"Whoa, J.P. You figure that if she is worth 16 million, then she could easily go to a bank and borrow money. Considering her financial status and all, I'd say she could have bought the magazine for 30 million, but not a whole lot more. Maybe if she knew the banker personally, but she would be a good risk in today's economy."

"That means she wasn't just blowing smoke when she was angry with Joey Malone for trying to sell the magazine without consulting her. Gives her motive to kill him."

"True."

"Who inherited the magazine?"

"Well, my search has revealed that there is a will and that Papa Malone is the only viable candidate to inherit anything."

"Only viable?"

"Yes. No one else is standing in line. Joey had no wife, no children. Just papa."

"You're forgetting Gretchen and Bimbi."

"Not for a minute. But they're not legal relations. He could leave it to them, but it would be contested."

"Papa?"

"You bet. The assets are too big to just give away to a former prostitute and her daughter. Come on, you think Craven Malone would do that?"

"He might, given the right incentive."

"And that would be, what?"

"Coercion."

"Ah, yes, friendly persuasion."

"Keep your wheels spinning. I'll check with you later."

The shock had worn off by now and I was hungry. I heard Gretchen in the shower, so I called room service and ordered us a full course breakfast. I told them to bring everything they had on the menu considered breakfast food. For two.

After she finished, I jumped into the shower to refresh before my day full of police reports and lots of questions. I also planned to do some investigating, just in case I needed to. I told her to be on the lookout for the room service. I gave her twenty dollars to tip the bellboys.

When I emerged from the refreshing shower, there were two carts heavy laden with everything imaginable from the breakfast kitchen.

"Somebody comin' to join us?" Gretchen said.

"I hope not. I'm hungry. You?"

"Yes, ma'am. I like being with you. You eat so well."

Suddenly I had this tinge of guilt for having lavished this young girl with so much luxury. I had forgotten that she worked in a soup kitchen and spent many nights in a homeless shelter helping the poorest of the poor. My appetite was waning.

"Perhaps I did overdo it a bit. Sorry 'bout that," I confessed.

"Well, I don't mind being spoiled a little now and then. But I try not to get used to it. Daddy used to spoil me when we would go on trips, or he would have me and Mama over to his place. But the real world is not like this, Miss Evans. My friends are very poor, but I love them anyway. I usually eat what they eat. Sometimes I go to bed hungry at night. It's not because I can't afford to eat regular food, or eat lots of food, it's because I feel for them so much. I want them to trust me, and I want to know what they are feeling. I know that sounds crazy, but I really care about them."

"Doesn't sound crazy at all, Gretchen. I admire you for the work you do. You help more people than I help. You're showing empathy."

"I don't know what *empathy* means," she said.

"It means you're a genuine human being full of compassion."

"Thank you, Miss Evans."

We ate our bounty in silence for several minutes. Despite my guilt feelings, the food was delicious and I was enjoying it.

"You wear that gun all the time?" Gretchen interrupted our silence.

"Not all the time, but I have to wear it a lot. Sometimes I have to investigate difficult situations. Sometimes there are dangerous people around. I use it to make sure I make it through the day."

"I wouldn't like a job where I had to wear a gun. I couldn't shoot anybody."

"I understand. I don't like shooting people, but sometimes…." I didn't know how to finish that sentence that sounded wholesome.

"You have to, is that what you were going to say?"

"Sounds horrible to say it, Gretchen."

"Yes, ma'am. It does sound horrible to say out loud. Sometimes the truth is horrible, I suppose."

We finished our meal without discussing guns. I was pleased that our subject matter shifted. She talked about her work and about her mother.

It was close to noon when I hailed a cab for her. She was

going to the soup kitchen to work. I told her that I would still be working to get her mother released. I asked her to trust me. She said she did.

I took a cab to the police station and spent several hours with Morland and the rest of the boys. I saw a few policewomen around the station, but none of them had anything to do with me.

"You know who Scarletti was working for?" I asked Morland.

"Not a clue. I figure it was LeFoy, but we have no proof."

"What next?"

"Lots of new cases. No rest for the cops. What about you?"

"Working on loose ends. Lots of loose ends. Like your cases."

He handed me my gun. I checked the cylinder. It was empty.

"That's an interesting gun you have."

"Ever fire a .357?"

"Oh, I don't mean the caliber. Sure, I've fired many .357s and lots of other models. I mean that gun. It's registered to a government agency in Washington, D.C. and you have a permit on file to carry it."

I tried not to look as surprised as I was.

"And you thought?"

"Black market. Street gun. Some hooded figure sold it to you after you stepped off the plane a few days ago. So how did you get the gun, Miss Evans?"

"What did the permit say?"

"Didn't say how you got it."

"Issued, wasn't it?"

"Well, if you are asking if everything was in order, then yes. But, you and I both know you are not allowed to carry guns on an airplane. At least not private detectives. You must have some friends in high places."

"Sounds reasonable."

He smiled wryly, but his eyes told me that he retained a few more questions.

50

It was after four o'clock when I entered the office building on McComb Street. It was a short walk from the police station. Miss Flair was still hard at work. Today she was wearing some bright aqua colored dress that was two sizes too small. Her neckline plunged on this one revealing more cleavage than I could ever hope to have.

"Mr. Conroy has left for the day," she said.

"I'd like to see the editor."

"I'll check to see if she is in," she turned a little sideways and punched a button on her yellow phone.

I thought about walking away to give her some privacy. That would make it easier for her to lie to me and say that Miss Dilworth was not in after she had spoken with Miss Dilworth. I decided against moving away from my vulture-like position. Mean and deadly.

"She's not seeing anyone today. Perhaps you could ...."

"She'll see me," I said and walked through the doors into the publishing world once more.

Memory served me, and I found B.A.'s office without getting lost in the maze. I knocked.

"Come in," her voice said.

I entered and closed the door. Confrontation time.

"Who let you in here?" she said.

"Me."

"You can't barge into my office."

"Didn't' barge. Just entered when you said 'come in.'"

"Get out."

"Need some information."

"What do you want?"

"Just a few questions. I'm still on the case."

"The case is over, or don't you read the papers. They have arrested a whore for the murder."

"You and I both know that she didn't do it."

"I know no such thing."

"Sure you do. Think about it. If you take Conroy's position and believe that Malone was gay and preferred little boys, then there is no way that he would be sleeping with a prostitute. But if you take the other position, the all-knowing position, where Malone was completely heterosexual, had no interest in boys or men, and was madly in love with a woman who used to be a prostitute, fathered her child, and lived a secret life, then you have to admit that her killing him would be odd, to say the least. She had a gold mine with him already. Joey took care of everything for her and the daughter. Everything. She didn't work. She wasn't doing tricks. Hadn't done tricks in years. He was a sugar daddy. Why kill the golden goose? That would be stupid. Are we communicating here yet?"

"You should write fiction. That stuff makes for a good story. But in real life, well, Joey Malone was a queer."

"I can see you are tolerant of alternative lifestyles."

"Get out of my office."

"One more question, then I'll go."

"You'll go now," she walked across the room and opened her office door.

I stood in front of her desk facing her. She was standing by the door.

"Why wouldn't Joey sell you the magazine?"

I saw a flinch, but nothing more. Her facial expression remained placid. Angry, but placid.

"Get out."

I left.

Miss Flair was just leaving herself when I entered the reception area. We walked out the front door of the office building together.

"You have a way back to your hotel?" Miss Flair asked.

"I'll get a cab."

"Come on. My car is just across the street in the lot. I'll give you a ride. It's no trouble."

Sometimes my work is full of genuine surprises. People. Go figure.

She drove a dark green Taurus. Apparently, they were everywhere. She paid the parking lot attendant and pulled out onto McComb.

"I'm Marlene. We haven't formally met yet. Marlene Streeter," she said as we pulled out into traffic.

"Clancy Evans, Marlene. Thanks for the lift."

"Glad to help."

"You work for magazine long?"

"Almost ten years now. It's a pretty good job. They pay me well for handling the phones and clients and traffic off of the street."

"That the whole job?"

"Sometimes I help Cyler do something special, like set up a party or a reception. Once I got to help out on a story that appeared in the magazine. I didn't like that very much."

"Magazine not your cup of tea?"

"Not really. But I say live and let live. If it floats your boat, hurray for you."

"Hurray."

"Are you really a private investigator?"

"Yes."

"And you are investigating Mr. Malone's death?"

"Yes."

"But they arrested that woman … who was with him."

"They did."

"And you don't think she's the one who did it?"

"I don't."

"You think somebody at the magazine did it?"

"Don't know. That's why I investigate. Tell me, what kind of relationship does Cyler have with Miss Dilworth?"

"Well, she says jump and Cyler says, 'How high?' Does that help you?"

"It helps. Dilworth like that with everyone?"

"Let me see. I think the answer to that would be yes. All except Mr. Malone. Cyler told me that years ago she tried to handle him like she does the rest of us, did it in a subtle way, but he was too shrewd for her. Never gave in. He just let her run the magazine, but not him. He seldom made suggestions to her, as far as I know."

"Does she have any other interests?"

"Interests?"

"Yes, things outside of the magazine. Hobbies, social events, clubs, stuff like that."

"None that I know of. She might have some hobbies, but I know she doesn't do the club thing. She does social events that help the magazine. She's not into charity functions, at least not around here. I think she gave away some money a few years ago to something down south."

"You recall what?"

"Uh … no. That was before my time. There was quite a

buzz about it around the office, but I never did hear all the details. I was new then and it wasn't my place to be nosey. Besides, it was her money. She could give it or burn it."

"She have any romance?"

She laughed.

"I'm sorry. But that was a funny question," she said.

"Funny?"

"B.A. Dilworth is a lonely, wealthy, mean woman. She hates men. All men. She told me that once. Said it like I would say I hate asparagus. No passion, just hatred. Except for her position at work, she's practically a recluse. You know where she lives?"

I shook my head.

"If you have time, I'll show you."

"Forge ahead," I said.

Marlene took I-75 and headed north out of town. We drove for about an hour, maybe more, then she turned off. I loss track of the turns she made. Eventually we stopped in a secluded area. She turned onto a paved road that had no houses. At the end of the paved road was a small house set off in the woods. Small and private.

Marlene shut off the engine.

"This is it?" I said.

"Her estate."

It was certainly not the home I would have imagined for B.A. Dilworth. I had some sort of large, gated, high-walled mansion on a hillside in my mind.

"How did you find this place?"

"Cyler. He drove me out here to show me this."

"Why?"

"I think it was the day that she told him off in front of everyone in the office, and he was really mad at her. I think he thought that showing me this would belittle her in my eyes."

"Did it?"

"Not really. I felt sorry for her. Oh, don't get me wrong. I don't like her, but I do feel sorry for her. Besides, this place is still larger than my apartment back in the city," she smiled.

"And you're not lonely."

"Naw, I have a boyfriend. We might even get married soon. No date, but he's talking serious-like finally."

"If that's what you want, then I hope it happens."

"Thanks. It's what I want. You have a boyfriend or spouse?"

"Not what I want."

51

Marlene dropped me at my hotel. I offered to buy her dinner, but she had a date with her boyfriend and had to keep moving.

As I approached the elevators, one of the women behind the reception desk motioned for me.

"You have a call. You may use that phone on the table by the chair."

It was Cyler.

"You remember how to get to my place?" he said.

"I do."

"Then get over here right now. I need your help."

"What's wrong?"

"Can't talk. Just come, for heaven's sake. Come now."

He hung up. I could hear some loud knocking in the background.

I hailed a cab and arrived at Cyler's place twenty minutes later.

The front door was hanging on one hinge. The living room was in disarray. I heard moaning coming from one of the back rooms.

I found Cyler on the floor in his bathroom. He had been badly beaten and was unconscious. I called 911 and waited for them to arrive. I called Morland to see if he could help. Morland didn't come, but sent some uniforms to handle the situation.

The police arrived just as the emergency medical team was taking Cyler out on a gurney. After I answered the few questions I could, they let me go.

I was sitting in the emergency room waiting for some word on Cyler. The chairs were comfortable, but the magazines were all outdated. Old news is good news. At least the shock had worn off.

I walked outside and called Rogers. I updated her on all of my recent interviews and discoveries.

"You got leads, Snookems?"

"Snookems?" I responded with mock surprise.

"Came across that term recently. Still expanding," she said.

"Expand in another direction. No leads."

"Hunches."

"Plenty, but nothing strong. At this point I would say that B.A. Dilworth did old Joey in because he wouldn't sell her the magazine."

"Well, I doubt if job security is really something she concerns herself with. She has more money than some cities. What does she care if he sells the magazine?"

"You're right. It's not about the money."

"Power?" she said.

"Perhaps. She's definitely a control person. Tell you what, dig up what you can on Big Bob LeFoy. Go back as far as you can on him. See how he came to power in Detroit. See if you can find someone back at the time Dilworth became the editor, someone at the magazine who knows what happened. Maybe a secretary who worked in the office who was fired.

Axe to grind. Something. Anything. My trails are running cold, except for this Conroy event. If he survives, maybe I can learn something from him."

"Well, if whoever beat him to a pulp wanted him out of the way, why didn't they just kill him?"

"Point for you. Maybe they just were angry as hell at him and wanted to send him a message."

"Just to the point of death, huh?"

"Maybe they got carried away. Homophobia. It happens, Babe."

"Say, you're finally getting the hang of it. I call you sweet names, you call me sweet names. Cool, huh?"

"I refuse to answer that. Anything on Morland yet?"

"Nothing showing up in my search so far."

"As always, do call me when you find anything worth reporting."

I walked back into the ER and sat in the waiting area. Busy night. Noisy and full of bodies. Could be a full moon out.

After a couple of hours, I caught a passing nurse and asked if she could tell me anything about Conroy. She checked her records and told me that they had taken him to ICU about an hour ago. Thanks for telling me, I wanted to say. I refrained.

I got off of the elevator on the fourth floor. There was a lady wearing a pink jacket sitting at a desk in the large lounge for the ICU waiting area.

"I'd like to see Cyler Conroy, please."

"What's the name?"

"Clancy Evans."

"Family?"

"No."

"Clergy?"

"No."

"Can't let you in."

"I'm as close to family as you get for him."

"I'll call the doctor."

"Good idea. Ask the doctor to come out here if the answer is no."

She frowned at me but said nothing. I waited. It took longer than it should have, but finally she hung up the phone and smirked at me.

"No."

"Is he coming out?"

"She. In a few minutes."

So much for public relations.

"You work for the hospital?" I said to the pink lady.

"No. This is volunteer work. I enjoy giving my time to help people."

"I can see that you are a real asset for the hospital."

Her badge said Marge Abbott.

"No need to get sarcastic with me," she changed her tone immediately. "I have to follow the rules."

"Marge, no one would know whether I am family or not if you let me in there."

She looked stunned. It was an idea that had not surfaced for her. I think she was about to let me go in, when a short, thirty-something, business-like woman came into the lounge looking for someone's head. My guess was that this was the doctor who had come to make some strong suggestions about what I could do and where I could do it.

"The person who wanted to see Cyler Conroy?" she said to Marge.

Marge pointed to me.

"What relation are you to Cyler?"

"Double first cousins, twice removed on my mother's side."

"That's family," she said while looking in Marge's direction. Marge was aghast that I would lie to a doctor.

"Distant," I said to the doctor. "Very."

"Come on. I'll show you where he is."

I followed the doctor and smiled at Marge as I left. Marge smiled back. Apparently she was okay with my subterfuge, or she was pleased to learn that doctors were not omniscient. I was just glad to finally be able to see Cyler.

The lady doctor stopped at the door to his room. She eased it open and motioned for me to enter.

"He's stable, but he's had severe head trauma. It might take him a while to come around. Or, he might not come around at all. Could stay in the comatose state for a long time. Hard to call. We've treated his cuts. Had a few stitches, nothing too serious. Fortunately, he didn't lose much blood. But whoever did this to him hit him hard several times in the head. My guess is that they used their fists and they were very strong."

"Thanks," I whispered to her.

She closed the door and left us alone. I held his hand and stroked it for a few minutes. Too bad that God is the only one who loves all of the children. Whatever God has, right now I'd recommend that we start spreading it in Detroit.

52

IT WAS EARLY IN THE MORNING AND I WAS SITTING UNDER A grove of trees somewhere near the hospital. I had spent the night with Cyler. Some time before dawn, I left the room for a break. Thus far, no consciousness for Cyler. His vitals were all stable, but the head wound was the culprit. I was hoping he would come around and tell me something.

I was tired, managing to doze off now and then during the night, but I decided against going back to my hotel suite. I didn't want to leave him just yet.

The sunrise was refreshing. I heard some birds fussing over my head. My cell phone rang.

"Yes, ma'am," I answered.

"How'd you know it was me?"

"No one else calls me."

"You need to get a life, Kid. Should I give your number out to some folks?"

"Internet friends?" I said.

"Acquaintances. They sound nice."

"No. What's up?"

"Got some low down on Big Bob LeFoy. Born Robert Elwood LeFoy, December 3, 1951 in Detroit. Grew up on the streets and was simply a hoodlum until some guy named Nelson Cannel came along and influenced him. Must have taught him the ropes because Bob took over some businesses for Mr. Cannel. All of this was strictly small time stuff it appears. Nothing really serious going on. But, because of all of these business interests that Cannel had, Bob became well known in Detroit by the time he was twenty-something. Overnight Bob became Mr. Big."

"Reason?"

"Can't say. Influence, maybe. Someone died and left him King. I don't know."

"What happened to Cannel?"

"Died in 1970. Killed in the line of business. Nasty stuff. Maybe Bob just naturally assumed he was the heir apparent and moved into Cannel's shoes."

"And he has been Big Bob LeFoy ever since?"

"Yes and no. He's been big. Bob was overweight as a teenager and got bigger after that. Well over six feet tall and weighs 300 plus. But the problem with all of this is that Bob LeFoy is not smart enough to run a big city crime syndicate. He's not dumb, mind you, but there is nothing in his past that would indicate Bob had the brains to do this. Cannel was a small time operator and gave Bob some good advice. I'm guessing here. But you can't make a silk purse out of a sow's ear. Like that one?"

"It's been around."

"Hey, I just found it. Thought it was a good one."

"Priceless. So, Big Bob does not fit the model for crime boss of a city. How does he do it then?"

"You want my opinion?"

"I generally do."

"I think he's a figurehead. He works for somebody else.

He's a good front, but he just ain't got the smarts to handle the whole package. Crime is sophisticated these days, as you know. You have to be shrewd in order to avoid both the local police as well as the Feds. Don't believe that Bob has the wherewithal to do that."

"Why would some guy allow this Mr. Fatso to be the Featured Attraction?"

"Maybe this guy appears to be lily white, some political figure, or someone connected to the authorities. Big Bob is a good front for him."

"You find anything to support your theory?"

"Nothing in politics or the local law. Bob has a group of people who work with him, but he doesn't have too many friends in high places that I have come across."

"When did you say Big Bob mysteriously took control of things in Detroit?"

"Cannel was killed in 1970, so ... by 1971 Big Bob LeFoy was the man."

"Hmm."

"Hmm?"

"Thinking."

"About what?"

"About why I'm here in Detroit working on two cases. I'll call you back."

I dialed Rosey's private number for emergencies. I was hoping that he wasn't somewhere in Mongolia consulting.

"Washington, here."

"Where are you?"

"Well, well, the prodigal daughter has finally checked in. I was beginning to worry."

"About me? I'm touched. You stay out of my life for twenty-eight years and now you're worried about me."

"Sarcasm is not as lovely a trait as you think. What's up?"

"I need some honesty and candor."

"Call someone else."

"Not joking here. I need to know specifically what you came across that gave you the clue that Craven Malone Industries had something to do with my father's murder."

"Can't divulge my sources."

"I know that. I'm not asking for sources. I'm asking for substance. You never told me what it was that made you think they had something to do with his death."

"We ran an investigation into Malone Industries, every company they owned. We checked all of the books, files, whatever data we could get our hands on. I was reviewing some of these because one of our guys was out sick at the time. Purely accidental. I was checking the info on the magazine, *Lusty*. Came across an expense item in the early seventies. Overnight accommodations at a motel for four people. Dan River, Virginia."

"That's it?"

"Mostly."

"Give me the rest," I said as I coordinated the dates with my father's murder.

"The nights' lodging was on August 24, the year Bill Evans died. Four men. The line item was an expense check paid out to Bob LeFoy."

"How could you remember that?"

"I'm intelligent. And I take good notes. I wrote that one down. Then I checked back and found that your father had been killed August 25th."

"Could be a coincidence," I said not really believing an ounce of that.

"You're kidding."

"Yeah."

"Bob LeFoy has developed into a hard-to-reach crime figure. Just thought you might want to check into it."

"And why didn't you check it out?"

"No reason. The books balanced. We found their records to be legal. I was the only one who was suspicious of that entry, for obvious reasons. Had nothing to go on. Seems to be all on the up and up as they say."

"Was that the only entry with Big Bob's name attached?"

"As far as we found. I figured that a good PI could run that one down."

"But you didn't tell me that. You simply parked in front of Craven Malone Industries and let me go wandering into the night looking for ghosts."

"True. But you must have found something or you wouldn't have called and asked the question."

"I don't think I like you."

"Sure you do. We're friends. We kill for each other."

"That sounds horrible."

"It does. But it's true."

I was silent, reflecting on his statement.

"You need anything else?" he said.

"You have any business in Detroit the next few days?"

"Might. You need me?"

"Might. I'll call. Thanks for the info as well as the candor."

"You're welcome."

He hung up.

I called Rogers.

"You have the name of the accountant for *Lusty* magazine?"

"Hold on."

Seconds zipped by.

"William R. McGinnis."

"How long has he been with the magazine?"

"Two years."

"Who was before him?"

Seconds passed.

"Malcolm J. Wheesely, III. Retired in 2001."

"How long did he work there?"

"Started in 1963 … close to thirty-eight years. Long enough to suit you?"

"He's my man. Get me an address. I'm going to see Malcolm."

53

I RENTED A WHITE CHEVY BLAZER FOR MY VISIT TO MR. Wheesely. It was late morning and I was indulging in a sausage biscuit from somebody's fast food chain as I followed the directions Rogers had given me to Malcolm Wheesely's house in Oak Park, a little north of metro Detroit. Wheesely lived in a medium sized home on Westhampton Street in a tranquil neighborhood.

Rogers told me that Mr. Wheesely worked for Joey Malone until he was 80 years old. He retired in 2001. I expected some old, white-headed geezer to totter to the door and yell at me because he was stone deaf.

I pulled into the drive and there was no other vehicle in sight. The garage door was closed, so I had to assume that there was something in there. Two cats sat in the large picture window of the house, like bookends. The one on the left was all white. The other one, on my right, was black. They watched me all the way from my car to the door. Lookouts.

A short, balding man opened the door. This man did not

appear to be anywhere near 82 years old. Maybe Wheesely had a housemate. He seemed distantly polite.

"Yes?" the man with large, black eyeglasses said.

"I'm look for Malcolm Wheesely."

"You found him. How can I help you?"

"I'm doing a story on the history of *Lusty* magazine and I wonder if I might talk with you about your years there," I lied. Sounded plausible.

"I don't like to be quoted. I'm retired from there. Talk with someone else."

He started to close the door.

"But you would be very helpful to me, if I could just have fifteen minutes of your time."

"Not interested, lady. There are plenty of others who will talk with you about that magazine."

He began to shut the door again.

"Wait! Let me start again."

"You look like a nice lady. I am trying to be kind to you. I am not interested in talking with a reporter who is doing a story on my old employer."

"I'm not a reporter," I said. "I'm a private investigator looking for the person who killed Joey Malone. I'm also investigating the murder of my father more than thrity years ago."

His whole expression changed. I detected a faint smile, but nothing that I could have sworn to.

"You're a real detective?"

"Yes."

"Should have said that right off. Come in."

I followed him past a living room that was immaculate, down a hallway and into a back room where he obviously spent most of his time. It was paneled with dark, knotty pine and had a large sofa with matching chairs. There was a stereo system on one wall and a collection of compact disks on the shelves around the stereo. In the center of the stereo components was a television. He was listening to Beethoven's Ninth Symphony.

This room was just off the kitchen, separated by a counter with three bar stools on the den side. It looked homey. There were paintings of ducks on the walls.

"Have a seat, Miss –?"

"Clancy Evans, Mr. Wheesely."

"Call me Malcolm. Now, what do you want to know?"

"Why are you willing to talk to an investigator and not to a reporter?"

"I do not like reporters. Look around. Do you see any magazines?"

I looked. No magazines.

"I do not like magazines. I read books. I used to read books about accounting. Now I read novels. A man like me has few pleasures in life. I was a number cruncher, a name that is a misnomer for my profession, but I understand what is intended. I was dedicated to my boss, Mr. Joey Malone, not to the magazine. He hired me in 1963. I had just lost my job and then found out about the interview with his magazine. I was really desperate, but I tried to act professional. It was tough to play it cool, as they say, but that's what I did that day. And, I got the job. It was a good job, all things considered. I am indebted to him for giving me a job that lasted longer than anyone would have a right to expect. If I can help you find who killed him, then that would be the least I could to repay him what I owe him."

"Tell me about B.A. Dilworth."

"Oh, old Bad Ass Dilworth, I used to refer to her. Not to her face, mind you. I would have been fired for such indiscretions. I said it to myself mostly."

"I take it you don't have a high regard for her."

"Have you met her?"

"Yes."

"And I need to explain this to you?"

"No explanation, but I would like to hear your story."

"Forgive my manners, Miss Evans. Would you like some water to drink?"

"Water would be fine, thanks."

He walked into the kitchen area and took two glasses, filled them with water from the sink.

"Ice?"

"Please."

He returned with the ice water, handed me one, and then sat back down on the sofa. I noticed a brown cat sitting on an ottoman next to the back window of the den. The cat was watching me intently.

"That's Asset," he said.

"Pardon?"

"The cat's name is Asset. She's my oldest. She has allowed me to live with her for close to twenty years."

"A real asset."

"That's funny," he said without laughing, "for a private investigator. I will just bet that you are real witty when you want to be."

My eyes met his and noted some type of twinkle in them. I raised my glass of water to him to acknowledge the compliment.

"So, tell me how B.A. got to be editor."

"Oh, that story. Okay. Michael Yarks was the editor when I came along in '63. He was a good editor in terms of layout and stuff like that, but he was no good at finances. Then along comes this feisty woman named Barbara Anderson Dilworth, fresh from her divorce settlement with Reginald Oswald Dilworth, Jr. and she wanted a job with the magazine. She was trained in journalism, but didn't have much experience. She received a lot of money in the divorce with

R.O., Jr., from the big Chicago newspaper family, and with her family connections, she was able to come on board with us as Assistant Editor."

"What family connections?"

"Oh, some uncle of hers knew Mr. Malone. This uncle needs a favor and Mr. Malone obliges. Plus, B.A. Dilworth made a generous gift of $200,000 to the magazine. Since we were struggling then, that was a sizeable gesture on her part. Between family ties and giving that kind of money, it was easy to see that they would hire her and give her an office. They did. Mr. Malone did."

"Recall the uncle's name?"

"No. I have it in my files somewhere. I can look it up for you, if you like."

"That would be good. You can check on that later and give me a call."

I took out a business card that read Clancy Evans and had a phone number underneath the name. I wrote the name of the hotel and my room number on the back of the card. I handed it to him.

He examined it closely, reading every word, at least twice. Methodical and complete.

I drank some of my ice water and noticed that another cat, a gray one, had wandered into the den. It walked around with an air that belied its lowly estate. I watched it circle carefully behind the furniture, making its way over to my chair.

"Meet Balance. She's my baby. Only had her about two years now. Got her when I retired. I thought Balance was a perfect name for her and for me at that time in my life. I still have balance, too."

"Clever. So what happened to Michael Yarks?"

"It took her two years, but with astute manipulation, she was able to undercut Mr. Yarks and finally Mr. Malone fired him. She did everything legal, mind you, just mean and hateful. She has always been mean and hateful. What she wants, she gets. Always. Behaves like a spoiled child, if you ask me. But then, no one ever asked me."

"Except me."

"Yes. You are the first," he raised his water glass to me and offered a faint smile. A man of few pleasures.

"Michael was desperate to hold on, so he did some questionable things, trying to cut costs. It all backfired on him, and then when she found out, well, it was over. She told Mr. Malone, and Michael was out. She was in."

The gray cat was now sitting on the window ledge above me and to my right. She was looking out the window at the birds in Malcolm's back yard.

"Say, Miss Evans, you want to make an aging man happy?"

"Before I answer that, give me the devious idea you have."

"Oh, nothing French, mind you. I was thinking how nice it would be to go out to eat with an attractive young woman once before I die."

"You dying any time soon?"

"Closer than I like to think."

"Sick?"

"No, nothing like that. Just old. How about an early supper?"

"Or a late lunch?"

"Whichever you prefer."

"Sounds good to me. You name the place and I'll drive," I said.

"I'll name the place and drive," he said. "I want you to go in style."

"What do you drive?"

"1963 MG."

54

MALCOLM DROVE US TO GEORGE AND HARRY'S BLUE CAFÉ. The other kind of music Malcolm indulged in was jazz. The mid-afternoon crowd was light and the music was that slow, blues-side-of jazz that sounds so painful at times. If you were depressed, it was the type of music that would make you go home and load the gun.

"May I order for both of us?" Malcolm said.

It had been a long time since anyone had said that to me. In fact, the question took me all the way back to my childhood when my father took me to a really nice restaurant in Richmond and made the same proposal. Of course, I trusted my father and the meal was a delight to a young girl of nine. I didn't know about Malcolm and his tastes.

Oh well, you only live once.

"Sure thing, Mr. Wheesely."

"Please, Miss Evans. Call me Malcolm. This is as close to a date as I shall ever come."

"Go for it, Malcolm."

He ordered the Red Snapper Key West for me and the Great Lakes Whitefish for himself. Then he told them to bring out both of the main entrees on serving dishes and to provide each of us with large, empty dinner plates. He ordered a bottle of White Zinfandel.

"Now, while we wait, we can continue our talk. Next question."

"Okay. So B.A. gets Yarks fired and now she is in complete control."

"Not complete, just mild control. The next few years are hard ones. The magazine is growing, but not doing great. Mr. Malone paid a lot of attention to his personnel and the word in the office was that B.A. was a bitch. Excuse my language, Miss Evans, but it was true. Still is."

"If this is to be a date, Malcolm, you've got to call me Clancy."

"Clancy. Good name. Strong name. I like that name. Make a good name for a cat."

I hoped that was a compliment.

"So, the office personnel were not overjoyed with the leadership style of Dilworth."

"An understatement. She was good at what she did. Better than Michael Yarks. But everyone hated her. Everyone. So, Mr. Malone decided that he would bring in some new people, interview them and get rid of her. He wanted to do this quietly."

The waiter brought our wine and some warm bread fresh from the oven.

"Dilworth found out."

"Hard to keep the personnel quiet. I think they got so excited at the prospects of having another editor that, well, somehow she found out."

"Was Cyler Conroy working at the magazine by that point?"

"Oh, yes. He's been Mr. Malone's assistant for a long time."

"You think he might have told Dilworth about the potential coup?"

"Clever aren't you?"

"Not really. Just adding numbers, Malcolm. So tell me how she thwarted Mr. Malone."

"Specifics I do not know. I can only provide you with bits and pieces."

"Bits and pieces it is."

Our dinners arrived. The portions were extremely generous and they smelled wonderful. Maybe I was hungry.

"Now, here are the rules. We will share everything. Like an old country buffet type meal. You have to try both the Red Snapper and the Whitefish. You will have to trust me, Clancy. Both are exquisite."

"Who am I to break the rules?"

I noticed that the twinkle was back in Malcolm's eyes. The man was not altogether humorless.

He was also a good judge of seafood. The snapper and Whitefish were excellent choices. The wine was perfect with them. I would never have paired the White Zin with the fish. Live and learn.

"The bits and pieces, Malcolm?"

"Oh, yes. I was enjoying this food so much I nearly forgot we had business to finish."

"Don't make it sound so pleasure-less."

"You are right. It is a most enjoyable afternoon. Business and pleasure can be mixed."

"Often."

"Something happened down south to one of our photo suppliers. All I know is that I stopped sending money to the account marked 'Virginia.' Dilworth had a meeting with Mr. Malone. When she came out of that meeting, she was smiling, and I can tell you from firsthand experience, that was a rare thing to see around the office. Piranha as a rule do not smile." He took a mouthful of Red Snapper and chewed with delight.

"Unless they are about to eat someone for lunch," I said.

He nodded and pointed his fork at me without speaking. He was eating and enjoying it. Good to see a person with few pleasures so happy.

"All this happened in the early seventies, right?"

He stopped chewing for a moment and seemed to be deep in thought.

"I would have to check my files, but I think you are right. I'll need the specific date, if you have it. You know, so I can check through my records. But I do recall that this happened around the same time that Mr. Malone announced to the company that B.A. Dilworth was the permanent editor of the magazine."

"Amid cheers and great joy."

"Exactly. The office was crushed, but I figured we had endured it for a few years, we could endure it longer. I could anyway. Some of the folks quit, of course. There were a few like me who stuck it out."

"But none as long as you."

"No. I have great staying power."

"Plus you didn't work directly for Dilworth."

"Plus that. I did have to deal with her, but I never really had many serious run-ins with her. She did her job and she allowed me to do mine. We were mutually exclusive, and I preferred it that way."

"Bet you did."

We finished our meal without talking business. He told me a little of his life story. It was a short story, despite his 82 years. Lifelong bachelor who loved numbers and keeping books. He had no family except for his five cats. I only counted four. One of them had failed to acknowledge his or her existence to me. He also added that he hated dogs, did not smoke or drink anything but wine. Solid citizen.

He insisted upon paying for the meal. I indulged him.

It took longer to return to his house in Oak Park because we caught the five o'clock traffic. It was close to seven when we pulled into his driveway. The black and white cats were keeping vigil in his window.

"You didn't meet Credit and Debit," he said.

"True accountant, huh Malcolm?"

"That's me, Clancy."

"Debit would be the all black cat, of course."

"Has to be."

"One of your cats failed to meet me," I said.

"Better clarify something. They're not my cats. They live in my house. I feed them. I take care of them, but they are not my cats. I am their friend, but not their owner. You don't own a cat, Clancy. I must learn to co-exist with felines. They permit me to live with them."

"Like you and Dilworth?"

"That was a much tougher relationship. I happen to like cats. I enjoy their independence, I admit. Might be their live and let live attitude. But I also enjoy their companionship when they choose to grant me the privilege of sharing the room or bed or whatever. We have an understanding."

"You and Dilworth never reach that understanding?"

"Only tolerance, I'm afraid. I tolerated her and she tolerated me."

"Any other bits or pieces for me?"

"Well, she became more and more powerful. She did whatever she wanted to with the magazine. And usually whatever she did worked for the success of the magazine. Of course I did not benefit first hand from any success of the publication. I was paid by Mr. Malone exclusively. I took care of all bookkeeping, both the magazine's and his personal stuff as well."

"Oh, I thought Cyler Conroy took care of his personal stuff."

"Cyler made some of the payments to individuals, but I kept the records."

"So you knew about Bimbi Love and her daughter?"

He got out of the Blazer and walked around to my side.

"Let's go inside and meet the other member of the family."

I followed him inside. He led me to a back room that had separate beddings for each of the five felines in the house. An orange cat was lying in her bedding. Above the soft bedding was the name Profit. Malcolm was consistent.

"He's mentally retarded. He's been here for over ten years. The other cats are friendly with him, but no one gets too close, except for me. He lets me stroke him and I come in here and we talk some. But he can't get out and do what the other cats do. He's a bit clumsy and awkward, but in this environment, he gets by. We all have our secrets, Clancy. All of us."

We knelt down and he guided my hand over to Profit and stroked the cat's back with my hand.

"He likes you."

"How can you tell?"

"He didn't attack you when we entered the room."

55

I WAS LYING ON THE BED SORTING THROUGH WHAT I HAD learned from Malcolm Wheesely and the others when the room phone rang. It was Malcolm.

"I checked my files and the name of Dilworth's uncle was Flowers, Homer Flowers. Don't know much about him, but he was Mr. Malone's contact in Virginia. Apparently Mr. Flowers knew the people who supplied the photos we used in the magazine."

"Imagine that," I said.

"You've heard of him?"

"A long time ago. Some ghosts never go away."

"I know about those kinds of things."

"Malcolm, would you verify something for me?"

"Sure."

"Somewhere in your records, the books for the early seventies, would you check to see if you had a single entry of a payment to Bob LeFoy?"

"Funny you should ask for that. I just came across that entry while looking up the name of Homer Flowers. Yes, I issued a check to Robert LeFoy for five thousand dollars in September of 1972."

"Damn."

"That must mean something to you."

"The end of a long quest."

"You don't sound too happy at arriving at the end."

"Oh, I haven't arrived at the end just yet. But I see the end, and I see where the road is taking me. You can't imagine how much help you have been to me, Malcolm. I am forever indebted."

"Nonsense. You have lighted up the life of an old man with simple pleasures. I shall forever remember fondly our afternoon delight at the Blue Café. I must say that you cannot imagine how much pleasure you have brought to a devout bachelor. Too bad we didn't meet fifty years ago."

"How romantic of you to say so."

"You are a dream come true, Miss Evans. Thank you for joining me for lunch. Oh yes, that Robert LeFoy entry was the only one for that year for him. However, there have been numerous ones since then. In fact, regular payments."

"Every year?"

"Yes, but not directly traceable to Robert LeFoy. You know of course that we are talking about Big Bob LeFoy, don't you?"

"Yes."

"Well, there were two accounts set up for what Dilworth called 'discretionary' accounts, number one and number two. Number one was the business account she used for magazine stuff. Number two she used to keep Big Bob on the payroll."

"On the payroll. What did Big Bob do for the magazine?"

"I have no idea. You'll have to ask either Big Bob or B.A. Dilworth."

"Count on it."

"I was kidding, Clancy."

"Not I. I'm an investigator. Therefore, I investigate."

"LeFoy is a dangerous man."

"And Dilworth is a piranha."

It was mid-morning and I was dining at a restaurant near the hotel enjoying a hearty breakfast. I figured if I had to wrestle with Dilworth and LeFoy today, I should at least put some calories inside of me. I had both guns with me, the 9mm in the small of my back and the .357 in the shoulder holster. Despite the heat of late August, I was wearing a sporty jacket to help conceal the weapons and carry some extra rounds in my coat pockets. I always like to be prepared when I dance with the devil.

I was just finishing my second cup of high velocity java and silently cursing my luck at confronting both Dilworth and LeFoy alone when Rosey walked through the door of the restaurant and came over to my table.

"What a glorious sight for my all-too-weary-yet-fearful eyes," I said.

"What do you have to afraid of?" he said.

"We're all going to die sooner or later."

"Philosophic this morning, are we?"

"Mellowing, I think. How did you find me here?"

"What I do."

"Consult with, shoot at, and search for people."

"In a nutshell. So, what's on the docket for today?"

"Time to confront."

"You find the missing pieces?"

"I know who killed my father. I know who hired him to kill my father. I know why. That's enough for now."

"What about Joey Malone?"

"Dead end on that one so far."

"Could be the same people."

"Motive is all wrong. Let's go see Dilworth. You got something for us to ride?"

"Rental Jeep. I'll drive and you can tell me what I need to know."

Rosey drove us to the magazine's offices on McComb. Marlene was working the reception area as usual. I provided a quick update so that he would know most of what I knew. Concise but meaningful.

"Editor in?" I said to Marlene.

"Sure, let me buzz her."

"No, we want this to be a surprise."

She started to object, but I winked at her and she put forth no effort to argue with me. I was an old hand by now for walking into the office area as if I knew what I was doing. A good act.

No one paid any attention to me, but some eyes followed Rosey as we walked through toward Dilworth's office.

I stopped at the desk of a young, dark-haired woman who looked friendly. I hadn't seen her there before today. I asked her about Conroy and she said that they had received no word this morning. He was still in a coma as of late last night. I thanked her and we moved on.

I knocked gently on Dilworth's closed door. We went inside when she invited us to do so.

"You're not welcome here," she said to me. "This your bodyguard?"

"Among other things."

I sat down in front of her desk. Rosey stood to the right of the door hinges, just in case Dilworth might be fretful of our presence.

"Who's this?" she said to me while looking at Rosey. "He looks familiar. I seldom forget a face."

"Roosevelt Washington," he said to her.

"Name doesn't mean anything to me," she said.

"It will," he said.

"What do you want?" she was talking to me this time.

"Revenge, but I'll settle for justice."

"What are you talking about?"

"You hired Big Bob LeFoy along with three other fellows to kill my father back in the early seventies."

"That's absurd. I'm the editor of a magazine. I don't go around ordering murders."

"You did at least once."

"Even if I did do it, you can't prove it."

"Line items in your books. Payment to LeFoy and for a motel room in Dan River, Virginia."

"That could mean anything, could be for anyone."

"Could be, but it's not."

"Who was your father to me?"

"Nothing to you. Small town County Sheriff in Virginia. You thought he was the one who stopped your source of pornographic pictures of little children, and the one who killed Uncle Homer."

Her face turned pale at the mention of Homer, and I thought I could detect a hint of sweat bead on her forehead.

"You're the daughter of that hick sheriff who should have minded his own business years ago?"

"In person."

"You expect me to believe that you tracked me down after all these years for some murder that happened in Virginia when you were a little girl?"

"I don't care what you believe, Dilworth. I don't even care if you accept the fact that I know all these details about you, how you got this job to begin with, and how you dealt with Joey Malone to keep it. I don't care what you believe. You're going to jail, but before that happens, I just wish you would do something really stupid right now. If there's a gun in one of your desk drawers, I wish you would try to get it and use it on me."

"I don't have a gun in this office."

"That's too bad. Would it help if I loaned you one of mine?"

"You can't arrest me," Dilworth said to me.

"I can," Rosey said.

"And who are you?"

"I work for the United States Government. Contracting a murder in another state is a federal offense. You're under arrest."

Rosey walked over to her and lifted her out of her chair by the arm. We had no handcuffs.

"Where is your proof?"

"In a safe place," I said.

"Where are you taking me?"

"Police station just up the street. Detective Morland would love to talk with you."

"I want to call my lawyer."

"Maybe at the police station," Rosey said.

56

"You'd better have solid evidence against her, Evans," Morland said to me after he had Dilworth locked in a cell.

I told him everything I had to connect her to my father's death.

"I thought you came here to find out who killed Joey Malone."

"Still working on that one," I said.

"I'll have to call Virginia. They'll likely want Dilworth down there. Know any good state attorneys who will work hard on this?"

"One or two."

"This will be a hard one to get a conviction."

"Even with the evidence?"

"Thirty-two years is a long time, Evans. Most of what you have is circumstantial. It certainly looks like she went after your father. Points to her, but a trial is a different animal. You need LeFoy to admit that she hired him."

"Not likely, huh?"

"Not likely at all."

"Let's go talk to him," I said to Rosey.

"Tell me again what agency you work for," Morland said to Rosey.

"Didn't tell you the first time. Covert activity."

"How can I verify all of this?"

"You're the arresting officer," Rosey said to Morland. "That's why I suggested that you give her the Miranda ritual."

"She call a lawyer yet?" I said.

"Yeah, just before they put her in the cell."

"Who'd she call?"

"Don't know. That's private, you know."

"Sure."

We started out the door.

"You want some help talking to LeFoy?" Morland said to us.

"Thought you'd never ask," I said.

Rosey drove and we followed Morland. LeFoy had been on my list of people to see. We were in the vicinity of the Rattlesnake Club. I recognized some of the streets so I knew that we were close to the river. That was the extent of my knowledge.

We were on Franklin and then turned onto Walker Street. LeFoy's building was on the right. There was a modern office complex next to a large warehouse. Morland and the four squad cars that followed him parked in front of the warehouse. Rosey and I parked near the office building.

Morland sent two cars around to the back of the buildings. He joined Rosey and me as we entered the office complex. No one was working the lobby desk. We walked down the hallway and knocked on some doors, but no one answered. The doors were all locked. Apparently, no one was home.

"Whattaya bet that B.A. Dilworth called Big Bob LeFoy and not a lawyer?" Morland said.

"I never bet on a sure thing," I said.

"LeFoy had to know we were coming. He's always got people in this place working their buns off. His operation is too large to shut down unless he is really frightened."

"Dilworth might have encouraged him to be frightened," I said.

"Would he leave the country?" Rosey said.

"Not likely, but he might go into hiding for a very long time. Either way, it would be tough to find him," Morland suggested.

"Wait," I said, "let's not assume that Dilworth is giving up and that LeFoy is gone into hiding just yet. If they could destroy the evidence and me, then the state of Virginia would have no case against them."

I realized that Wheesely was in danger.

"We've got to go, Morland. We'll call you later," I motioned for Rosey. We ran to his rented Grand Cherokee and headed for Malcolm's place in Oak Park.

"Where are you two going now?" Morland yelled after us.

"To protect my sources," I yelled back.

Despite the steady flow of traffic, it still took us twenty-five minutes to get to Wheesely's place. No one was home except the cats. Credit and Debit, the bookends, were stationed at their usual positions in the front window. I assumed that the rest were in hiding. There were no signs of forced entry, and the MG was not in the garage. Perhaps Wheesely had just gone out to pick up something at the grocery store. All appeared calm.

"Where to now, Madame?" Rosey said.

"Options are thin."

"But not exhausted."

"It's a big city."

"Intuition?"

"Running on empty these days. How about a hunch?"

"Hunches are okay sometimes."

"I have a hunch that Big Bob has been working for Dilworth nearly all of his life. She has made him into the figurehead we all see. But the truth is, she's the real criminal mind and money behind the whole operation. He was a front for her, and her job was a great cover."

"You making this up as you go?"

"Yeah, but it does sound plausible. When Tony Scarletti was dying, I asked him if he worked for Big Bob. He shook his head."

"But he never said who he was working for."

"True, but let's assume that he was telling the truth. He did not work for Big Bob. By all appearances, LeFoy would be the natural one to work for if you are a dirty cop."

"Appearances."

"Try this on. Dilworth sends Big Bob to Malone to buy the magazine. Dilworth hears through Conroy that Malone is wanting out anyway, so she sends in the figurehead. The front guy. Mr. Kingpin. She must have known that Malone did not like her all that much and that he would not sell the magazine to her. So, she goes through another door. Then, to seal the deal, she goes to Malone and fakes an argument with him over the selling of the magazine."

"So, you don't believe she killed Malone."

"No. She wanted to own the magazine. If Malone is dead, she loses her opportunity to buy it. Big Bob's offer and her great acting skills were about to close the deal. Then someone killed Malone."

"Too bad for the mean lady."

"Yeah, really."

Rosey was driving us back into the city.

"Where are you taking us?" I said.

"Don't know. You haven't given me a direction nor place."

"Find I-75 and go north. I know a good place that LeFoy might hide."

"Another hunch?"

"Nothing less."

57

It was close to five o'clock when we turned down the empty paved road that led to B.A. Dilworth's modest home.

"She lives here?" Rosey said.

"At the end, in the woods. House is visible from the road, so I suggest we park here and walk."

"Why is it you and I seem to end up in the woods together a lot?"

"Hansel and Gretel?"

My cell phone rang.

"Yes, ma'am," I said.

"Morland here."

"Thought you were someone else. I don't get a lot of calls."

"Giving you a heads up. Dilworth is out. Her attorney got her released. Maybe an hour ago. I was discussing procedures with my chief when I got the word."

"She's fast. You barely had time to do the paperwork to get her in."

"She's tightly connected. Friends in higher places than I can go."

"Me, too."

While Morland and I talked, Rosey prepared himself for a potential conflict.

He was at the back of the Jeep checking his stash of weapons. He took out a Winchester 70 with a scope. It was a 7mm with good range. He then put on a 9mm Glock 34. I walked around to the back with him and watched. I told Morland where we were, that we were following nothing more than a hunch. He laughed and hung up.

"You want a long gun?" he said.

"Got anything light in there?"

"The Weathermaster 7400 is not bad," he handed me the 30-06 made by Remington. "Only has four rounds, so shoot wisely."

"My number one goal."

"Mr. Morland have any good news for us?" Rosey said.

"Dilworth's out on bond. Good lawyer and well connected."

"Imagine that."

We walked along the road until we could partially see some of the house in the woods at the end. I entered the woods on the left and Rosey took to the other side. We circled deep into the forest area until we were adjacent to the house. There were two guns out front leaning against a late model Lincoln Town Car. I guessed it was Big Bob's. I moved slowly to position myself adjacent to the back of the house. Two more. One on the back porch appeared to be wiping his gun. The other was standing near a large pine smoking a cigarette.

Rosey and I had predetermined our strategy. My task was to enter through the back while he created chaos and confusion in the front. I waited for the chaos and confusion, and for the two guns out back to go around to the front. The silence was deadly. I knew what was coming.

The sound of Rosey's 7mm rifle echoed throughout the surrounding woods. The man sitting on the porch cleaning his weapon dropped his rag and hurried to the front to enter the action. The cigarette smoker grabbed his automatic weapon and went the other way to the front of the house. The back was empty and open, but still dangerous. I had no idea how many were inside.

I moved toward the back porch by going from tree to tree for protection.

Another shot came from the front. Since Rosey didn't often miss, I could assume that the outside force was now reduced to two. I heard a volley of return fire from the opposition. I took the opportunity to enter the screened-in back porch hoping that all eyes in the house were focused out the front.

A window to the left of the back door gave me a partial view of the inside. I was looking in the kitchen window. No was eating or fixing. I could see one man a bedroom kneeling down looking towards the front of the house. I could see a leg and a foot of another person in the living room. Neither of them appeared to be Big Bob. Wrong size.

I waited for another volley of gunfire and then entered carefully through the back door. Just my luck that the man in the bedroom decided to move from his window position. As he turned to come out of the room, he saw me. I didn't have time to draw either of my handguns, so I fired the 30-06 in his direction. The force of the blast sent him airborne and into the front window. Glass and debris were flying everywhere as he landed in the front yard.

I ducked back into the kitchen area. I had no protection in there since it opened into a den with nothing separating the two areas except furniture. From my vantage point, the living room opened off to the left, the bedroom with the large hole in the window was to the right. There was a short hallway further off to my right. I couldn't forge ahead into the living room where the other gunman was for fear that there might be someone in another room down the hall to my right.

I heard another rifle shot from the front of the house. Maybe three down and one to go before Rosey could come help me. I leaned the 30-06 in the corner of a bottom set of cabinets next to the sink. I wanted a handgun in close-quarter combat.

The .357 was in my hand as I waited for my next move. Sometimes instinct is all that helps you when you are in a dangerous and vulnerable position.

I was pushing my left shoulder into the front of the refrigerator that sat along the only wall that separated the kitchen from the living room. I could hear a single volley from an automatic weapon coming from the front. A sound to my blind-side left gave me the strong impression that the gunman in the living room was coming for me. I dove from my only cover towards the back of the sofa some fifteen feet away. I fired the .357 while I was in the air where I thought the gunman might be standing. He fired, too, but only as a reaction to my surprise attack. A bullet caught me in my left thigh just before I hit the hardwood floor.

The gunman from the living room went down, but he was not dead. He looked up just in time to see me fire once more into his body. He stayed down this time.

All was quiet, inside and out.

I used the sofa to help me to my feet. My leg hurt, but I could at least stand and limp towards the front door. I wanted to check on Rosey.

I had the .357 in my hand as I limped along.

"Drop the gun where you are standing, or I'll drop you."

I decided to do what I was told. I let the .357 fall as gently as I could onto the hardwood floor. I turned my head a little to see a large, fat man pointing a 9mm at me.

"You must be Big Bob LeFoy," I said.

"You have the advantage, but I suspect you must be the broad Andy told me was making some heat."

"Andy?"

"Yeah. B.A. Dilworth. My partner."

"Partner, huh? Fifty-fifty?"

"Yeah, more or less. I do okay. See that car outside, all mine."

"Impressive. You're the brawn and she's the brains."

"What does that mean?"

"Excuse me, you're the muscle and she's the brains."

"Oh, yeah. Good way to say that. Plus I get all the credit. Everyone thinks I'm in charge."

"But we know better."

"Hey, you ain't gonna mess with my mind. I've had a good thing goin' for years now. Don't think I ain't given a lot of thought to this. I got money, power and people moves over when me and the boys come callin'. I don't care if folks don't know the truth. Ain't hurtin' my wallet none. But you, ... you're here to mess things up. That won't do."

"So why didn't you shoot me?"

"Orders."

"Andy?"

"Who else?"

58

It was time for Rosey to come charging through the door and rescue me from Big Bob. The situation was not playing out exactly as I had hoped.

I decided to limp back over to the sofa in the den in order to put Big Bob between the front door and me. It was a perfect plan. Rosey would have a great shot at a target nearly impossible to miss.

The front door opened and Rosey came in. He had no gun. B.A. Dilworth came in behind him holding an assault rife and looking meaner than usual.

Now I really was worried. This was not the plan I had conceived.

Rosey saw my leg bleeding and came over to help me.

"You don't need to do that. You'll both be dead in a few minutes," Dilworth said.

"Can I kill her, Andy?" LeFoy said.

"She's all mine, Bobbie. All mine. You get the black dude."

I heard a car pull up outside.

"Hey, Ms. Dilworth?" a voice that sounded like Wheesely yelled out. "Ms. Dilworth, you in there?"

It was Wheesely. He came walking into the living room as if he did this all the time. He looked around at the dead bodies, then at the weapons that were aimed at Rosey and me. Then he saw my injured leg. His expression never changed.

"I have the books you asked for, Ms. Dilworth," Wheesely said.

"Thank you, Mr. Wheesely. You can put them on the kitchen table. We'll destroy them after we destroy these two meddling people. All will be right with the world after that."

"What do you mean destroy these two? You can't kill them," Wheesely said.

"Sure we can, Mr. Wheesely. This is a part of the business I wouldn't expect you to understand. Sometimes people have to die."

"I can't let you do it, Ms. Dilworth," Wheesely said and stood in front of me.

"How are you going to stop me?" she said.

"I'll stand here and protect her. You won't shoot me," he said to Dilworth.

"Get out of the way, Wheesely," Dilworth said.

"No. I won't move."

"Wheesely, come on. Move out of the way. This is not your affair."

"I can't just let you kill her, Ms. Dilworth. It's not right," Wheesely said rather calmly.

The gun shot surprised everyone but LeFoy as he fired his 9mm. Wheesely began falling to my left, and I grabbed him as he fell and guided him to the floor. Rosey, trained to act quickly, immediately kicked Dilworth in the face and she dropped her weapon. LeFoy shifted slightly to the right to shoot Rosey, but his gun jammed.

Just like that the tables had turned to our favor. LeFoy kept fiddling with his 9mm to get it to fire. No avail.

"Put the gun down, LeFoy," Rosey said.

LeFoy ignored him and kept working on the jammed gun.

I was on the floor holding Wheesely who was semi-conscious. He had been shot in his right side and was in some obvious pain, but not showing signs of undue stress. He was remarkably calm for an 82 year old man who has just defended a fair maiden perhaps for the first time in his life. Chivalry was not dead.

"Put it down!" Rosey said louder this time.

LeFoy looked at him with eyes of desperation, but continued to fiddle with the useless gun. Then he saw my .357 next to the wall to his right. He dropped his gun and reached for my weapon on the floor. Rosey fired a volley of rounds that hit LeFoy in his hand, arm and lower leg. He went down to his knees and sat motionless for a few seconds. He was bleeding profusely.

"You can't kill me, I'm Big Bob LeFoy. I'm the Main Man of Detroit City."

There was a wild gleam in his eye, almost as if he had just decided to go mad that instant. He picked up the .357 and Rosey fired a few more rounds into Big Bob. They all hit him but he held onto my gun and turned it in Rosey's direction.

Rosey then engaged the automatic with a volley of shots that seemed to last a lifetime. I turned my head and leaned over against Wheesely to protect him even though we were safely out of the way. Some things you just can't watch. Despite the speed at which the rounds came out of the automatic, they had a familiar sound to me. I was transported at that moment back through time to that horrid day when I was in my room getting ready to go to Mr. Joe's house to celebrate his homecoming from the hospital.

The sound was familiar and awful. I knew that death was at the end of the sound. There was no point in looking over at Big Bob LeFoy. I knew that he was not with us any longer.

I suddenly realized I was crying.

"You okay?" Wheesely said as he looked up at me.

"I'm okay."

"You weren't hit, were you?" he said.

"Only my leg from an earlier shot. I'm okay. How about you?"

"I'm great. I think I saved your life."

"I think you did, too. The knight and the maiden. Thanks."

Wheesely and I were both taken to the hospital and treated. His wound was not as bad as I had first thought. The bullet had entered his side at an angle and had exited his back, missing anything vital. My wound was a clean shot that didn't look so clean to me. But there was nothing to dig out and that was good news. A faster healing time.

Several hours later I was ready to leave the hospital. Rosey came into the room with the doctor.

"I want you to remain overnight, just as a precaution," Dr. Milo Herauldi said. "You're a strong person, but you lost some blood. Besides, you look as if you could use some rest."

Rosey nodded in agreement with the doctor's advice, so I decided not to fight the collective medical opinions of the room. The doctor left.

"Get a wheelchair for me. I'm going to visit Wheesely."

Rosey started to argue, but finally decided it was futile to do so.

Wheesely was all the way down the end of the hall from my room. He was sitting up in the bed when we entered.

"How are you, Miss Evans?" he said before I could ask him.

"Clancy, remember?"

"I'm sorry. I suppose when you rescue damsels in distress, you should sound as if you know them on a less than formal level," he said.

"I'm okay. I get to spend a night here resting, so says the doctor."

"Good. Perhaps we can pass the time. I get to spend a day or so here likewise."

"Thank you again for what you did for us, Malcolm," I said.

"Glad I could help you."

"What you did was extremely dangerous. You could have been killed. I don't think you should make a habit of doing things like that."

"What, at my age?"

"No. At any age. A person holding a gun is more likely to use it than not."

"Too much violence in the world," he said as he adjusted the covers around him. "It has to stop. We're all going to kill each other unless some of us take a stand. I was just doing my part to slow down some of the violence."

"We're grateful," Rosey said. "Sorry you got shot."

"This? Ah, it's nothing. Like Matt Dillon used to say, 'It's only a flesh wound.'"

59

It was very late when Rosey rolled me back to my hospital room. We had a long visit with Wheesely, even dining together on hospital food. It's wasn't quite up to what I had been eating of late, but then my own cooking wasn't up to the ritzy standard of the places I had visited during my brief stay in Detroit.

An unfamiliar nurse came into my room just as Rosey was about to leave.

"Clancy Evans?" she said.

"That would be me."

"Do you know Mr. Cyler Conroy, he's a patient here?"

"Yes."

"He regained consciousness and was asking for you. I just happened to see the entry log and noticed that you were also in the hospital. Thought I would let you know."

"Thank you," I said trying to cover my surprise. "Thank you for coming to tell me."

"You're welcome," she said and then she left the room.

"More visiting?" Rosey said.

"You tired?"

"Yes, but we have to go, right?"

"We have to go."

Cyler was in another wing of the hospital and it took us nearly ten minutes to find his place from mine. We knocked gently and entered the room when we heard someone speak. We couldn't understand what they had said.

The room was empty except for Cyler. He smiled when he saw me.

He looked like he had been run over by a truck. An eighteen wheeler. He was being given oxygen through his nose and had patches all over his face. There were more bruises than I cared to look at. I was sorry for him.

"Welcome back," I said.

"Thanks," he whispered. "Nice … to be … back."

I smiled as Rosey wheeled me to the side of his bed. I gently took his hand and held it.

"Glad … you … could come. What…," he gestured gingerly toward my wheelchair with his left hand, his only uninjured limb.

"Oh, this. It's nothing. Injured while hunting vermin."

He arched his eyebrows as a way of questioning my word.

"Pests," I said.

He smiled, then looked at Rosey.

"Who's … this?"

"Old friend. Came along to save my bacon. Wouldn't be here without him."

"I … would … not be …. here … with…out ……. you," Cyler said.

I smiled and gently cupped his hand in both of my hands.

"I … need … to …. confess," he spoke with some obvious strain.

"What?"

"I … killed …. Joey."

"Why?" I said with some shock. "I thought you liked the man. Thought you were like kindred spirits."

"Me, too. ... But ... he lied .... to me... He .... was ... straight ... and .... never ... told me."

Then I realized what Malone had done. He had kept his darkest secret from someone who had loved him. Some injuries run too deep for words. Deception is hard to accept.

"You found out about Bimbi," I said.

"And ... Gretchen .... That's ... why... I ...framed...Bimbi," he shook his head slowly. "For ... over ... twenty .... years....." his voice trailed off and he turned his head away from us to keep us from seeing the tears.

I held on to his hand while he sobbed softly. I felt badly for him. I wanted to crawl into the bed beside him and comfort him, like a mother. He finally stopped crying and turned back toward us.

"You ... tell .... the police, okay?"

"They'll need a statement from you."

He nodded and then closed his eyes. He was exhausted.

I was set free from the hospital by mid-morning the next day. Rosey drove us to see Morland. We told him what Cyler had confessed and he sent a couple of detectives over to get a statement from him.

"Think he'll survive?" Morland said.

"Hard to say. Some of his injuries are pretty severe. My guess is that he'll be a long time recovering," I said.

"We'll wait. In the meantime, I'll put a police officer over there to protect our interests."

"No more Mr. Nice Guy, huh?"

"Huh," he grunted with slight exasperation.

"You'll let Bimbi go now?" I said.

"Paper work is already in the system. Should be cleared this afternoon," he said over his shoulder as he walked away.

"He could have said thanks," I said to Rosey.

"For what?"

"I don't know. All the meals I paid for, the hours of help I gave him. I don't know. Common courtesy."

"What meals? I thought Craven paid for everything."

"Details. You're always concerned about details."

60

Rosey and I were on a plane the next day heading home. I convinced him to come to Norfolk and spend a few days with Sam, Blackie and me. I wasn't ready to tell him about Rogers. Besides, he was smart enough that sooner or later he might figure her out.

"You take care of the guns?" I said.

"I did."

"I'm sorry we had to use them."

"I'm glad we had them to use. Death without them."

I made no comment. I thought about what Wheesely had said about the violence. My life and work was a part of that violence. It left a bad taste in my mouth. It wasn't from the peanuts I was eating.

"Any loose ends?" Rosey said.

"Yeah. I'm concerned about Bimbi and Gretchen."

"Joey's girls."

"Yeah. They could have it rough with Joey gone."

"Life's a bitch."

The bad taste was still with me. I drank some ginger ale hoping that would help. It didn't.

"I called Morland and thanked him for his help. He said to thank you, that he enjoyed all the meals that Mr. Craven Malone provided," Rosey said.

"I'll bet he did. You trying to make me feel better?"

"Is it working?"

"No."

"I'm not good at failing," Rosey said. "What can I tell you that'll help?"

"Can't have everything, Mister."

My cell phone rang. Rogers had some breaking news.

"Thought you'd like to know what just happened."

"This good or bad news?"

"You'll have to decide that one for yourself, Dearie."

"Go ahead."

"Don't scream."

"I'll contain myself."

"No shouting either."

"Talk to me."

"Okay, I'm reading now. Headlines from the morning's newspaper: 'Craven Malone, CEO and President of Craven Malone Industries, Incorporated, passed away at his Virginia Beach home late yesterday afternoon. The cause of death was not immediately determined, but the Medical Examiner has ruled out foul play. Mr. Malone was 90 years old. Funeral arrangements are still being made. Please contact J.C. Whitmore for further information.' How 'bout that?"

"I shouldn't be surprised with his age and all, but I certainly didn't expect it. Any speculation, like maybe a heart attack?"

"Whitmore sent an email to somebody in New York saying that it was a heart attack, but that's all I've been able to pick up. Looks clean, no 'foul play,' … isn't that a riot? …. nothing unseemly involved, apparently."

"Looks like I will have to converse with J.C. Whitmore one more time, just to get my expenses paid."

"Looks that way. Everything kosher on your end?"

"One or two things not to my liking, but I can't solve all the problems of the world. A long journey has ended. It feels good to be coming home."

"It'll be good to have you home. The canines miss you."

It was slowly becoming her line. Made me wonder. How far can AI go with computers?

She hung up before I could respond. Progress was being made. At least she expressed some sort of farewell word. It was a start. I'd have to work on her bluntness.

Rosey took a few days off and stayed with us. I felt obligated to attend Craven Malone's funeral since the man still owed me money for the work in Detroit and some expenses. J.C. Whitmore had done an excellent job on the funeral arrangements, so Big Daddy's service was better than son Joey's. Only an opinion.

Rosey accompanied me to the Virginia Beach affair. J.C. had a reception at the waterfront cottage. There must have been a few hundred of the elite, high-brow, society types all doing the cheek-to-cheek stuff which had no appeal to me at all. I wondered if money was the cause of this insanity, or just plain old pretentiousness. I was at the bar staring out over the Atlantic Beach and silently criticizing my very weak Martini when Whitmore came over. She ordered a Martini.

"Nice of you to come," she said. "I heard that you finished your work in Detroit. Sorry that Mr. Malone went to his grave not knowing who killed his son."

"Better that way."

"Who did do it?"

"Not who, but what."

She looked puzzled. I sipped my very bad Martini. It

made that bad taste in my mouth even worse. Whitmore took a sip of her drink.

"Bad decisions in life," I said.

"We all make bad decisions, Miss Evans."

I nodded, "And sometimes they cost us dearly."

She swallowed some of her Martini and acted as if she enjoyed it. My standards were higher.

"I suppose you want your money."

"Whenever you have time," I said.

"I have time now. Let's go to the study."

I followed her into Craven's beach home. It was larger than the mansion in Linkhorn Park. She guided me through the maze to a large study on the first floor. The walls were all mahogany matching the desk, the chairs and the credenza behind the desk. Consistency. The room was beautiful.

Whitmore moved a painting attached to the wall with hinges. Behind the painting was a safe. She played with the dial for a few minutes and then it opened.

"Trusting, aren't you, to let me see where the money is kept?"

"You a thief, too, Miss Evans?"

"Not yet."

She took out a large, manila envelope, closed the safe, spun the dial, and moved the painting back into position. I took the envelope from her when she offered it to me.

I turned to walk out the door and back to reception. I wanted to go home and see my people.

"You aren't going to open it and count it?"

"Why, you cheat me?"

"Hardly."

"Then there's no reason to open it now."

"You mean you trust me?"

"No. Just means I know where you live and where you keep the valuables. I can always come back."

"Wise ass."

I waved and turned to leave again.

"You want to hear a funny ending to a bad story?"

"What bad story?"

"My life."

"Okay, shoot. Tell me the funny ending," I said.

"Craven had no relatives, so he left everything to me."

"Everything?"

"Well, he gave a hundred million to some charities and some lose change to a few local things around Virginia Beach, but I got the rest of it."

"Enough to retire?"

"Two hundred million. What do you think?"

"I'd hate to pay the inheritance tax," I said.

"I'll still be set for life."

"Good luck to you. I hope you'll be happy. What about the other holdings, the companies he owned?"

"The old geezer did something most unusual. He gave each company to the employees, each one becoming an equal owner of the company. So, if the companies continue to do well, then each employee will do well. Some incentive, huh?"

"Good gesture. And the houses here in Virginia Beach?"

"Mine, too. Both."

"Good for you, J.C. Don't let it change your sweet disposition."

"Go to hell," she said. "Oh, one more thing. I'm getting married again."

"Now, you are joking, right?"

"Giorgio Leoni. How does that grab you?"

"A match made in, well, not exactly heaven."

"Not exactly, but it's a good start for me."

"Think Giorgio can handle you?"

"Are you asking me if I'll kill him?"

"Crossed my mind."

"Only if he tries to take liberties not freely offered."

"He know about your ex?"

"Every detail. I wanted him to know what I am capable of."

"Good luck," I said and left.

"I'll invite you to the wedding," she called after me as I walked down the long hall of the beach house.

EPILOGUE

I WAS HEADING TO VIRGINIA BEACH FOR A LITTLE R&R WHEN the phone rang. Uncle Walters had a favor to ask.

"Ask," I said without hesitation.

"This is a big favor," he said.

"There is no way I could ever repay you for all that you have done for me. But, I can certainly try. What is it I can do for you?"

"I need to borrow one of your dogs," he said.

"Borrow."

"Yes. I know that this might appear to be a strange request. I can assure you that it is a little important. Goes to public relations of a sort."

"A little strange," I agreed. "PR?"

"That would be a way to explain it."

"Do you have a preference as to which dog?"

Sam raised his head when he heard my question. Blackie remained deep in dreamland. His eyes penetrated deep into mine.

"As a matter of fact, I do. I need the one I gave you. I need to borrow Blackie."

"Should I ask her or do I just tell her it's in the cards, so to speak?"

"So she's like Sam and answers questions?"

"Not quite that conversational. However, she does have opinions."

I noticed that Sam turned his still raised head to look at Blackie sleeping at the other end of his couch. Then he shifted his gaze back at me.

"You think she might not want to come stay with me for a few weeks?"

"Personally, I believe she adores you. Just an observation. But if you prefer, I can ask her about a road trip and a long visit with you there in Boston."

"Better ask," he said.

"You wanna wait while I wake her and ask?"

"I need an answer fairly soon," he said without hesitation.

"This PR gig ... does it have anything to do with the fellow who gave you Blackie before you gave her to me?"

"No wonder you are such an astute detective with powers above those of normal human beings."

"I can put you on speaker so you can listen in to the request," I said.

"That would certainly be informative."

Rogers changed the setting without my asking. Uncle Walters could now hear everything that was about to occur.

"Blackie, sweetie," I said as I approached her sleeping position, "I need to ask you something."

Blackie shifted her head without raising it. She merely moved so that she could look into my eyes from her prone position.

"Uncle Walters would like for you to come visit with him for a few weeks. You up for a road trip and visit to Boston?"

She wagged her tail but said nothing.

"She'll be happy to come," I said for Uncle Walters benefit.

"I heard nothing," he said.

"The answer was in her eyes and in the movement of her tail," I said.

"You want further explanation," he said.

"Not unless you think I need to know."

"How about a story at the end of the visit?"

"Sounds like a plan," I said.

We made plans for Uncle Walters to drive down to Norfolk and retrieve Blackie for the soon-to-be visit. I offered to bring her to Boston, but he would not hear of such a thing. He planned to drive down in two days, so I had ample time to pack her a bag full of treats and toys and her favorite blanket when she didn't utilize the couch.

In the meantime my little family of canines had a road trip of our own to the Atlantic Ocean at nearby Virginia Beach. I was lying on a towel on the beach in the sun enjoying my Labor Day retreat. It was now a month after Labor Day and the beach was not crowded at all. Sam was out playing in the water and Blackie was sitting under the umbrella on the blanket. She was asleep and likely dreaming of chasing or being chased by something, or perhaps she was creating some fanciful memories of her time upcoming with Uncle Walters in Boston. Who knows what dogs dream?

The waves were rolling back and forth in that rhythmic cadence that lulls one into a state of tranquility, if not sleep. I was just about to pass into sleep when my cell phone rang.

"Clancy?" the voice said.

"Clancy Evans here."

"This is Malcolm, Clancy."

"Malcolm Wheesely?"

"The one and only."

"Well, great to hear from you. How's life in Detroit?"

"I wouldn't know. I seldom go into the city. Life in Oak Park is pretty good these days."

"So, tell me what's happening."

"Well, I was named as the Executor of Joey Malone's estate and the will was probated at the end of September. Thought I'd let you know what happened to the stuff Mr. Malone owned."

My curiosity was not peaked, but I played along as if it were vital information, pertinent to national security.

"I'm listening, Malcolm. Did he leave you anything?"

It was a dangerous question, since I had my doubts that Joey would do anything like his father had done for the employees of the companies he had owned.

"A little. Paid me a hundred thousand to be the executor."

"Wow. That's a nice piece of change."

"Yeah. Now I can fix some of the things around the house. I gave each of the cats new bedding and got some expensive medication for Profit."

"Good for you. You need to be careful, though. Now that you have money, the women of Oak Park will likely come around and bother you."

"Already happened. Some old bag from down the street, she must be sixty-five at least, she's been down with bread and pies and all kinds of junk. Can you believe some people?"

"Keep 'em at bay, Malcolm. You have your children to think of."

"Well, that's not what I called to tell you. I called because I knew you might be interested in knowing that after Mr. Malone took care of me, he left everything else to those women."

"What women?"

"Oh, let me see. I have it written here, some place. Just a moment. I can't find the paper. Hang on."

He left me for a few minutes. I really didn't want to know all of this. One of the cats must have come over and inspected the phone while Malcolm was searching for the paper he needed. There was a constant meowing in the receiver. Wish I could speak cat.

"Okay, I'm back. Sorry about that. I tend to get more and more forgetful these days. Aging is not for sissies. Couldn't remember their legal names. Sorry. Darlene Sledge. Darlene and Gretchen Sledge. Darlene was the one you asked me about. She went by Bimbi. Anyhow, they got it all. There was a trust fund set up for Gretchen so that she'll have plenty the rest of her life. I have to manage the trust fund. Only stipulation was that Darlene must not work anymore and that Gretchen had to continue her work with the homeless. I have to keep tabs on them now and then, but I doubt if I have any problem. We've talked. Sweet deal for them, right?"

"I suppose. But you can't make people bow to your will by money. Sounds like he's still trying to control things."

"Maybe, but one could also say that he is encouraging Bimbi to find a life for herself and not resort to old habits. Could be just good old-fashioned discipline," he said.

It occurred to me that Bimbi, Darlene, was a few years past her prime for that old profession to really work again. Still, sometimes it's easy to return to the default position whenever life gets rough.

"You're a nice guy, Malcolm. Always looking for a positive spin on life and people."

"I hope so, Clancy. I think Joey Malone had some good traits, but they were buried pretty deep. Still, he had this will drawn up nearly ten years ago. He hadn't changed one sentence from that time. Sure, he was an eccentric with lots of money. But I also think he had a small place where he reserved some love for a few people."

"Everyone's capable."

"And I sold what was left of the magazine. The office building, the supplies, the printing equipment, that sort of stuff, it's all gone. Another publishing company wanted it.

Frankly, I was glad to get rid of it. Never liked the trash they printed anyway. It surprised me, but all of that stuff went for one point five million. You believe those numbers?"

"Prime real estate."

"That's what they told me. Anyhow, that was in Mr. Malone's will, too."

"Ten years ago Joey Malone had plans to sell out and get rid of the magazine. That's really interesting," I said.

"But not as much as what he stipulated in the will for that money."

"What did you do with it?"

"Half went to some Gay rights group and half went for the work with the homeless in Detroit. Gretchen was given the responsibility of managing that second gift. Along with my help, if she needs it. Can you imagine that?"

"The nerve of some people," I said.

A LOOK AT MERCY KILLING (A CLANCY EVANS MYSTERY)

Clancy Evans is asked to help a young clergyman. One of his elderly members knows more than he's saying...but who cares about a murder in 1933? Ancient history! Clancy cares. Clancy and Sam, her black lab, travel to Riley Corners to investigate. Straight talking and direct, Clancy wastes no time in riling this small town, including the law. She enlists an old friend, a former Navy SEAL, to help her strip away some of the secrets of this Southern community...and there could be hell to pay, for both of them

AVAILABLE NOW

ABOUT THE AUTHOR

M Glenn Graves has been writing fiction since graduating from college in 1970 but did not begin to work on novels until 1992. Born in Mississippi, he has lived in Tennessee, North Carolina, Missouri, Virginia, Costa Rica, and the Dominican Republic. He graduated from Mars Hill College with a BA in English and Religion. He received a Master of Divinity in 1977 three years after he finished his four-year tour in the United States Navy. Married to Cindy, they have three grown children – Brian, Mark, & Jenn. They also have three grandchildren – Jonathan, Matthew, & Phoebe. Glenn, Cindy, and Sophie, their Lab, currently reside in the mountains of western North Carolina where he is the pastor of a local church.

www.ingramcontent.com/pod-product-compliance
Lightning Source LLC
Chambersburg PA
CBHW030637020726
47493CB00006B/1759

* 9 7 8 1 6 4 1 1 9 5 3 2 4 *